A Tasty Way to Die

By Janet Laurence

A TASTY WAY TO DIE
A DEEPE COFFYN

A Tasty Way to Die

JANET LAURENCE

A CRIME CLUB BOOK
DOUBLEDAY
New York   London   Toronto   Sydney   Auckland

A CRIME CLUB BOOK
PUBLISHED BY DOUBLEDAY
a division of Bantam Doubleday Dell Publishing Group, Inc.
666 Fifth Avenue, New York, New York 10103

DOUBLEDAY and the portrayal of a man
with a gun are trademarks of Doubleday,
a division of Bantam Doubleday Dell
Publishing Group, Inc.

Library of Congress Cataloging-in-Publication Data
Laurence, Janet.
A tasty way to die / Janet Laurence. — 1st ed. in the United
States of America.
p. cm.
Previously published: Macmillan, U.K., 1990.
"A Crime Club book."
I. Title.
PR6062.A795T37 1991
823'.914—dc20 90-41089
CIP
ISBN 0-385-41491-9
Copyright © 1990 by Janet Laurence
All Rights Reserved
Printed in the United States of America
February 1991
1 3 5 7 9 10 8 6 4 2
First Edition in the United States of America

A Tasty Way to Die

CHAPTER ONE

The demonstration was slipping out of control. As Darina removed the custard from the microwave, she could see a large, pulsing scab disfiguring its smooth surface. Even before she drew the plastic spatula through the mixture, she knew it would contain large flecks of overcooked egg.

"This is a curdled custard," she told her audience gravely, stirring it so they could see the damaged dish in the overhead mirror.

A slight gasp came from the thirty or so women sitting in front of the demonstration area.

"I never did trust microwaves," sniffed a plump matron. The gilt buttons on her braided Chanel suit and a slave's purchase price in gold chains hanging round her neck sparkled and winked in the bright lights.

"I'm afraid the fault was mine, not the machine's," Darina forced herself to keep calm. Tall, immaculate in a white overall, a thick plait of fair hair running neatly down the back of her head then looping underneath itself, she presented a picture of efficiency, a white bow at the nape of her neck adding a grace note. Nothing betrayed the brilliant imitation of a tumble drier her stomach was performing. She lifted her chin a little higher and said with a fine air of confidence, "I allowed the custard to cook too long, that's all, the oven may be more powerful than mine."

"You had it on full power for that last burst," there was an accusing note in the thin woman's voice and she gave her neighbour a satisfied smile.

Darina controlled an urge to ask her why in heaven's name she had not pointed that out when the programme had been punched in, and reached for the Magimix. "Luckily all is not lost," she said, pouring the curdled mixture into the bowl and giving it a good whizz, "Isn't that magic?"

A little murmur of delight came from her audience as the smooth, pale gold mixture poured into a clean bowl.

"What are the tiny black flecks?"

The question came from the back of the room and Darina relaxed slightly; all this girl's comments had been truly interested.

"They come from the vanilla." A long, slim black pod veiled in custard was picked out of the bowl that had been in the microwave, "You remember how we split it before infusing it with the milk? Those tiny flecks give a wonderful, deep flavour. The pod can't be used for this recipe again but it still has enough strength to scent caster sugar for cakes or biscuits. Just wash and dry it then pop it into the sugar jar." She was back into her stride and the tension between her shoulder blades eased.

"Look at the savarin!" gasped a woman at the side of the audience. At the end of the demonstration island, yeast mixture was overflowing the top of its tin and slowly dripping down the side like some sci-fi primaeval ooze.

"Ah," Darina picked up the tin and reached underneath the counter for another bowl, "That is overproving." Keep calm, keep calm, she repeated to herself, don't panic. "The savarin should have been baked before it reached this stage. Now we shall have to deflate and set it to rise again." She neatly scooped the mixture out of the tin, giving it a few quick beats by hand to finish the deflating process. Once more shiny and elastic, the yeast batter was poured back into its tin, now washed and regreased by her assistant. Darina set it back on the counter, giving a little prayer of thanks that the apples to fill its centre hole had already been cooked in cider and the orange segments and crystallised peel prepared, she could not have borne it if the fruit had collapsed or she had cut herself whilst segmenting the oranges.

She put the cider juices from the apples to cook with sugar for the savarin syrup then went to a small freezer to take out a flat swiss roll loaded with melted chocolate and a chestnut ice cream. The ice cream had been too soft to roll successfully when Darina had first spread it. She had hoped a quick rest in the freezer would firm it up slightly. Now she saw with a heart that thudded down like a severed counterweight that the layer of chocolate was as solid as a pavement. There would be no rolling of that ice cream gateau. What an idiot she was!

Why had she ever agreed to do this afternoon's session? She had told Eve she could not handle it, that she had done very little demonstrating.

"Of course you can handle it," her friend had been supremely confident. "It's only 'Desserts from the Freezer,' darling, nothing particularly tricky, and they're all pussy cats. Half of them will fall asleep after lunch anyway and the rest just want a few ideas for their next dinner party. They're not taking diplomas. Anyway, you've got to do it. I shall be at the television studio and with Claire ill and Jo away, there isn't anyone else."

Darina had been carelessly walking along South Audley Street when she had literally bumped into Eve Tarrant coming out of Hobbs & Co., the Mayfair delicatessen and wine store, loaded with carrier bags. "Watch it!'', the other girl had said sharply, clutching her parcels more closely, then she had looked at her assailant and given a cry of delight, "Darina Lisle! Darling! Where have you been! Come on, it's lunchtime, let's eat."

They had gone to an Italian trattoria on the next corner. Darina helped dispose the bags underneath the table, admiring the way Eve took command of the best corner in the restaurant, summoning waiters with the ease of royalty. Then she looked properly at the friend she had not seen for some eight years.

The other girl was tiny, she had always made Darina feel every one of the inches that totalled a shade under six feet, a giantess beside a fairy princess. Only Eve's eyes were on a grand scale; bright blue, they sparkled like sapphire chips and lit her pointed face. The rest of her features were small and slightly crooked, the nose just off centre, the mouth pulled up at one corner, giving an effect that was somewhere between an elf and a monkey. A wild tumult of corkscrew curls the colour of old rope streaked with gold finished the picture. She was wearing what looked like an up-market designer's interpretation of a hunting outfit; only someone with no hips could have carried it off so successfully.

Eve flipped the menu over, read it rapidly, gave the hovering waiter an order for both of them and handed it back. She played restlessly with the cutlery, adjusting the position of the knife and fork, moving on to turn over the china, scanning the maker's name. Then the enormous eyes looked intently at Darina.

"I haven't seen you since our cookery course days. You went off to bury yourself in the country, are you still there?"

"No, I've been running a catering business in London for the last few years, but I've just handed it over to a friend." Darina felt reluctant to explain why, somehow the bequest of an expensive house in Chelsea from a murdered cousin did not seem a topic to be touched on lightly. "I've seen you mentioned several times in the press. Haven't you got a smart catering outfit doing desperately expensive cocktail parties and dinners?"

Eve laughed, "As you well know, my sweet, you have to charge a packet to make it worthwhile. But we've got a new wrinkle now, short cookery courses. And it's really successful, the punters are queueing up to enrol. We're still doing the catering of course, that's our bread and butter. Jo Parkins looks after most of that whilst Claire Montague and I concentrate on the courses and breaking into the media. Though it's desperate at the moment," Eve broke off and looked across the table at her companion, "Did you say you'd just handed over your business to a friend? What are you going to do now?"

"Oh, I'm just looking around," Darina was deliberately vague. "How come you have the time for a lunch out? Who's looking after the cookery courses?"

"They don't run every day. Our last course ended yesterday, the next one starts Monday. A photographer's using the demonstration theatre today and for once we haven't got a function. Claire's doing preparation work for tomorrow and I've popped out to get some special items we need." Eve paused as their food arrived then looked across the table at her friend, "Are you really at a loose end at the moment? Could you, would you, help us out for a couple of days or so?"

"With the cookery courses?" Darina was startled, "The only demonstrating I've done has been the odd evening for a local charity." She did not add that she had been terrified every time. Cooking was her life, she could produce a dinner for twelve, a buffet for fifty, cocktails for a hundred, but ask her to demonstrate a few simple dishes in front of an audience and it was as if she had been asked to perform the dying swan at Covent Garden.

"Not demonstrating," said Eve soothingly, her fork pushing the spaghetti around her plate, "On the catering side. Jo rang this morning. Her father's dying and she's got to go home to Leeds. Tomorrow we've got a fork lunch for two hundred plus a small dinner party plus a picnic lunch to prepare for a mushroom walk on Saturday, not to mention Lady Walden's cocktail party that evening. On Sunday I'm having a celebration lunch for forty, it's the first anniversary of The Wooden Spoon, that's what we call the cookery school, and on Monday, but I needn't go on, you can see we must have some reliable help until Jo gets back, it should only be a few days, and there's no one I'd rather have than you," she looked pleadingly across the table.

Darina thought for a moment. She had put the Chelsea house on the market, there were several people supposed to be coming to see it and she had appointments to visit two large houses in the country with a view to seeing if they could be converted into small hotels. There was no real reason why the estate agent should not look after showing her house and the visits to the country could be put off for a few days. Eve sounded as though she really needed help and Darina had enjoyed working with her when they did their course together. Why was she hesitating? It was, she decided, just a selfish wish to have a little more time to herself, enjoy her new independence. She had just come from the hairdressers and the unaccustomed luxury of an expert trim for her long hair. And she had been looking forward to a relaxed shopping expedition and the prospect of several more unpressured days before life once again needed to be tackled head on. But a friend was in trouble and it was no time to hold back, particularly if she was not being asked to demonstrate.

So how was it she was now in this pickle in front of thirty critically attentive upper middle class ladies? It was hardly Claire's fault she had gone down with gastric 'flu but it could not have been more ill timed. And what was she going to do about this culinary disaster?

Darina took a deep breath and laid the flat sponge with its layers of chocolate and marron on the working area under the overhead mirror. "I've got a little surprise for you now," she said to her audience, "We're going to finish this dish differently from your recipe sheets."

She picked up a large knife and began swiftly cutting the cake into equal-sized rectangular slices. She piled them on top of each other then cut the block into three narrow strips. Rapidly reversing the middle strip, Darina pressed all three back together.

"Now," she said, turning the block and cutting a slice off its end, "Look at the chequer board pattern. We'll just put the rest of the gateau back in the freezer, then I'll pass this slice around." She wrapped the block in tin foil and her helper returned it to its chilly home.

Darina breathed a sigh of relief as a wave of appreciative comments wafted across the demonstration area. Lightheaded with her success, she showed them how to defrost a frozen savarin and soak it in the warm syrup, then pile the poached apple mixed with orange segments in the centre, finally strewing strands of crystallised orange over the top. Nearly there, only the iced bombe to assemble now.

Behind her the ice cream machine stopped. Darina moved to get the bombe mould and the bowl of tiny chocolate curls she had so painstakingly created before the demonstration started by drawing a potato peeler down a block of chocolate. Panic set in once more as she realised she had left the bowl too near the hob. The chocolate curls were melting. Perhaps it would be best to come clean with this one.

"This is not my afternoon," she said, popping the little bowl into the microwave and carefully setting the controls to low, "I should have kept the prepared chocolate in the fridge." She swiftly lined the bombe mould with part of the ice cream, sandwiched the rest with the melted chocolate in the centre and drew a fork through with a final flourish. "So now we have a marbleized pattern in the middle instead of the more stunning chocolate curls spilling out as you cut into the bombe."

"And you have two ideas for a party pud instead of one." Eve Tarrant walked towards the demonstration island from the back of the room.

"A perfect demonstration of the importance of not panicking," she said. "When something goes wrong, there is usually something you can do to retrieve the situation but not if you are panicking. And if there isn't, well, what's the use of panicking?" She gave a comical smile that drew them into a little conspiracy against the gremlins that lay in wait for the unwary cook.

"Would you like to see what I did on television today?" She laid down the large plate she had been carrying and unwrapped it, revealing a selection of open sandwiches. The women crowded round to look, exclaiming at the way prawns had been lined up on lettuce, known as a "traffic jam" explained Eve, and garnished with two curls of lemon peel; at thin slices of rare roast beef rising in a wave over a little pile of chive-flavoured potato salad and neatly anchored in one corner with a small fan of sliced pickled gherkin; at cornets of smoked salmon stuffed with a herb flecked cream cheese filling and finished with fronds of green dill; at a complicated looking arrangement of sliced chicken and hard boiled egg on lollo rosso lettuce, its bronze-edged leaves a perfect foil for the pale flesh.

"You wouldn't believe the trouble I had keeping these for you, the crew wanted to wolf the lot. We shall be looking at making open sandwiches tomorrow morning with 'Easy Entertaining,' then in the afternoon we shall deal with 'Cocktail Parties,' " Eve conveyed the quotation marks with effortless ease.

"Now, if you are interested in any of the equipment Darina has been using for her demonstration, or need knives or saucepans, we've opened up the shop." Amid a flurry of chat and laughter, the women drifted out of the room.

Eve gave a quick look round, saw the last of the audience had left, and collapsed into a chair. "Well done, darling, I can see you'll be an old pro in no time." Her eye fell on the plate of chequered cake, chocolate and chestnut, "Another innovation, I see."

Darina explained briefly what had happened then asked how the television had gone.

"Not at all badly," Eve looked a tiny bit smug. "It wasn't difficult, those open sandwiches are just an assembly job and I kept them quite deliberately simple so there was no fuss." Darina took another look at the plate of elegant concoctions. If those were simple, what would Eve call complicated? But she certainly didn't seem at all strained by her efforts. An emerald green taffeta blouse with an upstanding collar and big sleeves was tucked into a green and blue tartan taffeta skirt that made the most of her minuscule waist. The effect was stylish and striking.

"The producer murmured something about more ideas for future spots so I think we may have an 'in' there now."

"How did you get asked in the first place?" Darina wondered how easy it was to get on television.

"The producer was at one of our party contracts and I made sure I got an introduction. I told him how simple it could all be made to look and before he knew it he was asking me to come along and demonstrate." Eve rose and stretched herself. "I must ring Claire and see how she is, you haven't heard anything, I suppose? Ah well, I expect the bug is running its course. I'll come and help with tonight's dinner in a minute, you know what we're supposed to be doing?"

"Individual spinach soufflés with anchovy sauce, pheasant with blackberry coulis, swede purée with pine nuts, carrots with pernod, scalloped potatoes, kiwi fruit with glazed sauce sabayon and savarin with apple." As she reached the end of her recitation, Darina looked at the tin with its now almost risen dough, "That was another of this afternoon's disasters. I hope Claire is all right by tomorrow, demonstrating really isn't my forte."

"All you need is practice, darling. There are always odd hiccups, what counts is an ability to cope and that you've obviously got. Cover up that plate and bring it downstairs, they'll do for our supper." She drifted elegantly out of the demonstration theatre.

Darina looked around. The washer up had finished and departed and all was clean and tidy. Four wall ovens ranged either side of the island unit sparkled brightly. There were four more at the other end of the room, with working areas and hobs in between. Below were shelves neatly stacked with pans and bowls. Four large and two small sinks provided water at convenient intervals and four fridges completed the equipment. The centre of the room was presently occupied by rows of chairs, the two rear ones on wooden daises. All these could be cleared away and two large tables erected in their place when demonstrations gave way to practical cookery.

Large posters of herbs, wild mushrooms, wine growing areas in France and Italy and the odd still life of fruit and vegetables decorated the walls together with bunches of dried herbs, strings of garlic and onions and bright red metal grilles holding spoons, scissors, spatulas, small sieves, ladles and other kitchen impedimenta. It was an efficient and attractive setting for the teaching and study of cookery.

Darina picked up the tin of risen savarin dough, balanced it on top of the plate of open sandwiches and made her way downstairs, past the little equipment shop by the front door where excited women were testing the balance of kitchen knives and buying ice cream makers, and made her way to the catering kitchen. It was time to leave the traumas of demonstrating behind and start preparing that evening's function.

CHAPTER TWO

Eve shut her office door and sank into a swivel chair with a crackle of taffeta. She flicked swiftly through the small pile of bills and letters left on the pale wood desk then tossed them impatiently into an overflowing rattan filing basket. She twirled herself round in the chair to face a window behind the desk. Through the slats of a white venetian blind could be seen the backs of large houses at the rear of their converted mews building.

It was a dull day and golden rectangles of light spilt out over the small yard and its array of dustbins. But those of the buildings opposite paled beside that streaming out of The Wooden Spoon's extension. This was the catering kitchen. Eve let her mind dwell for an instant on its satisfyingly professional equipment; the gleaming stainless steel ovens, hobs and sinks, the spotless white walls and working surfaces. Shortly she would be there, deftly preparing Daisy Delamere's dinner party, a meal that should add to The Wooden Spoon's already not inconsiderable reputation.

Eve wondered how she should organise the evening. Would it be better for her to serve the food and leave Darina looking after the final touches in the kitchen, or to stay there herself masterminding the presentation?

She looked at her watch, time to get changed but first she must ring Claire.

The telephone was answered after no more than a couple of rings. The soft voice was dull, exhausted, "Oh, Eve, how kind of you to ring, yes, I'm beginning to feel better. It's really been ghastly. I never dreamt gastric 'flu could make you so ill."

Eve twirled a corkscrew curl round her finger, "A friend of mine had it a few weeks ago and said it was absolutely grisly but she's fine now."

"You haven't heard that anybody else there on Sunday has been ill?" The voice was hesitant.

Eve frowned, "No, Monica rang to say how much she and Ralph had enjoyed themselves, she didn't mention either of them was under the weather. Kenneth was in earlier to make arrangements for another photographic session on Thursday and he looked perfectly healthy. I haven't heard from Elizabeth or any of the others but Joshua and I are fine. You don't think it could be food poisoning, do you?" Her voice was shocked.

"I just wondered about the mushrooms," the suggestion was so hesitant it was hardly audible.

Eve frowned again, "A poisonous one, you mean? Surely not."

"Well, there was that one Ralph told us to be so careful of," the words drifted through the receiver.

"But he destroyed that and threw away any others he was at all doubtful about. No," her voice grew firmer, "Ralph Cox is an expert, I'm sure it's just gastric 'flu. Keep warm, drink lots of water and don't think of coming in tomorrow unless you feel really well. Darina can cope."

"How's she doing?"

Eve chuckled, "Amazingly well, I can't begin to tell you what went wrong with her demo, it was almost classic, but she did some very nifty footwork and practically created a new dish. Must dash, we've got Daisy's dinner this evening."

She returned the cordless receiver to its recharger, remained sitting in her chair for a moment, motionless, then propelled herself out of it with a surge of energy and opened a door in the corner of the room, revealing a small shower room. Whilst she stripped, she thought over Saturday's mushroom walk.

It had been a glorious day, autumn sunshine at its best, so warm she had worn linen trousers and a crunchy linen sweater in an old gold shade she knew did great things for her hair. Joshua had run his fingers through it in a way she remembered from their early days. A shiver ran through her body that had nothing to do with the needle points of cold water that she had switched on.

Ralph had led them deep into a Sussex wood, pointing out inedible fungi on the trunks of trees and the dire looking ink caps with their long, pointed heads that only a fool, Eve thought, would have considered safe to eat but were apparently quite harmless when young. Ralph loved being in charge, laying down the law, displaying his knowledge. He was such a macho man, almost brutish, there was primitive animal under that veneer of civilisation. He'd looked at her across a sunny clearing as they broke off their hunting for lunch, an intimate look that made her blood race. Had Joshua noticed?

No, he had been helping Claire take containers out of the hamper Darina had brought, admiring the various salads their temporary help had prepared. There was no doubt but that girl had developed into an extremely good cook, Eve had done no more than show her what had been bought in and tell her how many there would be on the walk. The food had just appeared. Not looking as spectacular as she would have prepared herself but O.K. and tasting delicious. Pity Darina had not been around earlier, she would have made a good partner. Very resourceful, perhaps too resourceful? One of Claire's great advantages was she never tried to take over the driving seat.

Eve towelled herself down, rubbing hard with the shaggy bath sheet, feeling her skin glow with the friction. When was it Ralph had found that poisonous mushroom? After lunch? No, before. It had looked so innocent but he'd gone on and on about it and made a great song and dance over washing his hands thoroughly after throwing it away. Had even produced a little bottle of soapy water from a capacious pocket of his leather jacket. Deadly, he'd said it could be, even just that one little specimen. What a frisson had run through her at the time. Just to look at it and think it could end someone's life had given her goose flesh.

But the fungus had been destroyed, there was no possibility it could have been eaten with the other mushrooms that had provided the starter for her celebration lunch.

And what a successful lunch it had been. Eve thrust the thought of poisonous fungi away and spent a moment happily remembering the plaudits she had received the previous day. Then she dressed herself rapidly in chef's blue and white check trousers, added a white jacket buttoned hussar style and finger combed her tangle of hair, finally using a triangular white scarf to cover and hold it away from her face. She threw the damp towel into an ali baba rush basket, checked the office was tidy and went into the kitchen.

Later that evening, Darina brought the last of the dirty dishes through from Lady Delamere's elegant dining room into the cramped kitchen. Eve switched on an ancient washing up machine. "I'm afraid the rest will have to be done by hand, we can't wait for that cycle to finish." She picked up a fragment of apple from the remains of the savarin, popped it into her mouth and smiled ecstatically, "Bliss, darling, sheer bliss."

"Lots of appreciative comments on the food." Darina stacked dirty plates by the sink.

"Tell, tell, my darling, it's music to my ears." Eve filled the sink with hot water, added a generous squirt of Fairy liquid, and started washing the cutlery.

The other girl smiled. Eve was like a small child, knowing she had done well but desperate to have an adult confirm it. Carefully drying the silver, Darina repeated comments overheard whilst serving. "And someone said he could hardly bear to start eating, his plate looked like fine art," she finished, picking up more spoons. "I rather agreed with him, you have a genius for presentation."

"I do love it," Eve said artlessly. "When I arrange food something inside me quietens, becomes still. It's as though life is suddenly quite, quite perfect."

"What about tasting it?" asked Darina curiously, thinking of her continuous battle with her weight and how Eve looked as though she didn't know the meaning of a square meal.

"Oh, I love food, of course, but for me taste can't be separated from appearance. If it looks marvellous, it's going to taste marvellous."

"I can see I'm going to learn a lot working with you."

"Oh, darling, you're a wonderful cook," Eve sounded quite genuine and Darina felt unexpectedly complimented. "The food you prepared for Saturday's picnic was great."

And you hardly ate a thing, thought Darina, remembering the way Eve had picked her way through the various dishes with exclamations of delight that had sounded a touch extravagant when you realised just how little she actually consumed. Perhaps that was how she existed, a little bit here and a little bit there.

"But I wish you could have been at the lunch on Sunday, darling, that was truly delicious. The wild mushrooms were just divine."

Darina smiled, her small friend's enthusiasm was disarming, the tiny figure in its chef's trousers and white coat seemed far too insubstantial to cope with the preparation of a four course lunch for forty and act as hostess as well. Though, of course, Claire would have helped.

"Just what was the important engagement that meant you couldn't be with us?" Eve looked arch and Darina found herself blushing.

"It was only with a friend but I couldn't cancel, it had been arranged ages ago."

"You can't fool me, it *was* someone very special."

Darina protested but Eve merely looked smug and renewed her washing up water.

Was William Pigram special? Darina polished a fork carefully. She had to admit he had charms. He was taller than most men she knew, managing to top her even when she wore heels. And he had a keen intelligence with a wry sense of humour that was invigorating. But he was a policeman, a detective sergeant who had nearly had to arrest her for murder and it was no thanks to him she had avoided that fate.

When he'd rung and asked her out to lunch her first instinct had been to refuse. Then he'd explained he was coming to London from Somerset for a short holiday and if Sunday lunch was no good, perhaps dinner later in the week could be arranged. Lunch had seemed less threatening, less *committing*, than dinner, so she had agreed. Then she'd met Eve and the celebration lunch had offered a perfect excuse to ring William and post-pone their meeting. But she hadn't taken it.

She had sat waiting for him on the Sunday morning wanting to get the occasion over and done with. When the bell rang she had opened the door with mixed feelings in which reluctance surfaced uppermost, then experienced an unexpected lightening of her spirits as he smiled at her with obvious delight.

She asked him in for a drink. He accepted a glass of white wine, looking round the drawing room with interest.

"So this is your Chelsea house? Very nice, I like this effect." He placed a hand on one of the pillars supporting an arch that divided the room into two, then wandered around, peering at pictures, picking up one or two of the many small treasures displayed on the antique furniture, look-ing through french windows into the tiny garden with its stone paving, raised beds and two classical statues.

Somewhat shyly, she studied him as he moved through the familiar room she still found difficult to believe was hers. He seemed at ease, not aggressively so, more a case of fitting perfectly into the setting. He had an ability to absorb and reflect the atmosphere of a place that was disarming.

"It's a lovely room and it suits you, I shall like thinking of you sitting here, reading a book or watching television."

"I'm afraid you won't be able to do that for long, the house is on the market."

"You're selling it?" He sounded shocked.

"I couldn't afford to keep it, have you any idea what the running costs of a house like this are? And wasn't it you who suggested that I use it to finance my 'dream hotel'?"

He smiled, the dark curly hair making him look like a schoolboy about to suggest a particularly mischievous piece of behaviour. "All my fault, eh? Come on, get your coat, I've booked a table at the Connaught, you failed to come up with any bright ideas on where to eat Sunday lunch so I asked my uncle his advice."

With a pleasant sense of anticipation, Darina seldom got the opportu-nity to eat Michel Bourdin's food, she got her coat and allowed him to flag down a taxi. It was a bright day, almost as warm as the previous one and she found herself telling William about the mushroom walk.

"I never realised before how many edible wild fungi there are in Sus-sex, you should have seen what they collected and that was only before lunch. I believe they found more afterwards."

"You didn't join in the hunt?" He ushered her in the wake of the head waiter to their table and helped settle her so she could see who else was eating in the panelled room.

"No, I drove the picnic to them and then took the remains back afterwards, it meant they didn't have to return to their starting place until the end of the afternoon and Eve and Claire could get back to a clean kitchen."

"What happened to all the mushrooms?"

"Eve's using them as a starter for her celebration lunch today." Darina explained about the anniversary.

William looked at her with amused perception, "Don't tell me you weren't asked as well. I am flattered."

She laughed and his eyes narrowed ruefully, "I know, you thought if you cried off today I would pester you for dinner later in the week. No, don't say anything, I am properly put in my place but will rise above the situation. Tell me instead how you got involved with all this Wooden Spoon business, I thought you had your own catering company?"

Darina explained how she had handed that over to her assistant, so she could fulfil her ambition of owning a small hotel. Then found herself describing Eve's company and the food she had helped prepare on the Friday.

William gave a small grimace, "It sounds like the sort of food I dread, all looks and little substance. Now this is very attractive but looks as if it might be real food as well and, by heavens, it is." He raised a fork loaded with the chef's special Beef Wellington and ate with deep appreciation.

"Yes, I already had you tagged as a boeuf en croûte person."

"What sort of label is that?"

"Means you're rather more sophisticated than a plain steak man."

"But just as much a male chauvinist pig, eh? Don't try prevarication, that's exactly what you think of me, I just have to be grateful for the crust. I think I could like this game, let's see how I would tag you."

Darina waited whilst the herring grey eyes regarded her speculatively.

"I have it—crème brûlée, a struggle to get through the burnt topping but worth it to reach the rich cream beneath."

"I shall try to look on that as a compliment."

"It's one of my favourite puddings," he said with a flourish of his wine glass. "And how about your friend, Eve, can you play the game with her? From what you've told me, I see her as one of those complicated starters with a long French name that looks terribly chic and tastes of nothing."

"I've obviously been unfair, perhaps it's because her food really isn't my style, but I'm learning a lot. Eve makes me realise how little imagination I use in cooking. I don't think she would ever be content to present a chop as a chop, it has to be stuffed, or wrapped in pastry or cooked in something or other. And as for presentation, Eve's efforts make mine look like something out of the kindergarten."

"I remember your food as superb."

Darina thought back to the historical recipes she had prepared during that traumatic weekend when William and she had first met. "Ah, that was real food. And I think it's all coming back. The French call it cuisine gran'mère but it has a modern look and I don't suppose it tastes like the food your mother learned from hers."

"My mother's a hopeless cook, thank heavens she doesn't bother most of the time, she feeds dad on Marks and Sparks, says she's far too busy running the county to spend time in the kitchen. And she always hires help for entertaining. I suppose it's people like her that keep you and your friend in business."

"Let's drink to your mother," Darina raised a glass of the excellent wine William had ordered. She was thoroughly enjoying herself. The food was excellent, the ambiance of the restaurant seductive, somewhere between a gentleman's club and a manor house. It was crowded with interesting looking people but none more so than the attractive man sitting on the other side of the table. All her reservations about this meeting had melted away. Perhaps she had devoted too much time to her career, there were definite charms to socialising.

"We must do this again," William said, tucking into the Connaught's special Bread and Butter Pudding. "How about dinner during the week?"

"Where are you staying?"

"With my uncle and aunt just off Sloane Square, not far from you, in fact."

Darina looked at him speculatively, that would no doubt be the uncle who had recommended the Connaught for Sunday lunch. William might profess ignorance of the right place to go but he showed no awkwardness lunching in one of London's most exclusive hotels, nor had he blanched at the prices. Her first impression of him had been that he was not her idea of a policeman. What was it he had told her about himself? A career first in the foreign office and then in the city before taking up police work? No doubt that explained his unobtrusive sophistication.

"How about dinner?" he pressed gently.

Darina found she did not need to hesitate, "That would be fun, I don't know how long Eve's going to need me but I'm sure I can manage an evening sometime this week."

"I'll give you a ring tomorrow."

"It would be easier if I rang you, I think I shall be working most of the day and possibly part of the evening."

He gave her his uncle's number then suggested they walk through Grosvenor Square to Hyde Park.

"Oh, this is good," Darina said as her feet scrunched the layers of leaves lying beneath the enormous trees. "I do miss the country. I haven't been down to visit my mother for ages, how is Somerset?"

"Not much alters," he said gravely.

"How's the crime rate? Keeping up with the villains?"

"We've had nothing particularly dramatic, just the usual spate of thieving and juvenile delinquency."

"So the branch is managing without you for this week?"

"Just about."

They walked through to Knightsbridge, then down Sloane Street and along the King's Road to Darina's house, chatting of this and that, finding conversation easy and it was with a sense of regret that Darina heard William refuse her offer of tea.

"I'd love to but I promised to go with my uncle and aunt to a charity concert. Ring me tomorrow and let me know which evening you can manage." He gave a wave of his hand and walked back down the road.

"I bet it was the chap you want to go out with on Wednesday," said Eve now, swilling out the sink after the last of the saucepans had been scoured.

"You're sure that's going to be all right?"

"Shouldn't be a problem though we've got Monica Cox's party that night. She was there on Saturday. Her husband was the mushroom expert. He's a fruit and veg wholesaler, supplies most of the top restaurants and hotels in London. Monica always demands the best, and what else do we supply? But as long as you can help with the preparation, we'll be able to handle the actual event. Claire should be better by then and with any luck we'll have Jo back. You go and enjoy yourself."

CHAPTER THREE

Claire came in the next morning. She said she felt better but Darina thought she looked terrible, her eyes almost yellow above dark shadows, her round face drained and pale. Eve wouldn't let her assist with the demonstrations, setting her instead to help Darina prepare a large luncheon.

Claire started working swiftly and competently, making a trout mousse and using it to stuff roulades of smoked salmon, then arranging wild strawberries on the crème pâtissière stuffed almond tartlets Darina had produced. She worked in silence, reserving her energies for the job in hand, the way Darina herself liked to work. What a contrast, she thought, to Eve's non-stop stream of instructions, advice and gossip as they had cooked the previous night's meal.

Claire, in fact, was moon to Eve's sun, an opal beside a flashing diamond. It took a little time to realise how lovely she was. Puppy fat still obscured her good bone structure and her figure wasn't helped by being clothed in a gathered skirt and limp, lace collared shirt topped by a baggy cardigan. Her pale blonde hair was worn in a Sloane bob held back by a velvet band. Her eyes were the blue of a baby's bow. Where Eve fizzed and sparkled, generating excitement and ideas faster than the national grid, Claire offered quiet charm and efficiency.

But as Darina prepared countless lamb cutlets, neatly trimmed, sealed, spread with pâté de foie gras and wrapped in puff pastry, she began to worry. The other girl seemed far from well. Several times she grew confused over what she was doing and once she stopped and stood looking at the table as though she had been beamed up to a foreign planet. She was a very different person from the girl Darina had worked with the previous Friday. Then she had marvelled at Claire's speed in turning out items such as stuffed new potatoes, minced lamb kofte and miniature hamburgers in baby baps by the tray load whilst managing to maintain an aura of peace and calm.

Now Claire slowly glazed the last of the strawberry tartlets and placed it carefully on the tray with the others. She ran a tired hand across her forehead. "What's next?" she asked Darina, "I'm afraid I can hardly think straight."

"You're going to sit down, you should never have come in," the tall cook told her. "Emily and I can finish this off," Darina glanced at the young assistant who had been preparing the vegetables. "We aren't expected to serve this, are we?"

"No, they have their own staff for that, we just have to provide the food."

"Well we've just about finished and there's no function tonight, so go home. And don't think of coming in tomorrow, Eve and I can handle everything that's scheduled."

Claire smiled weakly, "She'll have to get on her bike and bring in some more business, can't have you hanging around with so little to do. I think, if you and Emily can manage to deliver all this food," she looked at the table massed with deep trays filled with the fruits of their labour, "I will go home, my legs don't seem too strong yet. I'll just put the kettle on, Eve will want a cup of her herb tea after the morning's session and how about one for you?"

"I'll do that." Darina was already busy at the tap. She switched on the kettle then turned round to find Claire holding out a box of little muslin bags tied with thread. Trust Eve to find an exclusive brand of herbal tea.

She took the box then went and found the cooking brandy, poured out a slug and handed it to Claire. "Sit still and drink this." She watched the other girl lift the glass in a hand that shook slightly then sip the amber liquid, closing her eyes as the fire hit the back of her throat. "I gather Eve's lunch was a great success?"

Claire produced a smile that contained a little of her normal composure, "Oh, yes, the food was marvellous and everyone enjoyed themselves."

"You must have been exhausted afterwards, no wonder the bug has hit you so hard."

Claire closed her eyes again for a moment, "It was hectic, but Eve had it all so beautifully organised I wasn't really all that tired. It was in the evening I began to feel so terrible."

"Who was there?" asked Darina hastily as the memory of her experience threatened to overwhelm the other girl.

"Oh, lots of interesting people. Mostly good customers with a few press and some friends." She grew almost animated, "I really enjoyed talking to some of them, normally one doesn't get a chance. I never realised Clive Thompson could be so charming."

"Clive Thompson?"

"Yes, he's some big wheel in the city, Eve says he'll end up owning all the food companies and he's used us for several do's. When I realised I had to sit next to him, I almost panicked, well, what do you talk about to someone like that? I'm sure he would have preferred Eve but he actually seemed to enjoy chatting to me."

"What did you talk about?" Darina watched the pale girl as she drew the back of her hand across her forehead again, shaking her head a little as though to clear it.

"Oh, nothing very much, food and the country, he lives not far from my parents." Her eyes closed for a moment and a brief spasm seemed to shake her body.

The kettle boiled and clicked itself off. Darina looked at her watch, "Stay there, I'll be back in a minute." She went off to the office, where Jackie, Eve's secretary, was furiously typing addresses on envelopes. "Claire is just about whacked, can you get hold of a taxi?"

"Oh, poor dear, of course, there's a rank just round the corner. And Jo rang a short while ago, her father's funeral is today and she'll be back tomorrow. I think she was going to ask if Eve could manage without her a little longer but as soon as she heard Claire had been so poorly, she said she'd return."

"That's good, will she be able to help with that big cocktail party tomorrow? I don't think Claire will be well enough to work."

"Oh, I should think so, she was going to start early." The secretary was a thin, intense girl with enormous glasses and a talent for pairing colours that should never be seen together. Today's choice was a dingy mustard sweater with a raspberry ripple skirt. But though she might have been colour blind, there was nothing wrong with her other faculties. Whilst she talked, she was dialling a number and within minutes she had organised a taxi.

During the telephone conversation, Darina picked up a slim brochure from a pile that was sitting on the desk. On the front was a full colour photograph of the demonstration theatre overlaid with a big wooden spoon tied with red ribbon. *Club Membership for Christmas,* it said underneath, in letters surrounded with holly. Darina opened the brochure. Inside were details of The Wooden Spoon Club, offering quarterly newsletter, recipes, advice on entertaining and discounts on kitchen equipment; annual fee to be £35.00 but special introductory offer until the end of year £25.00.

"It's Eve's latest gimmick," Jackie said as she came off the line. "Ever so many people have said they're interested. We've sent them to everyone on our lists, both for the courses and the catering. And to the press, of course. We're hoping for some mentions in the Christmas present columns."

There was a ring at the front door, "That'll be the taxi," she said.

A few minutes later Darina helped a desperately pale figure into the vehicle and stood looking at her for a moment, "Are you sure you'll be all right, wouldn't you like me to come with you?"

Claire forced a smile, "No, really, I'll be fine, I've just overdone it. I feel miles better than yesterday, all I need is more rest."

"Better get her a basin, miss," said the taxi driver, "Don't want no accidents."

Darina fled inside and fetched a large stainless steel bowl, covered it with a clean tea towel and thrust it at the hapless girl. "Are you sure you wouldn't like me to call a doctor? No? Well, let us know if you need anything."

The taxi drew away from the kerb and Darina went back to organise delivery of all the food they had prepared.

As she entered the small hall, chattering women came down the stairs followed by Eve, "Remember, back by two o'clock sharp," she called as they disappeared out of the door. "Two hours to get lost shopping, I wonder if I should cut down the lunch period but they do like their Oxford Street binges," she said. "How've you got on this morning, darling?"

"I'm just about to get the van out, does your secretary have the keys? Oh, and I've sent Claire home in a taxi, she seems to be all in."

"Silly girl probably should have stayed at home, those gastric 'flu attacks can really knock you out."

"Eve," called Jackie from her office, "I've got Mrs. Thompson on the phone, can you do a dinner for twelve tonight?"

"At this short notice? Really!" Eve moved quickly down the stairs and went to take the telephone, Darina following.

"Mrs. Thompson, how nice to hear from you. Your husband's done what? Really, aren't men *thoughtless.* Well, as long as you can manage with something not too complicated, we are so rushed at the moment, business is just pouring in, but as you're such an old customer, suppose we say a foie gras salade tiède, breast of chicken stuffed with crab and ginger plus mousseline of carrot in spinach leaves and pommes dauphinois, a cheese board, of course, with home made oat cakes, and how about finishing with three sorbets in tulip cases garnished with fresh fruits?" She finished by mentioning a price per head that had Darina reeling. If this was what Eve was charging, her own clients had been getting a bargain.

Eve severed the connection then started to dial another number, her eyes dancing with delight, "Well, that's a nice little commission. Darina, darling, you can handle that, can't you? Jackie will order the food and you can pick it up on your way back from delivering lunch. Ah, Joshua Tarrant, please," her fingers drummed a soundless tune on the table as she waited to be connected, then she tucked her hand under her armpit as she held the telephone a little closer to her ear.

Her voice changed, became softer, "Josh? It's me. Can you do me a big favour? You know I've got that invitation to discuss the local radio spot tonight? Well, Marina Thompson has just rung with a marvellous order, Clive is apparently bringing some colleagues home to discuss a hush-hush takeover. There'll be twelve of them. The business is great but, the thing is, Darina will need someone to help serve. You couldn't do your buttle act, could you, darling? No, Claire isn't well enough, we've just had to send her home, Jo's not back yet and you know how hopeless Emily is, she can't pass a vegetable dish without spilling the contents over the most important guest and I don't want to send Darina off with one of the irregulars, she'll have enough to cope with without checking their every move. I can trust you, you do it all so well. Yes, I must go, you know how important this spot could be, all London listens to that station. It's only just this one night, please, darling?"

There was a long pause whilst Eve looked into space, her arm pressed across her almost non-existent breasts, holding the tension inside her body. Then her eyelids dropped and she smiled into the receiver, "Oh, thank you, darling, I'll tell Darina, she'll be *so* relieved."

She gave an address then replaced the receiver. "That's all settled, Joshua will meet you at the Thompsons', darling, he's an ace butler, the two of you can manage the evening standing on your heads. Here are the keys to the van, you'd better get your skates on if that food's to be delivered on time. Tell Emily to bring me a herb tea and then start preparing my afternoon demo. Jackie, leave those envelopes and come through, I must deal with some letters."

Darina picked up the keys and went off to load up the van. "Helping Eve out" had begun to assume formidable proportions.

Joshua Tarrant replaced the receiver on a desk whose computer terminal was almost obscured by piles of paper. Bloody Eve! As usual getting everyone else to run her business for her. O.K., so the radio spot could be important but she didn't seem to consider that his research was equally important. She had been keen enough on the advance he had got for the book, now the delivery deadline was here and it still wasn't finished. Why couldn't she have got one of her free-lance butlers? But he knew why, because she would never pay someone if she could get him free. So why did he agree?

Because he could not resist that note in her voice. Despite everything, she could still turn him on in a way that— He stopped his thoughts abruptly and picked up a Ministry of Agriculture press release that after three readings still defied clear understanding of the government's position vis-à-vis rape production and the Meligethes beetle. There was a story down in the murk there somewhere; he considered possible contacts. There were a number of botanical specialists who would be delighted to advise the serious press's leading agricultural correspondent. Then there was that unexpectedly intelligent chap he had met at the National Farmer's Union do the other day, didn't he say he grew rape? Joshua got out his personal organiser and flipped through its notes section.

Then he dropped it back on his desk and sat staring at the telephone, resisting the urge to make an entirely different call.

A hand slipped over his shoulder and pressed it gently, coral tipped fingers caressing the hard muscle beneath soft cotton. "Do I interrupt genius at work or would a hungry hack like a quick lunch?"

"Why not?" He gave Elizabeth Chesney a quick smile and rose, picking up his jacket from the back of the chair. Together they left the busy office, now slowing down for the lunchtime break with a general exodus towards the few pubs the somewhat desolate setting of the new office offered.

They were an attractive couple, the man in his early thirties, medium height, with a strong face, beaky nose and eagle-yellow eyes, the somewhat craggy effect softened by luxuriant hair of a warm, russet brown. His companion was about the same height with an equally strong face; dark eyes set wide apart above well chiselled cheek bones, straight nose and generously curved mouth. Dark hair hung loose and waving to her shoulders. But the effect was handsome rather than beautiful, the mouth was compressed, lines etched either side, the nose a little sharp and the eyes had a hard gaze that missed nothing. When she stood in the daylight outside, her age looked closer to forty than thirty.

Joshua put a glass of beer and a whisky on the small table they had found and looked at his companion inspecting the inside of the wholewheat bread sandwiches she had bought. "Why you bother so much about the purity of your food and allow Eve to talk you into drinking herbal tea whilst consuming so much of this stuff," he pushed the whisky towards her, "I will never work out."

"Nonsense, it's a pure, natural product, much better for you than that synthetic beer you drink or liver rotting gin. And whilst we're on the subject of food that's good for you, are you going to that salmonella press conference this afternoon? I thought we might share a taxi." Elizabeth drank a generous measure of the spirit.

"Can't, I haven't got my story together yet for tomorrow and I thought I'd leave food poisoning to you, you're always saying it's the food editor who should write such stories, not the agricultural correspondent. You might pick me up a press pack, though, just as well to know the latest wool they're trying to pull over our eyes, it is being given by some chicken breeders' association, isn't it?"

"Thank God they're not giving us lunch."

"Which reminds me, you didn't suffer at all after Sunday's do, did you?"

"Only from making a pig of myself, I shall have to have one of my detoxification weekends soon. Eve really is a marvellous cook, I quite understand how she managed to seduce you away from me." The comment was only slightly arch and there was hardly a pause before she continued, "Why, there's no suggestion we had salmonella infected poultry, is there? I thought it was grouse, not chicken."

"Claire's been quite ill. Eve thinks it's gastric 'flu but I just wondered if it could have been something in the meal."

"Most unlikely if she was the only one affected. Unless a totally new food bug has metamorphosed, you never know these days. The government still needs to take much stricter measures over food production. They don't look closely enough at the food chain. You really ought to come to this conference, you know." She drank some more whisky then chuckled, losing her intensity, "But I'm preaching to the converted, fancy me trying to tell the author of *Danger Down on the Farm* he should find out the current state of salmonella poisoning in chickens. How's your new book coming along?"

Joshua grimaced, "The answer, if you're really interested, is not very well. I never seem to have time to finish the research and there are some vital areas I need much more information on. Any news on sales of your latest?"

"The publisher's delighted, according to my agent. I never thought Turkish food would be that popular but apparently everyone thinks it's going to go like hot baklava. Tell me, darling, just how well is Eve's little business doing?"

Joshua's laugh had a slightly hollow ring, " 'Little business' indeed. I don't suppose ICI has a more complicated infrastructure. Eve's chief problem, as I keep telling her, is that she is grossly understaffed. Now that they've got the cookery courses so well launched, they really ought to take on someone else to assist Jo on the catering side. How she copes so well I can't imagine, the only backup they've got is a series of none too reliable part-time girls: look at the state they're in at the moment with her up north and Claire ill. If Eve hadn't run into that girl, Davina or Darina whatever her name is, I don't know how she'd be managing. As it is, she's had to get me to help on an unexpected booking for this evening."

"Ah, now I understand. You're always bad tempered when Eve's managed to get you to do something you don't want to. You should just learn to say 'no' to her." Elizabeth gazed at her empty whisky glass, her eyes rueful, "Not that I'm one to talk. I agreed on Sunday to a free demonstration."

"Free?"

"Apparently they never pay demonstrators pushing books. The publicity, Eve says, is payment enough, that and the opportunity to sell copies. That's why I asked how the business is doing. I don't want to seem mean, I'm perfectly prepared to help her out, but if she's rolling in money, I don't see why I shouldn't get a fair wage. It's a lot of work putting on a demonstration, plus I have to catch up on my page afterwards. Still, I expect I'll sell quite a lot of books. People always love to get them autographed. And the profit will be mine. But Turkish food to her ladies—does she realise it's a peasant cuisine? I thought the high class housewives who came to The Wooden Spoon were only interested in refined dishes of the Roux variety."

"Another one?" Joshua picked up their glasses.

Elizabeth looked at her watch, " 'Fraid not," she said regretfully, "If I'm to make that conference, I shall have to dash. Oh, for the good old Fleet Street days." She picked up her large bag, checked it contained her notebook, and left, waving and exchanging badinage with other colleagues on her way out.

Joshua looked moodily at the pattern of froth on his empty beer mug for several minutes, then, refusing offers of more drink from several quarters, returned to his desk.

CHAPTER FOUR

Darina's alarm clock woke her early on Wednesday morning. With a small groan, she forced herself out of bed and under a hot shower. It was disconcerting to find out how quickly she had got out of the routine of a punishing day preparing food followed by a tiring evening serving and clearing it up. Three weeks of the soft life and she felt she needed a marine's training to get back into proper shape for coping with it all.

But she had to admit it was fun as well. She had thoroughly enjoyed the previous evening. Eve's husband had proved efficient and easy to work with. "I used to earn a few pounds hiring myself out as a waiter-cum-butler in my university days," he said when she commented on his expertise as they started on the clearing up.

"Is that how you met Eve?" Darina carefully placed a pile of Coalport plates in the dishwasher.

"No, that was at a press lunch, much later. I'd had several newspaper jobs by then and begun to specialise in agriculture. I was invited to a do for a new meat substitute made from field beans and Eve had been hired to show its possibilities." He brought over a load of cut crystal and placed it beside the sink.

"You took one bite of the delicious veggie burger and fell for the cook?"

"Veggie burger? You must be joking, Eve explored possibilities no meat substitute had gone before. But the food, good though it was, had nothing to do with it. It was," he paused, absentmindedly polishing the tray he was holding, "It was remarkable, I'd never felt anything like it before; *coup de foudre,* I think the French call it. And it was the same for her. We were married two months later." His face broke into a broad grin, "My mother thought Eve must be pregnant. First she was relieved, then disappointed when it was obvious no little Tarrant was on the way."

"Would you like children?" She studied his craggy, intelligent face, wondering how he would react to becoming a father.

Joshua put down the tray, picked up a cloth and started drying glasses. "God help the child with Eve for a mother! She hardly has time to be a wife, how she'd cope with a baby is hard to imagine." He placed the clean glasses on his tray. "I'll put these back in the pantry then I'll check the drawing room and see if they want more coffee, with a bit of luck I might be able to pick up an odd detail that would let me work out which company they're planning to take over."

He vanished leaving Darina to wonder whether Clive Thompson realised his temporary butler was a journalist. Then she remembered Claire saying he'd been at the celebration lunch. But even if he hadn't recognised Joshua, he must be alive to the dangers of indiscretions in front of catering staff. Sure enough, the part time butler came back disappointed. "Not the slightest hint could I pick up, they didn't even call each other by name so I've nothing to check with our City man. Pity, we could have made ourselves a nice little sum of money."

He was very quiet for the rest of the clearing up operation. Darina wondered if he was shifting around odd snippets of conversation, trying to make an identifiable pattern. It was, she supposed, a form of detection, like upending a detail to see if it would reveal something different if looked at from another angle. But there were no clues, nothing to identify which company it was the predators they had been feeding were intending to take over. How much money would Joshua have risked if he had been able to name it? And was his concern a real need for money or just his unstoppable journalistic instinct?

In her bedroom, Darina brought her wandering mind back to the present and dressed herself quickly in a working shirt and skirt, picked up a clean overall and let herself out of the house. She indulged in the unusual extravagance of a taxi. That was another reason to sell the Chelsea house, public transport was not one of its attributes. Buses were unreliable and it was too long a walk to Sloane Square tube station, especially today when time was so important. There was a directors' lunch for twelve and the cocktail party for a hundred this evening and the way things were going, it looked as though it would be just Eve and herself to cope with it all, plus the willing but basically unskilled Emily.

"She's a dear child," Eve had said that lunchtime she'd bumped into Darina, "Wants so much to learn, so I've taken her on as a trainee. Said I wouldn't charge her if she was willing to help whilst learning, works quite well, really."

"Unpaid skivvy," was the term that came into Darina's mind but she kept the thought to herself.

Eve was already in the catering kitchen when she arrived, weighing out ingredients. She sighed with relief as Darina came in. "Thank heavens you're early, darling. Claire's just rung, she'll come in if we really need her but she still isn't feeling at all bright, I told her we ought to be able to manage. But I only hope Jo arrives before this evening, otherwise I shall have to ask you to give up your evening off, I can't supervise everyone, not for Monica.

With a jolt, Darina realised she had forgotten it was tonight she'd promised to have dinner with William.

"Did you get anything settled about the radio spot last night?" she asked as she started making pastry.

Eve's face lit up, "We got on awfully well. No promises but he said they are definitely going to think about giving me a trial spot next spring and I'm to work on some ideas for it."

Cooking steadily with few interruptions, they prepared the lunch and sent Emily off with strict delivery instructions then started in on the cocktail party menu. Plus a large casserole for afterwards. "Monica is asking about twenty close friends to stay, what she actually means is Ralph's best customers. She wants it kept simple but it's got to be good; we're doing Boeuf Bourguignonne plus a couple of puddings and a cheese board. Check the deliveries, will you, darling, that man has a nasty habit of sending firm brie."

They continued working. Neither girl stopped for lunch. Around them grew trays of canapés carefully overwrapped with cling film. Mange tout peas stuffed with cream cheese lightly seasoned with nutmeg; tiny new potatoes hollowed out and filled with caviar sprinkled with finely chopped onion; quails' eggs stuffed with a mixture of yolks, cream and a little browned and chopped hazelnut, and by the time Darina had finished this fiddly job, she never wanted to see another quail's egg again; whorls of brown bread and smoked salmon, an easy task that allowed concentration to let up a little; tiny rounds of toast topped with a rosette of pâté de foie gras glazed with aspic; minute pizzas, each topped with half a black olive, another fiddly operation they did together as an assembly line job, quickly baking them before the base could rise too much; meat balls, which Darina insisted on using her own recipe for, begged from a Swedish chum many years ago and one of her great standbys; small queen scallops wrapped in bacon; little chunks of chicken marinated in spiced yoghurt and placed on skewers ready for grilling. What was the fastidious Monica's oven situation, asked Darina, watching the number of items that needed cooking or reheating mount up.

"Monica, darling, has the most up-to-date and well equipped kitchen you can imagine. Aga plus a double Neff oven *and* two microwaves, one plain and one combi. No need for us to take supplementary cooking equipment tonight."

At last it was all ready. Emily had been despatched to Monica's to check the drink deliveries and the arrival of two barmen organised by Eve. "And ring me if *anything* has been forgotten or there is any problem whatsoever. Do not try to use that tiny peanut you call your brain, just check, recheck then check again."

Emily's cheerful face remained its sunny self. Unskilled she might be but she never seemed to sulk or resent any of Eve's barbed attacks when her skills at the lowly jobs thrown her way proved inadequate. And she produced cup after cup of tea or coffee to help keep them going, grinding the beans before making a small cafetière for Darina, no instant allowed in Eve's kitchen. Wanting to save even that small space of time in the afternoon, she asked instead for one of the herbal teas and found it unexpectedly soothing and refreshing.

Darina checked the number of silver trays piled for delivery with the canapés then asked if Eve would like her to bring the van round for loading.

"Please, darling, that'll be great. It looks as though you'll have to help this evening after all, Jo still hasn't arrived."

Darina looked at her watch, "I'd better ring William." She was surprised at how disappointed she felt at the collapse of her evening.

Both girls went to the office. "Have you heard anything from Jo?" Eve asked.

As the secretary shook her head, the telephone rang, "She's standing right beside me," she said to the caller and handed the phone to Eve, "It's Jo, right on cue."

Eve took the instrument, "Where are you? I expected you back . . ." but stopped as the phone leaped with a torrent of words, their intensity if not their sense reaching the others in the room.

"But," said Eve, "No, listen, Jo, I had no idea. No, she seemed quite all right this morning. Well, not *quite* all right of course, otherwise she'd have been here, but not seriously ill . . . Of course I would have done something if I'd thought . . . Calm yourself for heaven's sake, you're not going to do Claire any good by getting yourself into a state . . . All right, ring Joshua later and let him know what's happening . . . Of course I can't come, it's Monica's party tonight. I really need you there as well but I quite understand you won't be able to make it. We'll manage." The voice on the other end calmed down slightly and after a few more words rang off.

Eve put the phone down and stood looking at it for a moment. Then she raised her head. "Claire's apparently quite ill. Jo said she found her in a terrible state when she called in to drop off her case and change before coming on here. She rang the doctor and he's arranged an ambulance to take her to hospital. Jo's going with her. She sounded quite hysterical, accused *me* of neglecting Claire," Eve sounded outraged, "As though I would, I had no idea she was so ill. She didn't look that bad yesterday, did she, Darina? You were the one working with her." The phrase sounded accusatory.

Darina felt worried. Should she have taken Claire home? "She looked groggy but not desperate. I didn't think it was that serious. How did she sound this morning?"

"That's it, not at all bad. I mean, she even offered to come in if we really needed her, so why the collapse?"

"What did the doctor think it was?"

"Jo wasn't making any sense, by the end she was almost totally incoherent. I'll ring Joshua later and see if he's heard anything from her. I asked him if he'd help this evening but he said he had to research. That bloody book, it seems to take every moment he has. Darina, darling, you'll have to help us out a bit longer it seems. Ring your friend, I'll bring the van round."

Darina checked her diáry for the number of William's uncle and reached for the telephone. She couldn't help feeling sympathy for Joshua. Once in a week should surely be more than enough for Eve to expect him to come to her rescue. And what could be the matter with Claire? She thought of the quiet, friendly girl and hoped it was nothing too serious. But once she was in hospital, the full resources of today's medicine would surely put her right.

"Hallo, can I speak to William Pigram, please?" The pleasant voice on the other end of the 'phone said he'd fetch his nephew. As she waited, Darina tried to relax. She hoped he wouldn't think this was a put off, surely he would understand?

He not only understood, he said, "What you need is another pair of hands. Why don't I come along and help too? What do I need to look the part?"

This was a possibility that would never have occurred to Darina. "Eve's waiters wear black jackets, grey striped trousers and a grey tie. But you can't, I mean, have you ever, that is . . ."

"Relax, I've been around enough waiters and parties in my life to know what the form is. Now, what's the address?" Darina got the details from Jackie and relayed them. "O.K., I'll be there as soon as I can." She found she was holding a dead telephone and put it down slowly. William was full of surprises. What was Eve going to say?

"I've got you another recruit," she told her as they loaded trays into the van.

"Great," was Eve's only comment, "As long as he's efficient and doesn't try to touch you up during the party, we can use all the help we can get."

CHAPTER FIVE

Forty minutes later, wearing striped city trousers and a grey tie borrowed from his uncle, plus his own dinner jacket, William drew up in the road outside a handsome Highgate house. Double fronted, with a neat half circle of grass inside a sweep of drive, its heavy front door was standing open and lights illuminated every room. Seen from across the street, it looked like a superb doll's house, with antique furniture and crystal chandeliers perfect in every miniature detail, except that live people could be seen moving through the rooms, arranging bottles and glasses on long, white-clothed tables, placing ashtrays strategically and moving the odd table and chair around the large reception rooms.

William waited a few minutes, automatically taking in the scene, noting the well swept drive, the neat bushes, the pristine paint, the beautifully swagged curtains. His policeman's mind noted that here was a house with money. If this was a case, he would be asking whose. But it wasn't a case and he didn't quite know what he was doing here.

Except that he wanted to see Darina and if this was the only way, then he was perfectly prepared to dress up and perform. It had been difficult enough to cajole her into having lunch last Sunday. He'd known exactly how she would look when she opened the door to him, her smoke grey eyes wary, her square shoulders braced, a polite smile on her firmly tucked, wide mouth. What he had not been prepared for was the way her face had relaxed into a genuinely welcoming smile as he'd said hello.

The encounter had been successful beyond his wildest dreams. And there was no doubt his dreams since that extraordinary weekend at the Abbey Conference Centre had been turbulent. She had got under his skin in a way very few women had managed and he was far from inexperienced in relationships with the female sex. But he had never before met a girl who affected him like Darina. He wanted to get behind that cool façade, make contact with her mind and light the fires he was sure smouldered somewhere within that marvellous body.

A van passed his car, turned into the drive and drew up outside the open front door. Out stepped Darina and a tiny girl with a shock of fair hair. They opened the back of the van, took out a laden tray each and disappeared into the house. William got out of his car, locked it and walked up the drive.

By seven o'clock, the party was in full swing. William wrapped a napkin round a freshly opened bottle of champagne and started refilling glasses. The more experienced barmen were dealing with requests for spirits and non-alcoholic drinks. There was little demand for the latter, though, the taxi trade was doing well tonight. This was a moneyed crowd. And not old money. Passing through the rooms, deftly pouring his champagne, expertly opening more bottles and circulating again, William assessed the guests.

There was a fair sprinkling of East Enders, tough faced men in Savile Row suits, exuding confidence and camaraderie, hands displaying heavy signet rings, ties the odd diamond, their wives expensively dressed and coiffured but lacking the same air of certainty. There was a contingent from the City, their eyes tired but razor sharp, the women with silk shirts dressing up their natty suitings, all swapping horror stories of missed market rises and volatile exchanges. There was what could probably be classified as the local Highgate intellectual set, not as slick or as smart, clothes subservient to conversation, with unquenchable appetites for the trays of small eats being passed round by Eve and her team of waitresses. There was a collection of smooth mannered men and women expensively dressed in a style which could be classified as internationally acceptable that, from snippets of conversation, William decided were hoteliers and restaurateurs.

"How is the champagne going?" The hostess was at his elbow.

"Such is the generosity of the commissariat, supplies are unlikely to be exhausted much before midnight." He refilled her glass, his face a mask of polite attention, his demeanour every inch the perfect waiter.

The look she gave him nicely blended amusement with slight distance, "Keep an eye on it and let me know if midnight approaches."

William watched her move through the room, expertly shuffling guests, breaking up small groups, rescuing bored women, greeting new arrivals. She was in her early forties, on the plump side with protuberant pale blue eyes, excellent skin and a lively expression. Her dress was unobtrusively elegant, a dark blue crepe that moved beautifully suggesting a ripe promise in the body beneath. She had that air of sublime confidence only produced by breeding and background.

And what a background she had created in this house. Here expenditure had been directed by excellent taste. Not that of an interior designer's, either. There was no painfully perfect matching of decor and furnishings nor was the magnificence of many of the pieces allowed to become at all intimidating. It was a home to be enjoyed.

He fetched yet another bottle of champagne, enjoying his role of nicely calculated service without obsequiousness. But he was beginning to resent his inability to catch a glimpse of Darina. He scanned the team of girls clad in black with lace edged aprons who were passing round silver trays of canapés but none was nearly six feet tall with a fall of hair the colour of jersey cream.

He discarded his latest empty bottle and picked up a tray. Passing swiftly round a room that was just beginning to thin out, he loaded it with discarded glasses then made his way to the kitchen.

It was a scene of organised chaos with Darina orchestrating a complex dance of deep frying, reheating, supplying waitresses with freshly loaded trays of eats and receiving empty ones, an exhausted looking girl assisting her. Darina herself looked remarkably fresh, her eyes bright, her face flushed but alert, her long hair neatly held back by a triangle of white linen. Her overall was spotless.

More than anything, William would have liked to kiss the little bare patch of neck revealed as she bent over a tray of skewered chicken pieces she had removed from a wall oven. But he restrained himself, this was neither the place nor the time.

"Right, Emily, these are the last, load those trays, please." She went over to the Aga, removed a large casserole, gave it a stir, replaced it then checked an array of baked potatoes.

William put his tray down and started unloading glasses, "Looks as though they're stuck here for the night. The champagne may run out after all. I have no idea who the hostess is but she can run a mean party."

Darina ran a hand across her forehead, "You mean they're not leaving yet? We were hoping to serve supper soon."

"Supper? Good God! I hope you've enough for a small army, the ranks are thinning but not by very much."

"Relax," said Eve, entering with more dirty glasses, "I don't know how Monica manages it but the message is getting around that the closed signs are about to be put up. No," she said to two waitresses coming in for new supplies of food, "don't serve any more, you'll only confuse the signals. Start clearing the glasses instead. Though you could take a tray down to the family room, Ralph is shunting the favoured few in there. You," she looked up into William's eyes, her own wide and confiding, "have been absolutely marvellous. Are you on for the rest of the evening? If so, I can get rid of the two barmen after they've finished clearing up."

"Eve, really," protested Darina, "William's done enough."

He looked at her, her cheeks even more flushed, adrenalin pumping sparkle into the grey eyes.

"Nonsense, I'll be delighted to stay on, I'll start washing up these glasses." He was damned if he was going to be banished back to the reception rooms if Darina was anchored to the kitchen.

Eve's eyes flashed in delight, "What a sweet William. Darina, darling, you must tell me where you found this delicious man." She threw him a flirtatious glance, picked up an empty tray and disappeared.

He looked after her retreating back, "And where did you find *her?* Not your type at all, I would have thought."

"Eve and I did our training together. She runs an excellent business." William thought a slight haughtiness suited Darina, lifting her deliciously straight nose to a particularly fetching angle.

"Where the hell's Claire?" The kitchen was suddenly taken over by a large man he'd last seen chatting up a group of restaurateurs in the manner of mine host. Definitely one of the original East Enders, but the first impression of easy camaraderie had vanished. His heavy, angular face seemed carved out of some weather-beaten stone, the brown eyes were more perceptive than warm and the mouth gave nothing away. Black hair was sleeked back in a cut which only just cleared the collar of his well tailored but unexceptional suit and a large cigar seemed permanently attached to his left hand.

At first sight he was an unexpected mate for the elegant Monica, then you realised that both exuded a lust for life that was as potent as extract of civet. William wondered what his business was. There was something of the pirate, the merchant adventurer about him.

"I've been looking out for her all evening, thought she must be tucked away in the kitchen." The powerful figure stood in the doorway puffing at his cigar, his eyes darting about as though Claire might emerge from behind the fridge.

"She's ill," said Darina, piling salad into two big bowls.

The host lowered his cigar, "What's the matter with her?" There was genuine concern in his voice.

"We don't know. She had gastric 'flu, couldn't work on Monday, came in yesterday morning but had to go home at lunchtime and apparently this afternoon she just collapsed and was taken to hospital."

"Is this true, Eve?"

Claire's partner put down the tray of glasses she had just brought in. William, drying up the first batch he had washed, saw a flash of annoyance in her eyes before she said smoothly, "I'm afraid it is, Ralph. If I may, I want to ring Joshua a little later, Jo was going to let him know what the hospital said."

"Of course you can, you know that. Let me know how she is." He left the kitchen abruptly, two deep lines pulling together his bushy brows.

"I hoped neither of them would notice Claire wasn't with us," Eve sighed.

"I'm sorry," said Darina, putting the salad bowls to one side with a jar of dressing, "I didn't realise he knew her well."

"Ralph and Monica are old friends, his Covent Garden company supplies all our fruit and vegetables. They were both at my luncheon party on Sunday." She whisked out of the kitchen like an actress leaving the stage on a good exit line.

William continued washing and drying up glasses thoughtfully.

Much later he was again at the sink. Supper had gone well. He had erected two round tables, clothing them in yellow, floor length cloths. Then Eve had laid them with cutlery, plates, cut crystal glasses and blue damask napkins. Yellow and blue flower arrangements had been fetched from The Wooden Spoon van as well as gilt chairs with yellow and blue squabs. The final picture was fresh, stylish and charming. He wondered, though, if it would have taken any longer to reassemble the long, D-ended Georgian dining table he had noticed in pieces in the back passage instead of this importation of no doubt costly-to-hire additional furniture. But it was none of his business.

Then he had helped ferry the food through, admiring the large glass plates of amazingly arranged fruit salad and the rolls of apple strudel dusted with icing sugar. The other staff had departed after the rooms had been cleared and it was Eve who had helped guests serve themselves from the sideboard whilst he filled glasses with an excellent burgundy. It was an assembly of people who knew each other slightly rather than well and William admired the ease with which Monica conducted the conversation at her table, changing the subject as soon as it started to drift in the direction of contention or boredom. At the other table, Ralph ladled out dollops of bluff good fellowship but the penetrating brown eyes were everywhere and no one was allowed to dominate the talk for too long.

Once coffee had been served and the port started to circulate, Ralph indicated William could leave them. By then, he noted, the host's attention had started to wander, he sat staring abstractedly at his plate whilst an exuberant cockney who apparently ran one of London's great hotels was allowed to take over the table with a series of outrageous stories. William thankfully left him to it.

In the kitchen Darina and Eve had restored a certain order. The tiled work surfaces were piled with dirty crockery but the stacks of empty, deep trays had been returned to the van and the cooking impedimenta had been cleared away. All that remained now was to finish the washing up.

William discarded his jacket, loosened his tie and rolled up the sleeves of his silk shirt, gently moved Darina away from the sink and plunged his arms in. The trio were too tired to exchange more than the odd word. If William had felt acting as a waiter would be a good way of getting to know Darina better, the evening could be counted a failure, yet working alongside her did seem to have developed the friendship he had felt grow during Sunday's lunch. She seemed totally at ease in his company now.

Monica came into the kitchen, looking as lively as when the evening had started. "A triumph, my dear Eve, everyone said how gorgeous the food both looked and tasted. And the Boeuf Bourguignonne was the best I've ever had." William could feel Darina relax beside him. "The supper went brilliantly, in fact, Ralph is very pleased."

"Can we clear the last of the supper things?" Eve smoothed down her lacy apron, she looked very fetching in the short skirted black dress that just stopped the right side of qualifying for a French farce.

"Ralph's seeing off the last guest and the room is all yours. Have you had something to eat?"

William realised with a slight shock that he had had nothing since the sandwich his aunt had pressed into his hand before he left that afternoon. "I know what waiters have to go through, you eat that, my lad," she said. Little did she know what policemen all too often also had to go through.

"Oh, we're fine," said Eve.

Darina looked conscience stricken, "William, you must be starving."

"My dear man," Monica came forward, started looking in the dishes left over from supper, "There's plenty here, do help yourself."

"What's the position on Claire?" Ralph's bulk filled the doorway, the frown was back.

"Claire? Is something wrong, I wondered why she wasn't here?" Monica stood with a casserole lid in her hand, her pale blue eyes bulging more than usual.

"Eve says she's in hospital. She was going to ring Joshua for news."

Eve put down her drying up towel and drew her arm across her forehead. She looked deathly tired. "I rang a little while ago. She's in a coma. Jo had no news on what was wrong with her and she's still at the hospital. Joshua wanted to go there but I told him to stay at home, there can't be anything he can do."

Monica sat down with a little thump on a pine windsor chair. Ralph ground the butt of his cigar into a dirty plate then leant against a bank of polished wood cupboards; all warmth had left his face. "Tell me again when she started to feel ill and everything that happened up until she collapsed."

Eve repeated the details of Claire's illness. Darina went on drying up, carefully placing the clean glasses in a set of large boxes. William placed a last goblet on the draining board then stood quite still. There was a deep sense of foreboding in the room, he could feel tension climbing like an acrobat towards the high wire.

The man leaning against the cupboards thrust his hands deep into trouser pockets and contemplated highly polished shoes, his face set into lines of granite. As Eve finished her recital there was silence.

"What is it, Ralph?" Her voice had an unfamiliar note of softness and entreaty.

Monica looked at her husband, "Yes, darling, what are you afraid of?"

William noted the choice of words.

The big man raised his head, "It sounds horribly like Amanita phalloides poisoning," he said.

"Amanita, what?" asked Eve.

"Phalloides, the Death Cap mushroom."

There was a little gasp from Monica. "But you said on Saturday . . ." His wife didn't finish her sentence.

He looked at her sadly, "I know and from what Eve has said I don't think Claire stands much of a chance, not now."

CHAPTER SIX

Claire died at noon the following day. Darina spent the morning preparing a series of complicated dishes for a directors' lunch. Jo, she understood, was still at the hospital. But as she organised Emily into sorting out what had been brought back the previous night and got on herself with the cooking, Darina's mind was on Claire.

It had been a very silent little group that finished packing up Eve's van. William had followed them back to the Marylebone base. They'd taken everything out of the van and stacked the dishes and trays neatly in the kitchen.

"I can't stay here another minute," Eve said as the last load was brought in. Her face was drained of all colour and animation. With its mobility gone, her quirky face lost much of its appeal; the corkscrew curls now belonged to a rag doll that looked as though its stuffing was leaking away. "I don't know what Kenneth is going to do tomorrow, he's so fond of Claire." She collapsed rather than sat onto a stool.

"Who is Kenneth?" asked Darina.

"He's a photographer, you met him on Saturday, he was on that mushroom walk. He's making a series of videos featuring me and Claire on cooking vegetables. Channel Four are supposed to be interested. He's booked the kitchen theatre for some more filming tomorrow." Eve's exhausted voice stopped as though the electricity that kept her going had been turned off. Even the mention of television possibilities failed to reanimate her.

William took both girls home, brushing aside Eve's half-hearted suggestion of a taxi. She and Joshua lived in Putney in a solid, late Victorian semi-detached house with charming stucco work on its façade. She sat in the car without moving as, following her directions, it drew up in front of the paved garden. "Well, that's that, I suppose," she said finally as William levered forward the driving seat. With an effort she manoeuvred herself out of the apology for a back seat, waved a limp hand in Darina's direction and propelled herself up the path, William following.

As Eve reached the front door, she felt for her handbag, realised it wasn't hanging on her shoulder, glanced helplessly around, then rang the front door bell. Darina looked in the back, saw a bag lying on the floor, picked it up and arrived at the front door just as it was opened by Joshua.

"Oh, darling," cried Eve, with the wail of a child overcome by events and emotions she cannot understand, and fell into his arms.

Joshua held her close and buried his face in her hair. But not before Darina had seen how transformed the alert, sardonic countenance she had worked with the previous evening was. Now it was ravaged, the eyes hollow and the beginnings of a stubble giving the skin a pallid, unhealthy look.

William gently drew the door closed, shutting out the sight of the two figures locked together in a shared agony.

Whilst he drove back towards Chelsea, Darina told him what little she knew of Claire, her voice catching as she spoke. "She's one of those people you like immediately, would trust with anything. One of life's carers. She'd make the most wonderful wife and mother. To think of her lying in hospital dying in agony is unbelievable."

"I think Eve said she was in a coma," said William prosaically.

"God, you policemen, so literal! You know what I mean."

His voice softened, "Yes, and I agree, it is bloody. All because of a careless selection of wild mushrooms."

There was silence for a little as he negotiated Putney Bridge. Then he said, "I suppose it was carelessness?"

"What do you mean?" There was shock in Darina's voice and a hint of aggression.

"Just that it's odd no one else was affected. I would have thought if the mushrooms had been cooked together, the toxins would have contaminated the rest of the dish. How were they prepared, do you know?"

Darina thought back to Saturday's picnic, "Eve said she was going to sauté then dress them with a light walnut vinaigrette and serve them cold accompanied by warm chicken livers cooked in Madeira and a tiny mixed salad."

"Did she give the recipe as well?" Sarcasm edged his voice.

Darina sighed, "Everyone on the walk was interested in food and we were all dying to know what she was going to do with them. We asked and she told us, there was nothing odd about going into such detail."

William gave her an affectionate glance, "No, I suppose to you foodies, there wasn't. Well, if she does die, and we mustn't assume that just because Ralph Cox believes it she will, there will have to be an investigation and inquest."

"Inquest?"

"Sudden death," he explained patiently. "It might only be a matter of routine but it will have to be gone through."

"Claire isn't even dead yet and already you're planning the inquest," said Darina crossly, "It isn't even certain that she *has* been poisoned by a deadly mushroom, Amanita whatever it is."

"Phalloides. Didn't you see Ralph's face as Claire's symptoms were described? He was someone seeing Dante's hell opening before him. I hope for everyone's sake it was something else but I wouldn't take any bets on it."

"But are you suggesting Claire might have been deliberately poisoned?"

"Hold on, I only said it was odd no one else had been affected."

"We don't know that."

"How many were at the lunch?"

"About forty, I think. I know Monica and Ralph went and they looked fine tonight. Then there was Joshua, of course, and the photographer; if he hasn't cancelled the booking for tomorrow, he must be all right. I don't know about the rest but surely they would have rung if they were suffering from food poisoning?"

"Didn't Claire think she had gastric 'flu?"

"So someone else might think that too?"

"It's a possibility, though I think if I'd been eating wild mushrooms and got ill, I'd suspect poisoning. I'm surprised Claire didn't, she must have trusted Ralph's judgement implicitly."

"I think that's the sort of girl she is. I suppose the police will have to check on all the guests. Heavens, do you think others may be dying, too?"

"Who knows? I would think it depends on how many poisonous mushrooms were in the dish. If it was only one, maybe the toxins wouldn't spread too far and be less lethal in other portions. But if it turns out that Claire was the only one who suffered, I would think it a case that needed further investigation."

There spoke the policeman. Darina was silent for the rest of the journey. "I'm sorry," she said at last as they drew up outside her house, "You've been marvellous and it's been a dreadful evening for you."

"Not precisely what I had in mind originally but far from a total disaster. And look what Eve's given me," he reached behind his seat and flourished a bottle of champagne, "two of them in fact."

"Good heavens!"

The street lamp caught the silvery grey light of William's eyes, "I don't think she knew how to deal with my recompense and this seemed a convenient way out. It's good champagne, too, worth much more than a straight wage would have been. I wonder how carefully Ralph checked his wine returns? It hardly seems the right time to suggest opening bottles of bubbly, but I would like to see you again before I go back to Somerset on Sunday."

Darina sighed, "I'd like that too but I have no idea what the rest of the week is going to be like. It looks as though I shall have to help Eve out for rather longer than I thought. Can I ring you?"

"Of course. Come on, let's get you inside, you must be all in."

William had taken her key, opened the front door, put on the light, gave her cheek a brief kiss, said good night and left. Darina had gone to bed with questions circling around her mind. Questions about Claire, questions about poisonous mushrooms, questions about William. There were no easy answers to any of them.

The next day, Darina had to take prepared food to a directorial dining room, finish off the cooking in the excellently equipped kitchen and serve the meal. It was three o'clock by the time she returned to The Wooden Spoon. The catering kitchen was cleared up and Emily had disappeared.

Darina went to the office. Jackie's eyes were red and swollen, she was applying TippEx to a sheet of typing.

Darina sat down quickly, "Have you heard anything . . ." She couldn't continue.

Jackie gave a curious gulping noise, somewhere between a sob and a hiccup, "She's dead. Jo rang a little while ago."

"Where's Eve?"

"In the demonstration theatre with Ken." She gave another gulp and a large tear fell onto the typescript.

The theatre looked like a harvest festival. Tumbled on work surfaces were large shiny red tomatoes; golden corn on the cob, the ears unwrapped from their papery green husks, silky floss still clinging in places to ribbed rows of kernels; slim green courgettes, some sporting limp ochre-coloured flowers; enamel bright capsicums in shades of green, yellow, black and red; deep purple aubergines; orange and green gourds knobbly and indented; and onions with skins subtly streaked in Rembrandt tones of cinnamon, umber and sienna brown. On the main demonstration counter were half-prepared vegetables, in the mirror were reflected the contents of several deep pans that held various stages of ratatouille. In front of the counter stood a video camera on a tripod.

For a moment, Darina thought the theatre was empty, then, in a corner, she saw a figure sitting slumped over one of the work surfaces, head resting on folded arms. Sitting beside him, her arm over his shoulder, her face set and drawn, was Eve.

She looked across at the other girl, "You've heard?"

Darina nodded, "I'm so sorry. I came to see if there was anything I could do."

"I don't know what has to be done, I can't think straight."

The man raised a blotched face and turned himself round. "I can't believe it, I didn't even know she was ill, someone should have told me." He drew a handkerchief from his pocket and mopped his eyes.

"Ken, darling, we just thought it was 'flu." Eve sat passively on the stool beside him, weaving the fingers of her hands together in a ceaseless series of patterns.

"She seemed so well at your lunch. We laughed together. To think that was the last time I saw her, and she should have sat next to me. Why did you change the seating?" The question came out as a kind of wail.

Eve put a hand on his knee, "I'm sorry, darling, but it was Claire who suggested we swop places so I could sit by you. I think," she hesitated, ran her finger along his thigh, then laid her hand firmly on his leg. "She thought we had been quarrelling, and that this would be a good time to make things up. I told her," she glanced at Darina, "it hadn't really been a quarrel; it was just a firm exchange of opinions. Anyway, she said it would be a good idea if we sat together. And we did have fun, didn't we?"

But Kenneth seemed hardly to hear her. He was twisting the handkerchief in podgy fingers, his face screwing up and working with the effort of not breaking down again. Thinning light brown hair was drawn back in a pony tail that hung below the collar of a leather bomber jacket worn over an open necked shirt and jeans. The clothes looked expensive, as did his trainer shoes. Darina realised she did remember him from the picnic lunch. He had been one of the quieter members of the party, sitting on the outskirts of the group, occasionally picking up a small camera to take a few shots. After helping serve the food, Claire had sat herself beside him and they had exchanged remarks with the casual ease of old friends.

Eve stirred restlessly and stretched her arms out in front of her, the hands locked together, palms turned outwards, "Why don't we abandon all this, Ken? Let's go and have a drink." As she slipped down from her stool, a tall girl with short, dark curls came into the room.

"Jo, darling!" Eve ran towards her.

After the telephone conversation between the two the previous day, Darina half expected an antagonistic response but the newcomer allowed Eve to sit her down in a chair, pull up another, perch beside her and clasp both her hands. "What an appalling time you must have had. Have you slept at all, had anything to eat? Can I get you something?"

Jo shook her head. There were dark rings under her eyes and the lids were red and puffy. She looked at Eve, "Didn't anyone think it could have been mushroom poisoning? They said if only she'd had treatment as soon as the symptoms appeared, she might have pulled through."

Eve closed her eyes, "She thought it was gastric 'flu and I know how ghastly that makes you feel."

"And you trusted Ralph?" There was a slight sneer in the newcomer's voice.

"You know how many times he's run these walks, what an expert he is. I can't think he'd make such a mistake. And he couldn't believe anyone would just have picked a mushroom without having it checked. I wish you'd heard him."

Jo leaned back in her chair and closed her eyes, "I did, when I rang him from the hospital. I wanted him to be the first to know he'd killed Claire."

Eve gasped, "Jo, you didn't say that!"

"Oh yes, she did." Ralph had entered the room unnoticed and stood quietly by a crate of vegetables marked Cox's Choice. Monica was with him, her pekinese face drawn, her only make-up powder and lipstick.

"We had to come," she said, "I can't tell you how upset we are."

"It's true, then?" asked Ralph, "She died of Amanita phalloides poisoning?"

Jo turned her pale face towards him, animosity had drained out of her, her voice was expressionless. "When I told the doctor she'd eaten wild mushrooms, he said her symptoms were classic. They're doing all sorts of tests but they seem convinced that's what it was."

Monica clutched her husband's arm, some of her poise had rubbed away. Strain strengthened the angles of Ralph's face, when he spoke, his voice was harsh, the cockney accent stronger than usual, "None of the fungi I passed were poisonous and I didn't see another Amanita phalloides after the one I destroyed. It's not that difficult to spot. Remember how I pointed out the sac at the bottom of the stem, the whitish gills and greenish yellow cap? Jesus Christ, I've been dealing with mushrooms most of my life, I just don't make that sort of mistake."

Jo opened her mouth, then closed it again as though it was too much effort to say anything further.

The door behind Monica and Ralph opened and in came Joshua and a striking woman with dark, shoulder length hair.

"Elizabeth and I have been at a Ministry of Agriculture briefing. Jackie's told us the news." His face, too, was strained, his eyes tired. Of them all, Elizabeth was the only one who looked as though she'd had a good night's sleep. Of them all, she looked the least touched by the tragic events. Her face was grave but her eyes were bright, keen, watchful.

Joshua turned to Jo and placed a hand on her shoulder and Darina watched a slight shudder run through the seated figure. "You must be all in. Is there anything we can do? What's happening to," he swallowed hard, "I mean, is the hospital, that is . . ."

"I rang her parents last night, they're at the hospital now but her body won't be released for burial until after a post mortem and an inquest."

"Inquest?" The sharp query came from Monica but each of them looked stunned.

"William said there would have to be one if she died," said Darina without thinking.

"William?" Eve's tone was puzzled and a little sharp, "What does he know about it?"

"He's a detective in the C.I.D."

CHAPTER SEVEN

"That new waiter you had with you last night was called William," said Monica slowly. When nobody said anything she went on, "May I ask what you think you were doing bringing the police into my house, uninvited?" Her voice was glacial, her poise bang back in place.

Eve looked terrified.

"We were supposed to be going out, but then I had to work and he offered to help." As Monica continued to look at her with icy eyes, Darina added, "Even detectives are allowed a private life."

Monica started to say something else but Ralph tightened the grasp of his arm around her, his big hand digging into the flesh of her upper arm, "Careful, my sweet, you are beginning to sound as though we have something to hide."

"How do you come to know a detective?" Eve's voice cracked slightly then her eyes widened, "Oh, I remember now, wasn't your cousin murdered and weren't you suspected of killing him?" The enormous sapphire chips managed to grow even rounder, "Was he part of the investigation?"

"It all sounds quite impossibly romantic," drawled Elizabeth, her narrowed eyes appearing not to notice Darina's involuntary shiver.

Joshua looked around, "I don't know about anybody else, but I could do with a drink. Why don't we sit down. Eve, what can you produce?"

She opened a cupboard in a corner of the room, revealing several bottles. Darina put on the kettle, "Just in case anyone would prefer a cup of tea," she said, feeling a strong disinclination herself to start drinking halfway through the afternoon. She was the only one.

It was a curious party, if that word could be applied to the assembly, sitting on upright chairs around the empty space in front of the demonstration counter, the video camera abandoned on the edge of their circle like some technological detritus. Eve, Elizabeth and Joshua were drinking whisky, Monica gin, Ken Campari and soda whilst Jo and Ralph had brandy. Darina tried not to feel too conscious of her cup of tea. Joshua's move had been successful in lancing the tension; with the production of alcohol the atmosphere had relaxed.

"What people don't seem to understand," Ralph said, "is how dangerous nature can be. We make no end of a fuss about farming with chemicals and talk a hell of a lot of baloney about how good 'natural' foods are for us. You see products marked only Natural Ingredients, Natural Additives, Natural Colourings. Coal tar is a 'natural' ingredient, so is cocaine, so is arsenic."

"Honestly, Ralph, you do distort an argument," protested Eve, "When we talk about 'natural' ingredients, we mean healthy products, growing naturally without artificial aids, unrefined."

"Amanita phalloides grows naturally without artificial aids, as you put it, and as for refining, what is it you do here? Talk about the torture of food." He glanced round the highly organised room. "No, basic education is what is needed. Take your country cottage, Eve my dear, where you go to 'get back to nature,' " his voice was scornful. "You talk of gathering 'nature's bounty' from the hedgerow. Have you any real idea what grows in your hedgerows? You pick nettles for a salad, make a few hips and haws into jelly and imagine you're into healthy living. If you're not careful, you could be dead within a few days. Have you noticed the hemlock growing within a few feet of your front door? Try making an infusion of that. Have you thought of making a nice salad with spring growths of bracken? I don't recommend it. Or what about . . ."

"Stop!" Eve put her hands over her ears, "I don't want to hear any more."

"I think that's enough, Ralph," said Monica, "We all know you're an expert and I don't think this is the right time."

"It's exactly the right time," his voice was savage, "Yes, I am an expert, I *do* know the country and what grows there and I did *not* allow Amanita phalloides to join the mushrooms we gathered on Saturday."

There was silence.

"Then," said Elizabeth slowly, "You are saying that . . ."

"I'm saying that someone thought they would do a little extra gathering and got criminally careless. Damn it, I made the dangers of uneducated selection quite plain enough."

"Carelessness, you think that's what it was?" Joshua's voice had an edge so rough it was barely recognisable, "Claire's lost her life through carelessness?"

"What else could it be?" asked Eve.

"It's unthinkable anyone would have *tried* to kill her," cried Kenneth.

So someone had at last put into words what had been hovering behind the conversation. Or, wondered Darina, had it only been her, watching the participants with the care of a centre court seat holder at Wimbledon, who had felt it was a possibility to be considered?

"Kill Claire?" Jo turned to him, astonishment all over her face, exhaustion stripping softness from the strong bone structure. "I can't think of anyone who would want to kill *Claire.*" She had taken very little part in the discussion so far, had sat slumped in her chair after tossing off the glass of brandy. Now she had been jerked out of her lethargy.

"*Did* anyone pick mushrooms without letting Ralph vet them?" she glared round at the little assembly.

They glanced at each other uncomfortably, heads were shaken, nobody spoke. Then Eve said, "Darina, you didn't take any back with you?"

She felt they were looking at her as at a last hope. Almost for a moment she wondered if by any chance she *had* picked the odd fungi to add to the brimming basket she'd taken back with the remains of the picnic.

"Only those Ralph had sorted out, the ones you wanted to cook that evening. I wouldn't have a clue which to pick and which to leave." Darina firmly dispelled any lingering hope they might have that they could place the blame on her.

"Is there a good book on how to identify mushrooms, that tells you which are edible and which poisonous?" a thoughtful-looking Elizabeth asked Ralph.

"A number, the best are by Roger Phillips, with excellent photographs. There's one over there," he nodded towards a bookshelf that held a collection of hardbacks. "But I wouldn't recommend anyone using a book as sole guide. Find an expert to go out with and learn from him."

Elizabeth studied the books then picked out a small volume, "Can I borrow this for a day or so, Eve? Thanks, now I must fly, I still have my page to finish for tomorrow. Joshua, are you coming back to the paper?"

He stood up, " 'Fraid so, have to write up a story on that MAFF conference. You working tonight, darling?"

Eve nodded, "I've got Monica's charity demo for next Tuesday to organise. I must get the recipes sorted out this evening so Jackie can type them up tomorrow."

"What about the Goldman dinner?" asked Jo sharply, "The one I asked you to quote for just before I left. Wasn't that for tonight?"

Eve laughed, it sounded a little forced, "Oh, they were quite hopeless, wanted the world for the price of Rutland. I told them to look elsewhere. But I tied up the Wethered press lunch for tomorrow, will you be able to help with that? Otherwise, even with Darina, I shall have to call in someone else."

"I'll be there." Jo dropped the matter of the lost contract and stood up. "If I don't get to bed soon, I'll drop where I stand. See you tomorrow." Her abrupt manner seemed to be accepted as normal by the others. But Darina noticed that the hand placing the empty brandy glass on the demo counter trembled and her eyes held a blankness that went beyond sheer exhaustion.

"Will you be all right?" Darina asked her. "Can I get you a taxi?"

"No!" Jo cut off the cry as soon as it came out, "Thank you, I'm O.K." Without another word she stalked out of the room.

Monica looked worried, "Do you think she should go back to that flat alone? You know how devoted she was to Claire."

"Jo will be all right, she's as tough as old beans." Eve walked over to the collection of half-prepared vegetables. "Ken, my darling, do you want to do any more work on these today? What's your schedule?"

The photographer had sat on his stool throughout the conversation with his head bowed, his arms resting on his thighs, his hands hanging limply between his legs. He looked at Eve with eyes full of misery, "I couldn't work today, not after . . ." His voice failed, then, with a visible effort, he pulled himself together. "What's happening tomorrow? I might be able to try then."

Eve considered for a moment, "I don't see why not, nobody's booked the theatre, we're not doing a course and I can probably get Brenda or someone to help with the press lunch. I'll ring her now. Monica, darling, thank you so much for coming round, you are an angel. Do hope you were pleased with how things went last night."

It was as though, Darina told William later that evening, she was a society hostess speeding parting guests. Within five minutes the room was clear of everyone but her and Darina, who was instructed to wrap all the half-prepared food in cling film and store it in the fridges.

Then she rang William and said she would be free that evening. She offered to cook him a meal but he wouldn't hear of it, so they went to a little restaurant just round the corner from Darina's. It provided well cooked, cheerful food with an ambiance to match, its predominantly young clientele letting their hair down. Afterwards they went back to Darina's for coffee.

"Not that I didn't enjoy the meal," she said as she opened the front door, "but the noise was reaching pollution level."

They had avoided the subject of Claire's death over dinner, continuing instead to build those bridges into each other's lives that construct friendship. But as they drank their coffee and sipped some of the excellent brandy bequeathed to Darina by her cousin along with his house and its contents she told him about the little scene in the demonstration theatre.

"So the possibility of murder actually came up?" he commented with interest after she had finished.

"Only really as an *im*possibility," she said. "Everyone seemed to think no one would want to kill Claire. But there was something Kenneth said earlier. He said Claire had originally been placed next to him at the lunch but that Eve had actually sat there. Apparently Claire had suggested they swop places as it would be a good opportunity for Eve to clear up some sort of misunderstanding or quarrel between her and Kenneth. And Claire told me she sat next to Clive Thompson, who's a big wheel in the City and a major client of Eve's. It would make sense that Eve had planned to sit beside him herself."

"Ah," said William, "You think that maybe nobody meant to murder Claire but that somebody could have wanted to kill Eve?"

"Doesn't she seem a much more likely subject for murder?"

"And I thought she was your friend."

Darina refused to be drawn.

"You may think Claire would be an unlikely murder victim but there could be a number of different reasons why someone might want to kill her. Finance, passion, jealousy, it's not necessary for someone to be unpleasant to generate murderous intent." He sipped the brandy absent-mindedly and stretched out his legs, looking very comfortable in the deep chair. "Motive, means and opportunity are the three linchpins of murder. All right, let's suppose this death was not a terrible accident. We haven't much information on motive but the means were provided during the mushroom walk on Saturday, the opportunity by the luncheon on Sunday. That, of course, narrows the field of suspects."

"To those attending both occasions?"

"Quite so, Watson."

"Yes, given a little luck, I suppose it could have been quite simple. Eve told everyone how the wild mushrooms were going to be served. All the murderer had to do was cook a poisonous one at home, bring it to the lunch and slip it onto the right plate. Kenneth said he had expected Claire to be beside him so the places must have been labelled and Eve's plate quite easy to identify, only it was eaten by Claire." Darina sat back in her chair with the air of a conjurer revealing a flock of doves.

William smiled at her but said, "Ah, but isn't there an objection? What would you, as murderer, do if you saw the wrong victim eating your carefully doctored meal?"

Darina's face fell, "Well, I could hardly call out, 'Don't eat that, it's poisoned!' " She thought for a moment then added, "But I might try to create a diversion, shout 'fire' or something like that, and switch the plates, or knock the poisoned one to the floor."

"You would have to be a quick thinker to stop Claire eating the mush-rooms if you weren't sitting beside her. Though I think we can assume that our murderer, if in fact it is murder, is a quick thinker. It seems that a poisonous mushroom is found and described in graphic terms, a group of people is told exactly how the mushrooms that have been gathered are going to be cooked and when they will be served. The crime is conceived and action taken, all within the blink of an eye. That's thinking on one's feet."

"Perhaps it was just taken on the off chance it could be used, the murderer having no more than a vague idea it might be useful," suggested Darina.

"An opportunist, then, who might very well have been able to create some sort of diversion. But suppose nothing occurred to him, or her. Don't you think they would have made sure Claire got the right treatment as soon as the symptoms appeared?"

"Maybe the murderer wasn't at the lunch? No, that wouldn't work, otherwise how would the mushroom have got onto the right plate?"

Darina had slipped from her chair to the floor and sat with her arms wrapped round her knees, looking into the leaping flames of the gas log fire she had switched on as they came in from the chilly autumn evening. There was a little frown between her eyebrows and her whole being was concentrated on the logistics of poisoning.

There was a sigh from William as he looked at her, then he said with a dismissive finality, "There are too many question marks at the moment but the police should be able to sort things out."

Darina fiddled with the fire irons that helped the illusion of a real fire, "Would anyone mind if I asked a few questions?"

William gave another sigh, "Is anyone going to stop you? Don't imagine you're going to get very far, though. What solves murders is detailed and patient sifting of the facts, scientific analysis of the evidence. I know you've solved one murder but I think you'll find that was beginner's luck."

Darina shot him a wicked glance, "You're only piqued because I broke the case under the noses of you and that starchy inspector."

William took another sip of his brandy and looked at her thoughtfully, "I can see nothing I'm likely to say is going to persuade you finding murderers is really a task for the police. I have a strong feeling I should leave for Somerset tonight. If anyone finds out I have any connection with you, my career could be finished."

He did not look seriously worried at the prospect.

"You wouldn't object to my discussing the case with you from time to time, though, would you?" Darina's tone was as soft and seductive as pâté de foie gras.

William put down his brandy glass, leant forward and gently ran his finger down the line of her cheek and along her square jaw, resting it on the corner of her wide mouth. "I would rather talk to you of other things."

Darina flinched and jerked her head back. She was not ready for this. Then she saw the hurt in his silver grey eyes, "I'm sorry," she said and placed her hand on his, "Don't pay any attention to me. I've really enjoyed this evening."

"I can't help feeling what you really enjoy is a good discussion about murder," he said ruefully, finishing his brandy in one swift gulp and rising. "I must go."

Darina stood also, wondering how to repair the damage, knowing she was not prepared to lay her emotions open to him in the way he wanted. "Will I see you again before you return to Somerset?"

He brightened, "Will your schedule allow it? What with cooking *and* detecting?"

She smiled at him, "I'm not going to let you tease me out of looking at the situation just a little more closely. I'm hardly likely to cut across the police."

She was standing so close they could have embraced without moving, her eyes kind but wary.

He squared his shoulders, "You're not going to like what I'm going to say but I have to say it. If you do find anything out . . ."

"Tell the police," broke in Darina. She grinned at him, "No need to sing your theme song, I know it by heart. Can I ring you when I know what time I'll have free during the next few days?"

"I'll look forward to your call."

She held his gaze with her eyes for a moment then led the way out of the room. In the hall she offered her hand, "Friends?"

He held it in his, "Friends, no matter what," he said dramatically, drew it to his lips with a theatrical gesture, then picked up his trench coat and left.

Darina closed the front door behind him and stood for a moment, the smile dying out of her eyes and her mind returning to the matter of Claire's death. She went and scanned the large food and cookery library in the study, locating a book on mushrooms without much difficulty. She found an entry for Amanita phalloides and read it through. The description of its deadly effects fitted the progress of Claire's illness exactly. She studied the illustration then flipped through the other pages; to her untrained eyes the Death Cap mushroom seemed very little different from other, innocent fungi.

She put the book back and cleared away the coffee cups and brandy glasses, her mind occupied with the details of Claire's death. Something told her it was murder, that someone had deliberately added Amanita phalloides, one of the most poisonous of all mushrooms, to a starter at Eve's luncheon party. She concentrated on the factors William had discussed.

First the means. Thanks to Ralph, everyone on the walk must have been able to identify that deadly mushroom. Had another been found? What, in fact, had happened to the first one?

Next the opportunity. Exactly how had the lunch been organised, when could the murderer have added the poisonous mushroom? Had the places been labelled, would it have been easy for a guest to find out before the meal where everyone was sitting?

Most important of all, had the intended victim been Claire or Eve? Darina was sure it was the latter but why, in that case, hadn't the murderer taken steps to ensure Claire got speedy treatment? Was it possible he hadn't known about the change in the seating?

Finally, what was the motive? Why did someone want to kill Eve?

Darina suddenly stopped in the middle of stacking the dishwasher and stood poised with a coffee cup in her hand. Was Eve's life in danger? Was it a case of a sudden impulse, a golden opportunity too much to resist, or was a murderer amongst them intent on killing no matter what?

Darina slowly fitted the cup into the top rack of the dishwasher. How much did someone want Eve dead?

CHAPTER EIGHT

Next morning considerations of murder had to take second place to cooking. In the catering kitchen Darina found Jo with Emily and Brenda, a part time helper who proved to be a steady, competent worker.

Jo was a revelation. Darina had never met anyone who worked as quickly as she did. Little individual quiches appeared faster than the eye could follow; mange tout were cooked, blanched and stuffed with the speed of a bank clerk counting notes; teriyaki chicken leapt onto skewers. The only sign of the last few days' strain was slightly reddened eyes. No wonder Eve had missed her.

Darina badly wanted to talk to Jo, get to know her, but the work was too concentrated to allow general conversation. And Jo did not allow shortness of time to excuse sloppy workmanship. Crudités had to be cut precisely, smoked salmon curls for little circles of rye bread evenly rolled. By the time the team had changed into their waiting outfits, the short black dresses with lace trimmed aprons that were The Wooden Spoon's signature, the pressure level had risen to the point where even Emily's usually cheerful face was strained.

They staggered under the loads of deep trays into the Wethered Ratchet Company premises then up to the board room on the top floor. An extremely worried looking press girl showed them to a small kitchen where they could off-load their food, then followed them in and closed the door behind her.

"If anyone asks where you're from, say anything except The Wooden Spoon," she hissed. "I've been frantic all morning. Thank God I never told Sir James who we'd got to do the catering. He's so nervous about the launch, this new Rocket Ratchet means everything to him. It's quite important to us, too, it's our first national account." She peered at the trays, "At least it *looks* all right."

Jo turned to face her, "What *are* you talking about? What's wrong with our food? We have a first class reputation."

It was hardly possible for the girl to look more worried but somehow she managed it, "Oh, I know, that's why we booked you. Clemmie said "It's got to be The Wooden Spoon, they're desperately expensive but they've got *the name."* And it was all such short notice. Wethered's got wind of a competitive launch and Sir James was determined to be first on the market. Friday is *not* the day for a press do but what alternative did we have?" The rhetorical question floated on the air.

Jo's teeth could be heard grinding. Darina was sure that any moment she would grab the girl by the arms and shake the information out of her. But she remained where she was and said, "If you don't tell me immediately what is wrong, I shall take these trays away and you won't have any food for your guests."

The PR girl stared at her as though she could hardly believe her ears, then said, "Haven't you seen today's *Recorder?* With the article on how one of your partners died from food poisoning?"

Jo and Darina looked at each other and then back at the girl. "Let me see it," ordered Jo.

The other girl whisked out of the room and was back within a few minutes with the newspaper.

TOP CATERER DIES OF FOOD POISONING, ran the headline on a short story prominently featured on the front page. The copy read:

Claire Montague, 26, died yesterday after eating a dish of wild mushrooms prepared by Eve Tarrant, 28. Both were partners in The Wooden Spoon, a well known catering company much patronised by top city firms and Mayfair hostesses. The dish was served at a lunch to celebrate the firm's first year in business. See article on Page 12.

Page 12 featured a long story by Elizabeth Chesney, food and drink editor of the *Recorder,* on Saturday's mushroom walk, ending with a warning against careless gathering.

"Typical press, tell half the story, blur the facts and throw in a few inaccuracies. It isn't our first year as a catering business, we've been going three. And the headline gives quite the wrong impression." Jo turned to the press girl, "Claire's death was an accident, it had nothing to do with our food. No-one is going to suffer from eating any of this unless they overstuff themselves."

The girl looked unimpressed.

"Wait till I get hold of Elizabeth." Without asking, Jo grabbed a telephone fixed to the wall and got through to the *Recorder* offices but Elizabeth was out and so was Joshua. Then she rang Jackie and told her to make sure Eve had seen the paper.

"Can't do anything else, we might as well get on with this function," Jo replaced the receiver and switched her attention to the food that Darina, Brenda and Emily were already setting out on silver trays.

By the time it was all over and they had returned to Marylebone, Eve was round at the *Recorder* offices, waiting for Elizabeth to return. Kenneth had gone back to his studio to edit some film. And three cancellations for next week had been received.

"Nobody said it was because of the article," Jackie said tearfully, "They all said they had to cancel due to 'unexpected circumstances.' "

"Do you think you should get on to a lawyer?" Darina asked Jo.

"That would only cost us a packet to be told there's nothing we can do. We can't dispute the facts. Come on, let's go and clear up."

Within a remarkably short time the kitchen was pristine with all equipment put away. "That's it," Jo said, wiping down the sink, "You can all go now." As Brenda and Emily left, she added the dish cloth she'd just used to the load of dirty tea towels in the kitchen's washing machine and turned it on. She stood by the gurgling appliance with her sense of purpose visibly draining away.

"Let's get out of here and go and have a cup of tea," suggested Darina.

Jo looked at her as if seeing her for the first time. Then, as though she had made up her mind about something, she said, "We should really start preparing for tomorrow's wedding but I'm finished. If we come in early, we'll manage. Let's go to my place."

In the little parking area she led the way to a rather battered cream estate car and drove competently through the busy London streets to Hammersmith, her route winding round under the carriageway that carried the remorseless press of vehicles out of London. Suddenly they were in a calm backwater. Jo switched off the engine. A small terrace of houses faced an oasis of green. As Darina got out of the car, the smell of the river drifted across. Behind her she could hear the ceaseless roar of the traffic but here all seemed quiet.

Jo locked the car, "Nice, isn't it?" She led the way to one of the houses and got out a key. "I found it a few years ago, couldn't possibly afford it today."

They climbed a flight of stairs to a door opened by another key, then entered a small hall. Jo shrugged off her jacket and hung it carefully in a cupboard with Darina's trench coat.

Darina followed her through the main room to a small kitchen. White cupboards and work surfaces gave a spacious feel; bright yellow food containers and notice board added a cheerful note as did a vase of large plastic daisies that should have been straight kitsch but instead were charming.

Jo put on the kettle, took a white porcelain teapot with a cane handle, warmed it, added tea from a caddy marked Earl Grey, found two mugs decorated with yellow flowers and placed it all on a white tray, looked at Darina and asked, "Milk or lemon?"

Darina declined either and they went back into the living room. It was decorated in the same spare, sparkling style as the kitchen. There was a white leather sofa, a couple of modern chairs of pale wood and slung canvas, a low coffee table of the same pale wood, nicely polished, and a wall unit to match which held a television set, a small hi-fi and a large collection of cookery books. In one corner was a round dining table with four chairs. On the wall were a couple of modern posters for art exhibitions, framed in chrome. The only touch that conjured up Claire was a low bowl on the dining table filled with an arrangement of dried flowers, their delicate, glowing colours and fragile stems contrasting with and setting off the stark lines of the other furnishings.

Jo placed the tea tray on the low table, poured pale gold liquid into the mugs and gave one to Darina.

Darina sipped her tea, wondering how to open the conversation. Jo was the one person connected with The Wooden Spoon who could not have picked the poisonous mushroom nor added it to Claire's plate that Sunday luncheon. Jo ran the catering side of The Wooden Spoon. She and Claire had shared a flat. She could easily hold some of the keys to the murder puzzle.

Jo sat back in her chair with a long sigh, bringing blue veined lids down over slightly slanting eyes. The mug of tea was held between her long, shapely hands as though they were cold. Still strained and tired but with the edge of exhaustion gone, her face was more relaxed than on the previous day and Darina could appreciate its fine sculpture, the high cheekbones, strong jaw line and straight nose. Short brown curls showed off a well shaped head but tailored trousers now covered the excellent legs revealed by the short black waitress uniform earlier in the day. An attractively patterned sweat shirt rose and fell, betraying a series of deep breaths.

Darina waited and after a few moments Jo opened her eyes and took a long sip of her tea. "That's good," her voice was slightly accented with the flattened vowels of the north.

"It's been a hell of a time for you, what with your father dying and then coming back to find Claire," said Darina sympathetically.

"You're right about Claire but the only regret over my father was that it didn't happen years ago." Jo looked into her mug and Darina said nothing. "I thought my mother would be glad to be shot of the bastard. I hardly expected singing and dancing but at least I thought she'd be relieved. Do you know she actually cried?" The hazel eyes looked bewildered, "All those years of hell and she actually *cried* because he was dead.

Perhaps it was the shock of realising she was free at last. I wanted to stay longer but when I heard about Claire it seemed I was needed more back here."

"What'll happen now?"

"God knows! That article this morning may be a nine day's wonder or it may close us. That bitch, Elizabeth, she's never forgiven Eve for taking Joshua away from her."

"She was engaged to him?"

Jo snorted, "Since when is anyone engaged these days? As far as I know, it was an office romance that would have fizzled out anyway. She's years older than him. He'd have been looking for younger meat quite soon even if Eve hadn't come along."

"Were you working with her then?"

"No, I was running a restaurant with a chum in the home counties. We were doing very well until she decided to chuck it all and get married, but we'd built up the business and it sold at a good price. I invested my share in this. I needed some roots no one could take away."

Darina glanced round again at the modern, cheerful room. It had been put together with commitment and style. She remembered Jo's cooking, it showed as much flair for presentation as Eve's.

"How did you get involved with The Wooden Spoon?"

"They advertised for help, I took the job as a stop gap, I really wanted to get more restaurant experience but I needed a steady income to arrange the mortgage and then, I don't know, somehow I stayed. Partly it was the relief of working with other committed women, not having to battle to prove my competence in a man's world."

"You obviously all got on, I suppose it was natural for you and Claire to share together."

Jo looked at her, then said, "That was another thing that started as something temporary, her flat broke up and she needed somewhere in a hurry. I suggested she move into the second bedroom here until she found something else. So often you want to get away from the people you work with, at the end of a long day the last thing you want is to take it all home with you. But Claire was such a," her voice caught and she drew a hand rapidly down her face, dragging the skin under her eyes, "a restful person. It seemed so . . . *natural* to come home together." She put her mug down then got up as if unable to continue sitting still. She strode to the window and stood looking out over the river. Darina quietly helped herself to more tea.

After a moment, without turning, Jo spoke again, "I don't think I can bear it if the company collapses as well."

"Surely you'll be able to ride out this bit of bad publicity?" Darina asked a little curiously. "People forget very quickly, and not everyone can be stupid enough to think your food could be suspect if someone dies from mushroom poisoning."

"Want to bet?" Jo turned round. Exhaustion had reclaimed her like a policeman an escaped criminal. "It's not as though they can't find someone else, there's so much competition around these days. Well, they can hardly cancel the wedding tomorrow."

"Where is it?"

"Wimbledon, one of those large houses off the Common, finger buffet for a hundred at one P.M." As she spoke, Jo seemed to recover some of her lost energy, her shoulders came back and animation returned to her eyes.

"Are we serving tea as well?" Darina was wondering what the possibilities were for making a date with William for the evening.

"Yes but only éclairs, nothing else. We should be finished by about five o'clock, thank heavens. Not one of those interminable events with a disco in the evening. Though the way things are going, it's a pity, we could have done with the extra business."

Jo came and sat down again and poured herself more tea. "I wonder if Eve has managed to get hold of Elizabeth yet. Not that there's much she can do when she does, the damage has been done."

"What you need is an early night," advised Darina, "You must be all in. Things won't look quite so bad in the morning."

"I'm tougher than you think, but you're probably right." She hesitated then said, "The worst thing is getting used to this place without Claire. I can't believe she'll never come through that door again." It was as though she had to force herself to look at the chairs and the sofa, the table, the walls, the very air, knowing the other girl would never sit on the supple leather, never arrange another bowl of flowers, never sip another cup of tea. Never, the word hung inexorably above the coffee table.

Darina looked at Jo, wondering if she ought to stay. As though Jo had read her thoughts, she lifted her head and said, "Really, you don't have to worry about me. I shall have a quick scrambled egg and fall into bed. I'll be back on the job at crack of dawn tomorrow. See you then?"

Darina nodded and got up.

Jo followed her to the door and retrieved her coat then said, slightly awkwardly, "Thanks for coming back with me. It helped, coming in with someone else, you know?"

CHAPTER NINE

Darina started walking towards Hammersmith underground station, wondering what her next move should be. After a little thought she decided that returning to The Wooden Spoon would be a good idea. It was not quite 5:00 and Eve might very well be back.

But when she walked into the office, she found Elizabeth Chesney standing in front of the secretary's desk.

"I'm sorry," Jackie was saying, "I haven't heard from her since she went to the *Recorder* just before lunch. If she's not there now, I don't know where she is. I wish I did, I want her to check these recipes for Mrs. Cox's demonstration on Tuesday. I'll try her home if you like." She nodded a greeting towards Darina as she picked up the telephone and Elizabeth turned to see who had come in.

"Hi, do *you* know where Eve is?" asked the reporter.

Darina shook her head and they both waited whilst Jackie dialled. A machine answered. Jackie left a message asking Eve to ring the office then she replaced the receiver and covered her typewriter. "I'm sorry, I've got to get home now, I'm late as it is. If Eve comes back or rings in while you're here," she looked at Darina, "ask her to check the recipes on her desk and give her these messages," she nodded towards a little pile of white slips. "No good news, I'm afraid."

"More cancellations?"

Jackie nodded. She seemed to have made some attempt at dressing to suit the occasion. A fluffy mauve jumper topped a dark brown skirt and her tights were black. The mouse brown hair was tied back with black ribbon. Her face was pale and heavy eyed. "The 'phone's never stopped ringing. It's either been a cancellation or people wondering if the newspaper report was true." She turned reproachful eyes on Elizabeth, "You might have thought what that article would do to us."

"The front page story was nothing to do with me, that was the News Editor, I had no idea he was going to pick it up like that," Elizabeth protested.

It sounded far too ingenuous for an experienced reporter but Darina said nothing, she had no intention of antagonising this possible suspect.

"Do you want to wait a little?" she asked, "I'm sure Eve wouldn't mind if we used her office, would she?" She turned towards Jackie.

"Course not," the secretary said, taking her coat off a stand in the corner of the room. "Help yourself to a drink, Eve keeps a bottle of whisky and a couple of glasses in her bottom drawer, or there's a whole load of booze in the demo theatre."

"Whisky will do me," said Elizabeth, following Darina into the next office. She plonked herself down in the comfortable chair in front of Eve's desk and stretched out a pair of elegant legs, leaning back and running both hands through her shoulder length hair, lifting it away from the nape, then letting it fall and stretching her arms straight above her head in a gesture that lifted her breasts against the wool jersey of her dress. It was topped by a heavy knitted jacket that fell away from her body as she stretched. Both dress and jacket were in a vibrant red that did good things for her colouring.

Darina sat in Eve's chair and opened first one and then the other of the bottom drawers of the desk, finding the whisky in the second. She lifted out the bottle and the glasses. "Water?" she asked as she poured a good slug into each. Elizabeth shook her head and reached for her drink.

"Eve and I did each other a good turn, I introduced her to whisky and she made me try herbal tea and health foods. Oh, that's good." She took a long swallow then looked at Darina. "What you must think," she said ruefully, "I can't imagine. First Claire dying, now that story. I can only say in my defence, I thought I was protecting the public, not putting the knife into poor Eve."

Could she really be that innocent? Darina wondered. "Do you think Claire's death was an accident?" she asked.

Elizabeth ran a finger round the edge of her whisky glass. "Ralph was very certain he couldn't have let a Death Cap mushroom slip through."

"What happened on the walk exactly?"

"My article is a pretty accurate description."

Darina tried to remember the story she had read that morning, then saw a copy of the paper sitting in the middle of the desk. She picked it up, turned to Elizabeth's page and slowly started to reread the article.

HOW DEATH LIES AMONGST WOODLAND TREASURE

Last Saturday I took part in a mushroom hunt. It was a perfect autumn day. The sun shone, the trees bore the last remnants of blazing beauty, the ground was thick with fallen leaves, their russet and golden tones dried to a rich umber. We walked spread out through the undergrowth, shuffling the leaves, releasing the smell of dark earth, laughing and shouting to each other, a merry band. We knew little about wild mushrooms but had been promised a rare treat, a treasure hunt that would yield a feast. We little realised that death was lying in wait for one of us.

The hunt was led by Ralph Cox, a noted mycologist who has spent a lifetime studying fungi. He explained how carefully we had to look for mushrooms. How they hide under leaves, by the side of paths, on the trunks of fallen trees, or on growing ones, amongst the roots or in long grass. It seems they hate to display themselves, they are shy and need searching for.

We spread out, some walking in twos and threes, some alone. In the peace of the woods there was little sound beyond that of nature, the song of birds, the odd whirring cry of a disturbed pheasant, the crack of dry branches breaking underfoot. In that sun-dappled quiet it was possible to imagine oneself back in time without industrial pollutants or modern pressures.

Then would come the excited cry of a successful hunter and we would rush to see what had been discovered, scrabbling in the leaves to see if more examples were lurking near the same spot, picking fungi in generous handfuls. They came in all colours and shapes, from cream through gold, apricot, differing shades of brown, varying tones of green, grey and yellow, to dark woody tints and purple black.

I found Wood Blewit *(Lepista nuda)* under a pile of dead leaves, looking not unlike an ordinary field mushroom but with a mauvish flush. Almost amethyst was a fungi known as the Deceiver, because it varies so much in appearance. According to our expert it was edible but hardly worth picking.

The difficulty of mushroom identification became apparent when shouts heralded the discovery of the highly prized Chanterelle, an apricot coloured mushroom with a dip in the middle of its cap. Alas, our specimen proved to be *Hygrophoropsis aurantiaca,* known as the False Chanterelle because it so much resembles the much better flavoured real specimen. Not poisonous but it can cause hallucinations.

Fungi we thought looked sinister were, we were assured, highly prized, like the Green Cracked Russula *(Russula virescens),* rare and well flavoured. And great was the excitement when one of our number discovered some Horn of Plenty *(Craterellus cornicupoides).* Their funnel shaped black caps are greatly sought by those fungi connoisseurs, the French.

At midday we ate an al fresco lunch and Ralph Cox went through the baskets of specimens we had collected and sorted them out.

Many of the fungi we found were discarded as inedible through lack

of flavour, bitterness or heat rather than as poisonous. But some could
cause mild stomach upsets and warnings were given that a few could
lead to serious poisoning.

Some possibly innocent specimens were discarded because of too
great a similarity to inedible mushrooms. Anything our expert was at
all doubtful about was thrown out.

Ralph Cox had no doubts, though, over a mushroom he found just
before lunch. At first sight it looked not too dissimilar to some edible
specimens, then Mr. Cox pointed out the greenish tint to its cap, its
white gills and a little round sac out of which the stem grew. These are
the signs of Amanita phalloides, the Death Cap mushroom, so deadly
only half a cap has been known to kill. Mr. Cox scrunched it underfoot
after making sure we could all recognise it.

At the end of the day we had collected several baskets of edible
mushrooms, including a large crop of the Oyster Mushroom *(Pleurotus
ostreatus)*, found on some dead tree trunks, remnants of the great 1987
storm. The haul was divided amongst the hunters. There was to be a
celebratory luncheon party next day for the first anniversary of Eve
Tarrant's The Wooden Spoon cookery and catering firm. She was to
produce a dish of wild mushrooms as the first course and those of us
present lucky enough to be invited contributed our share of the day's
spoils.

Now it seems that, despite all Ralph Cox's care, a Death Cap was
included in the collection after all and Claire Montague, a partner in
The Wooden Spoon and present at the lunch, died yesterday of Amanita phalloides poisoning.

Eve's dish was delicious but I think that will be the last mushroom
hunt I take part in. I shall choose to buy my wild mushrooms from
accredited sources. We are told we ignore the rich treasure trove of
edible fungi lying free in our woods for all to pick. My message is we
plunder it at our peril.

Darina finished reading the story and looked up at the journalist, who
was nursing an empty glass with an ironical gleam in her eye.

"Is that an unfair description?" she asked.

"No, it seems reasonable. It's the front page story that's so damaging.
Though I don't suppose Ralph is too happy with the way your article
implies he could have let a poisonous mushroom through."

Elizabeth sighed, "No doubt there's a message from him waiting for
me at the office. But I have to tell things like they are and we only have
his word he's so infallible." She didn't seem too distressed at the pros-

pect of having to deal with Ralph Cox but Darina would not have liked to incur his displeasure. He struck her as a powerful man in every way.

"You say here he destroyed the Death Cap that was found on your walk?"

"Ground it under his size twelve shoes. No beetle is safe when he's about and you couldn't have done much with that fungi after he'd trodden on it."

"And no one claimed to have found another during the day?"

Elizabeth shook her head.

"Would you have recognised one if you had seen it?"

"I think so. He made such a point of its characteristics."

Darina looked at the illustration that accompanied the article. Even with the *Recorder*'s excellent photographic reproduction, in black and white it looked even more innocuous than it had in the mushroom book she'd looked at the previous night. No dramatic spots on its cap. But the base of the stem grew out of a distinctive sac like a small, round purse that lacked a drawstring.

"Do you remember if anyone in particular walked on their own during the afternoon?"

Elizabeth's eyes widened, "Are you trying your hand at a little detection? How about another of those whiskies whilst we join forces and see if we can solve the case?" She held out her glass and watched whilst Darina poured out another hefty slug.

"You see I have, in fact, been giving this matter some thought since yesterday. It struck me, and no doubt you, as strange none of the rest of us suffered from any adverse effects. I don't know much about poisonous fungi but I do know mushrooms exude a lot of juices when cooked. I can't see any way for toxins from one not to have contaminated others in the pan."

Darina remembered that Elizabeth Chesney was the author of several cookery books.

"So it seemed to me much more probable the poisonous specimen was cooked separately and added to a particular plate, right?"

Darina nodded slowly, watching her. The woman was as relaxed as a sleepy cat but very definitely wide awake.

"So I've been through that mushroom walk in my mind's eye again and again but I can neither remember anyone pocketing a mushroom nor disappearing on their own." She drank from her glass. When she started speaking again, it was not so much to Darina as herself.

"There were about thirty of us. Well, you know that, you came and gave us lunch. There were some who knew each other well, some who came in couples and a few who came alone. But we all seemed to get on

well and there was a lot of shuffling around. One moment you were
walking on your own, the next you would find something and a whole
group would be crowding around. Then after the mushrooms had been
picked, the pack would separate out again and you'd find yourself going
on with someone else or in a group of three or four."

"What sort of wood was it? I only saw that clearing."

"Quite large, mostly beech I think, and we got very strung out at
various times. There was undergrowth but it wasn't particularly dense, it
would have been hard for anyone to hide if they'd wanted to."

"Did anyone want to?"

Elizabeth shot her a glance that seemed pure mischief. "It seemed to
me Eve wouldn't have minded getting lost with Ralph."

"Really?"

"Haven't you noticed that look she gives him every now and then? The
one that promises rare delights if he cares to dip into her treasure chest?"

"What about Joshua?" Darina remembered Jo's comment, was this
wishful thinking on Elizabeth's part?

"Oh, theirs seems to be a typical modern marriage, when the chemistry wears thin, the participants start looking elsewhere for gratification."

Was Joshua looking in her direction again?

"And you think Eve was looking at Ralph. Was he returning her interest?"

Elizabeth gave a slow smile, "Can you see him resisting such an invitation?"

"What about Monica?" Darina brought to mind the cool, sophisticated
woman. She hardly seemed the type to sit back and allow another female
to ensnare her husband.

"Ah, Monica. One never knows with Monica. So self-contained, so
careful of her image, so fond of her designer clothes, beautiful home and
designer children."

"Children?" There'd been no sign of them the other night.

"Nearly grown up now, the girl's at finishing school in Switzerland,
the boy's travelling abroad before Cambridge next year. If you haven't
heard all about them yet, you will. I met them once, as charming and
well bred as herself. One wonders exactly how she found herself married
to such a rough diamond."

Darina looked at the attractive woman in the chair opposite, such a
keen observer of life with a journalist's memory for facts and the ability to
sum up any situation rapidly and graphically. Had she really not noticed
anything more during that mushroom walk?

"Have you any theories on a possible murderer?"

Elizabeth shook her head gently, "You won't draw me on that one. If it was murder, I have no doubt passion was at the bottom of it, it usually is."

"Have you been married yourself? You seem to have a pretty cynical view of the state."

"How many happy, truly happy, marriages do you know? But, yes, I was married. When I was a young reporter in Bristol I thought the world well lost for a teacher of English who could describe my beauty in the words of quite twenty or so poets. Then Fleet Street made me an unrefusable offer. Go, said my husband. A love such as ours could survive a few years' absence. He'd write the book that was going to make his reputation, we'd renew our passion at weekends and eventually make a life together again. Would you expect such an arrangement to last? God, was I naive. I had to spend as many weekends working as I could with him in Bristol and it wasn't six months before he met a young widow who was dying to lavish her home-making skills on someone, anyone, no matter that he shouldn't have been available." The ironic note had vanished, across a gap of what Darina reckoned must be some fifteen years or more came muted but real anguish.

"And you never met anyone else?"

Elizabeth made an impatient gesture, "What do you think, life without men is a martini without gin. But one learns to love them and leave them. The man who is as exciting as my career or who wouldn't be bored to tears with me within six minutes if I gave up work, or who could stand me for twelve if I continued as a journalist doesn't exist." She reached across and picked up the newspaper, glancing at her article. "Not one of my best efforts but a powerful warning, I hope, of the dangers that can lurk in natural surroundings. We are so battered with information on the dangers of modern civilisation, on additives, on pesticides, on preservatives, we tend to forget raw nature is not always benign."

So Ralph had at least one convert. Darina wondered if she was being unfair, perhaps Elizabeth had thought this way before his verbal lashing the previous evening.

The reporter looked at her watch, "I can't wait for Eve any longer, I've still got work to do back at the office."

"You really are dedicated, aren't you? Haven't you found someone in the same line who could share both parts of your life?"

A very old fashioned look came across the desk, "Been talking to someone, have we? Our embryonic detective has heard all about Joshua and me? Don't pussy foot around, dear, come out with it. Am I still hankering after him?"

"Well?" Darina returned her look squarely.

"None of your business, dear, and what it could possibly have to do with Claire's death in any case, I can't imagine. Aren't you becoming just a little prurient, all these questions about who's interested in whom, what's happening in which marriage?" With that she rose, placed her empty glass on the desk, picked up her big square bag and left the office with the unhurried ease of a stalking tiger.

For a moment Darina sat looking after her, wondering whether to feel embarrassed or angry. Then she laughed. There was something refreshingly straightforward about Elizabeth. Had they met under other circumstances, they might have been good friends. Now she felt she had been warned off.

Darina looked at her watch, it was after 6:00. Was Eve coming back? If not, how was she to lock up? She got up to go and look for some keys, then turned back as the telephone rang. It was Eve.

"Darling, I'm so glad you're there. I'm exhausted!"

"Where are you? You've just missed Elizabeth, she came round to see you."

"*Did* she? Well, she can wait, I'll catch up with her later. I'm at home, the police have been here most of the afternoon."

"Jackie tried there, she got the answering phone."

"I put it on so we wouldn't be disturbed. What did she want?"

Darina told her about the recipe sheets and the cancellations.

There was a short silence, then Eve said, "Darling, could you bear to bring them round here? I really should check those recipes tonight, the rest of the weekend's going to be so hectic, and I ought to find out what our future looks like."

Darina felt torn. She'd thought of calling William and suggesting they have a meal together, on the other hand, this was a perfect opportunity to inspect the scene of the fatal lunch. And maybe discover what Eve had told the police.

"Of course. I'll pick up my car and be with you in about an hour. What do I do about locking up the shop?"

She found the spare set of keys kept in Jackie's top drawer and followed Eve's instructions on setting the alarm. Then she walked to Wigmore Street and found a taxi. This was getting too much of a habit, she thought as she gave the Chelsea address.

CHAPTER TEN

The phone was ringing as Darina let herself into her house. It was William.

"Can you come to dinner tomorrow, my uncle and aunt are having some friends round?"

Darina was taken aback, she'd hardly expected to be asked to meet William's relations. "What time? I don't suppose we'll be back from a wedding in Wimbledon until at least six, maybe not until seven."

"That's all right, it's eight for eight-thirty. Black tie, I'm afraid, though."

The last thing Darina wanted after a hard day was a formal dinner party making polite conversation to a whole group of strangers, including William's uncle and aunt.

"Will it cheer you up if I say that two of the guests are Monica and Ralph Cox?"

"They're friends of your aunt?" Somehow, without meeting them, Darina had formed the impression William's relations were not the sort of people who'd be friendly with the nouveau riche Coxes, then thought that was hardly fair to Monica.

"Aunt Honor and Monica Cox serve on charity committees together, I get the feeling they aren't exactly bosom pals but Honor has a healthy respect for her fund raising abilities. Anyway, they're coming tomorrow and I thought you'd like the opportunity of meeting them away from The Wooden Spoon."

"It was your suggestion I be included then?" Darina asked a little stiffly, wondering what the unknown Aunt Honor thought about this addition to her no doubt carefully designed dinner table.

"Relax, she suggested it. She knew I wanted to see you and they thought it would be nice to meet you. And she had a couple fall out."

Ah, the most pressing of reasons to get one's nephew to ask a girl friend round.

"Wonderful, I look forward to it. What's the address?"

"I'll come and collect you. In fact, I'll pick you up at The Wooden Spoon, drive you home so you can change, then bring you on here. No, I insist, you'll be too tired to drive or find a cab and I haven't anything else to do. I'll be there at six, just in case you're back early, with a book to fill in time if I have to wait." He rang off before Darina could protest further.

She went to find the keys of her car feeling cared for, nay, cherished. An unusual state. When you're nearly six feet tall, people tend to assume you are fully capable of managing almost anything for yourself.

Eve opened the door almost as soon as the bell sounded. She was dressed in tight fitting jeans and a skinny sweat shirt emblazoned with the name of some pop group. Her legs made a stick insect look shapely and there seemed no curves to impede the fall of the jersey over her chest. Her tumultuous curls were drawn back and tied in a waterfall of a pony tail and her big eyes, anxious and brilliantly blue, swamped her pointed face. The total effect was of a teenager on the edge of nervous hysteria.

"Darling, thank God you've come. I don't think I could have stood being alone here for a moment longer."

She led the way along a narrow hall, through a door under the stairs and down to a large kitchen in the basement, startling in its brightness. It was furnished as a family room but there was nothing cosy about it. A counter in steel and white tiles divided off the kitchen area. The efficient looking equipment was rigorously stripped of any incidentals, the steel of the cupboards and white of the working surfaces only disturbed by one bright red bowl filled with yellow porcelain apples, carefully positioned under a spotlight.

The floor throughout was white ceramic tiling with a black fleck. Against a wall of the living portion of the room was a matt black metal unit, its shelves pierced with round holes. It held a large collection of pristine cookery books and some elegant white china bowls of eccentric shape. The centre of the floor space was occupied by a round table, its top of heavy glass, its lower half a glittering collection of chrome supports rising from a bulbous base like lily stems. It was surrounded by eight sinuous sided chrome chairs with seats and backs covered in black suede. In the centre of the table was a tall, cylindrical glass vase sprouting a number of white chrysanthemums. On the wall opposite the shelving unit was an armless black suede sofa. Two small glass tables flanked it with a black uplighter shining through each. Another shone through the leaves of a huge cheese plant sited beside the patio window that occupied most of the end wall. A recessed ceiling light made a dramatic statement of the flowers on the main table. Above the sofa was a huge still life of a fishmonger's stall, almost repellent in its verisimilitude.

Eve went into the kitchen half and put on an electric kettle.

"Tea? Or something stronger?"

"Tea's fine, thanks."

Darina leant against the counter and watched the other girl reach into one of the cupboards above the kettle and bring out a box of her herbal teas and a couple of mugs. The kitchen area was well designed, lighting shone where it was needed and no expense had been spared in its equipment. In addition to a gleaming black Aga, there was a double oven, the latest model of one of the most expensive makes. A six ring steel hob had two rings electric, the rest gas; on one side of it was a charcoal grill, on the other a deep fryer. A hood above concealed what was no doubt a powerful extractor fan, the only clue to its presence an unobtrusive batch of switches.

Eve brought over the mugs of pale yellow tea, gave one to Darina, then headed for the sofa, where she plumped herself down with a sigh and reached for the file with the recipe sheets and telephone messages.

She ran rapidly through the slips, a deep frown etching itself between her fine eyebrows. "All people who haven't used us before. With a bit of luck we ought to keep our old customers but since we put up our prices, there aren't so many of them. It's the new business I was really counting on."

"It'll be a nine days wonder," promised Darina.

"I wonder, public fancy is so fickle. If only Ken can get that TV video series off the ground, that could enable us to hang on. The bank mightn't mind a temporary loss of cash flow if we could promise lots of exposure in the future, and TV always brings the punters in."

"How much did you get done today?"

"Hardly anything." Eve sighed. "Just as we got set up, the police rang. Then no sooner had we got back to work than Jackie brought in Elizabeth's article and I had to dash down to the *Recorder* to tackle her. But of course she was nowhere to be found. I couldn't even get hold of Joshua. I had a right set to with the editor, though." Eve grinned with the satisfaction of a small boy whose catapult has found the right target.

"Will he print a retraction?"

The frown returned. "No," she said shortly.

"How did the interview with the police go?"

"God, I don't know, they seemed to be here ages."

"What did they want to know?"

"Oh, everything. How we'd picked the mushrooms, what I'd done with them, how they were cooked and served. And all about the lunch. They took me over the whole thing again and again. I was just about at screaming point by the time they'd finished." She shifted restlessly on the sofa, sipped her tea, ran a hand through the bunched tangle of her curls then picked at a small mark on the suede. "It was as if, as if they suspected *me* of deliberately poisoning poor Claire."

"Much more likely that they were keeping a completely open mind about every possibility."

"As it is, I don't know how we're going to manage without her, never mind about all this awful publicity."

"What did you tell them about the lunch?" Darina wondered if Eve would be reluctant to repeat her account yet again but she seemed positively eager for a sympathetic audience.

She ran through everything. How she'd brought back the mushrooms on Saturday evening and cooked them immediately. "I sliced and sautéed them in olive oil. They released so much juice, I drained it off then finished them in a little more oil. Then I tossed them in the vinaigrette and left them overnight."

Darina wondered if draining off all the juices had meant the toxins from a poisonous mushroom wouldn't affect the rest of the dish, then dismissed the thought. A mushroom that poisonous would be bound to affect others it was cooked with, even if only at a less potent level.

"Where did you all eat?"

"We had one table down here and two upstairs." Eve got up, "Come and see." She led the way upstairs and through a door at the rear of the hall.

It led into a large L-shaped room running the full length and width of the house, only the hall had been carved out. Ornate plaster work ran round the ceiling and elaborate roses decorated three ceiling light fittings. Wide doors of polished wood were folded back from a central opening that had obviously formed a feature of the original design. But the part of the room Eve had led her into must have been separate at one stage; gaps in the plaster cornice had been filled in with not quite identical copies. French windows opened out onto steps leading down to a patio. It was almost dark and impossible to judge how big the garden was but there appeared to be a lawn and a number of mature trees and shrubs screening the side walls.

Darina looked back at the room. It was furnished with a mixture of Victorian and Edwardian pieces, none outstanding but the total effect was attractive. The broad foot of the L, that part of the room overlooking the garden, was the sitting area, a chesterfield sofa and some easy chairs were grouped around a high marble fireplace. A desk and some book shelves in the part they had entered created a combination of library and study area. The other end of the room, beyond the partitioning doors, was for dining. It was furnished with a D-ended table, a set of ten chairs, a sideboard and a corner cupboard. The upper, glazed half of this displayed an assortment of glasses and decanters. Another, matching, fireplace was on the same wall as the first. Opposite was a door leading into the hall.

"We had twelve round this table," Eve walked towards the dining area, "We were going to squash in fourteen but then Jo had to go home and someone else cancelled. I brought in one of the round tables we used the other night at Monica's and put it there." She indicated the study area, "We moved all the furniture back and there was plenty of room for another twelve. And a larger top on the table downstairs meant we could fit fourteen round that."

Darina looked from one end of the room to the other and felt excitement begin to build. She thought she could see how it just might have been possible the poisoner never realised two of the original place settings had been switched.

"Where did you and Claire sit?"

Her friend pointed towards the book cases, "I sat about there and Claire was downstairs."

"In each other's places?"

"Well, yes. We all changed around anyway after the main course, I wanted to mix people up."

"But you had named places for the first two courses?"

"Yes, I had these dear little cards, found them in France, and we had such fun, Claire, Jo and I, with the seating plan. We did want people to enjoy themselves." Her face crumpled, for a moment it looked as though tears were coming, then she smiled resolutely. "And it was a terrific success, they stayed for ever."

Darina went and stood with her back to the book cases and looked across to the dining area of the room. The table wasn't visible. She gradually worked her way round the edge of an imaginary table until she was back where she had started. Then she went and sat at the end of the dining room table with her back to the road. From here the other table would have been completely obscured. She moved down first one side of the table and then the other. When she'd finished, it was clear that at least two thirds of the people sitting round each table could not have seen who was at the other one. Eve watched her curiously. Darina went back to the study area.

"Do you have a copy of the seating plan?"

"The police took it away, it was only a rough scribble. Why?"

"Oh, I just wondered. Can you remember who was sitting at the dining room table?"

Eve frowned and directed a concentrated gaze towards that half of the room. "Joshua was at the head and he had Monica on his right, I remember placing her there because they always get on together. And Elizabeth was on his left, I know they see a lot of each other at work but I always feel slightly guilty about her." She shot Darina a quick sideways glance, "They had a bit of a thing going when Joshua and I first met and I think she still hankers after him a bit. I like to show I'm not jealous in any way." She smoothed an unruly curl back from her forehead. "Ralph was at the foot of the table, it's quite long and I wanted someone there who could make the party go. He had two of my best clients on either side of him. One of them rang today cancelling the Christmas party I was to do for her. I can't remember who else was on the table."

"And Ken was beside you in this part of the room," said Darina as Eve paused.

"Yes, I'd put him next to a television producer, which was another reason Claire thought it would be a good idea for us to swap places, she said I was so good at chatting up the media and I might be able to get her interested in the vegetable series. As it was, she spent the whole time talking to Joshua's political editor, who was on her other side, he's a great chum and a good client. Turned out she had just been moved from daytime TV to a news programme and wanted him for a coming edition. Typical of our luck." She sighed deeply.

"What happened when people arrived?"

Eve put her hands in the back pockets of her jeans and walked over to the fireplace. She swung back to face Darina and glanced round the room. "They came in here and we gave them champagne cocktails. I had three of the part time girls serving."

Darina imagined how the room had looked with the extra table and seating, "Must have been quite a crush for thirty-eight people."

"Oh, we were so lucky, it was another gorgeous day and they all drifted into the garden. Which was good because then everyone went to see the kitchen as well. I wanted to show it off. I got a big reduction when it was installed as I said so many people would see it. I must send the makers a little list of who was there. You never know when they might be useful again, do you?"

Darina opened the french windows and went down the steps. The evening was damp and chilly, droplets of moisture seemed to hang in the air and lay on the leaves of the evergreen shrubs that brushed against her legs on one side as she descended. A wrought iron balustrade gave support at either edge then curved prettily round as the steps reached the patio. At the other end of the paving was a shorter flight of steps down to a lower terrace outside the large kitchen window. The construction work looked new.

She walked down the other steps towards the big window, then noticed a narrow path between the end of the house and the garden wall. It led to a steep flight of steps that ran up the side of the house to the front garden. At the foot of the steps, by a couple of dustbins, was a door. Darina went and tried the handle. It opened into the basement corridor just outside the kitchen door. She went back the way she had come. Eve had opened the patio window and was standing looking at the room.

"Did anyone use that side door?"

"I don't think so, apart from the girls taking out rubbish."

Darina looked back at the garden then entered the kitchen eating area. "So everyone was moving around from that room upstairs into the garden, then into here, and then back again. Did they check the place names?"

Eve followed her into the room and closed the window behind her, shutting out the chilly night air. "Oh, yes, I hadn't had time to do a proper plan and so everyone had to find where they were going to sit. And lots of people wanted to see the kitchen, we've only just finished doing all this," she gave a gesture that encompassed the entire room.

Darina tried to visualise the scene: guests wandering around the garden, coming into the kitchen, looking round the table, admiring the cooking area, going back out into the garden and up to the main room. Thirty-eight people in all. With the waitresses moving around with trays of glasses and bottles of champagne. Lots of activity. Little opportunity to add a poisonous mushroom to a particular plate. Or, she thought suddenly, perhaps quite easy to do so without drawing attention to oneself? How would she take a poisonous mushroom to a party? In a plastic bag? She tried to imagine getting it out of a pocket or handbag unobtrusively. Then thought that perhaps if one went to the loo and got it out there, it could be held in the palm of the hand. One or, at the most, two Death Cap mushrooms, sliced and sautéed, wouldn't be much to carry like that; hold the hand over the right plate, lean forward to see the place name, open the fingers and let the slices fall onto the plate. Then back to the loo to wash off any poisonous traces left on the hand.

"Exactly how did you serve the mushrooms?"

New life entered into Eve and her eyes lit up. "Oh, you would have loved it, the plates looked so pretty. There was a small pile of the wild mushrooms,"

"Not moulded in a dariole or anything?" interrupted Darina.

"No, just heaped, I wanted it all to seem quite simple. Then a little pile of tossed mixed salad in a walnut dressing balanced the mushrooms, curly endive, radicchio, lollo rosso, lamb's lettuce, the larger leaves torn quite small. And round the mushrooms were placed pieces of chicken livers that had been marinated in madeira and just briefly sautéed, you know?"

So it would not have been difficult for a little extra mushroom to have been added to a particular plate, a deft touch and it would have blended in beautifully.

Darina looked up from the table, the vision of it laid with Eve's "simple" starter fading as she focused on the kitchen area.

"What about the serving of the meal, wasn't it a little tricky having the kitchen in full view of this table?"

Eve gave a bubbling little laugh, "All it needed was proper organisation and you know how people love to see the wheels turning. We had boned and stuffed grouse, they were done in the Aga at the last minute, just needed dishing up, with pommes dauphinois, cooked in the serving dishes of course and kept hot, and mange tout. Minimum amount of dishing up needed. Then a pear Tarte Tatin and my special syllabub trifle were placed on each table for dessert after the cheese board."

"And you had the wine on the tables?"

"Right, and the vegetables were placed for guests to help themselves as well. It all went very smoothly." As anything organised by Eve would.

"All these questions, darling, are you just interested in the meal or do you really think Claire could have been deliberately poisoned?" Eve stood with her head held slightly to one side, the worried frown back between her eyebrows, her body tense, like a wild animal poised to face possible threat.

Darina ignored the question. "Did you switch the place names before the meal?"

The blue of Eve's eyes appeared even more startling as she opened them to the fullest possible extent, "No, Claire didn't suggest we switch until just before we sat down." She gave a little gasp, "Do you think, are you suggesting," she swallowed hard, "that someone could have wanted to poison *me?*"

Darina said nothing.

Eve continued to stare at her for a moment, then sank onto the sofa. A long blink rather than a closing of the eyelids shut out the piercing blue for a brief instant. Slowly the shock faded out of her face, she picked up the tea mug, realised it was empty, got up and went to the kettle, refilled and switched it on. Darina sat at the round glass table and watched her.

"You know," Eve said slowly at last, gazing at the kettle, "I was nearly run down about a week ago."

"What happened?"

"I was coming back here, quite late, after a cocktail party we'd done. I got the tube as I usually do and walked up the hill then down our road. There wasn't much traffic about but as I crossed the street, this car rushed at me. If I hadn't caught a glimpse of it out of the corner of my eye and then moved faster than I've ever moved in my life, it would have had me."

The kettle boiled, Eve made herself another mug of tea. Darina refused, herbal teas could be refreshing but she found them unsatisfying compared with a good cup of Earl Grey. She concentrated on what Eve had been saying.

"Did you see what sort of car it was?"

"Not really, it was dark and I don't know much about cars, it seemed very ordinary, I think it was light coloured and sort of large, an estate car perhaps."

"You didn't recognise it as belonging to anyone you knew?"

Eve looked thoughtful, "I didn't think about it, just that it must be some drunken driver; it was such a shock, all I could think of was getting home. But now, I wonder, do you think that could have been an attempt on my life?"

"What did Joshua say when you told him?"

"He wasn't in, there was some press do on that evening, I don't remember what, I don't think he ever told me in fact. By the time he got back I was in bed with a strong drink and almost asleep. He was full of some story or other and I never told him. By the morning, I'd almost forgotten about it."

Darina felt another surge of excitement. Could this have been an earlier attempt on Eve's life? If so, it could prove very useful in eliminating possible suspects. Then she controlled herself, as Eve had said, it might just have been a drunken driver.

"Which evening was this?"

Eve thought, sipping her tea, "Must have been last Wednesday because it was after the Beamish do."

"Were you all helping at it? You, Claire and Jo?"

"Me and Jo. It wasn't a very big party and we try to see no one has to work more than two evenings a week. It was Claire's turn to be off."

Darina thought for a moment. "What about Ken and Monica and Ralph, would they have known what you were doing that evening? Or Elizabeth?"

Eve looked shocked, "You don't think any of *them* could have been driving that car, surely?"

"I'm just working on the assumption that *if* anyone tried to kill you on Sunday, it must have been somebody present both then and at the mushroom hunt on Saturday."

"Ah," Eve was working it out, "Because they would have known what I was going to serve, you mean, and they could have picked the poisonous mushroom?" She paused. "So that would have been Ralph and Monica, Elizabeth and Ken," Eve continued.

"And Joshua," added Darina, looking at her carefully.

Eve brushed aside the suggestion as ridiculous, "For heaven's sake, *Joshua* couldn't want to kill me. We're very happy and, even if we weren't, what reason could he have for murder? I wouldn't chain him to a marriage he didn't want. He could just walk out."

"Can you think of any reason why any of the others might want to kill you?" Darina set aside the question of a possible motive for Joshua.

Eve came forward and sat on the sofa again, placed her mug on one of the low side tables and looked at Darina with astonishment. "I can't think *any* of them could want to do away with me. Oh, I know Elizabeth would like Joshua back but I can't think it's that grand a passion. Monica and Ralph are just friends of mine, there couldn't be any reason there. I know Monica thought at one stage Ralph had a bit of a thing for me but I think she's over that now, anyway she'd never treat it as that important, and as for Ken, he wouldn't harm a fly."

Darina thought of the quiet man. Still waters and all that, she wasn't prepared to dismiss the photographer from consideration without a good deal more information about him even though he had known exactly where Eve was sitting.

"No," Eve spoke with decision, "We've got this all wrong. No one could want to kill me, it's just been coincidence and a tragic accident." She paused, "You don't look at all certain," she said, doubt lacing her voice. "What do you think I should do?"

"Just be careful, if it was coincidence, no harm done, if it wasn't . . ." Darina left the sentence uncompleted. "What are you doing for the rest of the weekend?"

Eve's face was as pale as the fillets of fish in the picture behind her. "After the wedding tomorrow I'm going down to our cottage in Sussex, we usually try to get there at weekends if nothing else is on. I thought I'd go straight from Wimbledon, it could save me a couple of hours driving time."

"Anyone know you're going there?"

"I should think most of our friends assume we'll be there."

"Is Joshua going with you?"

"He'll take a train down in the morning."

From upstairs came the sound of the front door opening and Joshua's voice calling "Eve?"

She stood up and Darina caught her arm, "Don't say anything," she whispered.

"But," Eve started, then caught her breath, "surely you don't think?"

Darina said quickly, "It's better not to say anything to anyone."

Then Joshua opened the kitchen door. There was a moment's hesitation before Eve ran to him, lifting a face to his that was bright with delight, "Darling, I'm so pleased you're back, the police were here for ever."

He put an arm round her shoulders and looked enquiringly at Darina. "Nice to see you again," he said, "Not still working are you, how about a drink?"

"I've just brought Eve some stuff from The Wooden Spoon," she said, gathering up her handbag, "I must get back home."

Eve followed her to the front door, "I'm sure you must be wrong," she hissed as she opened it, "but if you think I shouldn't tell Joshua, of course I won't. After all, you must know so much about murder."

CHAPTER ELEVEN

"Monica, my dear, and Ralph, how good of you both to come."

Monica allowed Ralph to help her out of her mink coat. Whilst he handed it to the waiting maid, she greeted her hostess, kissing the air lightly beside her cheek, feeling the paper-fine skin dry and warm against hers, cool from the night air. The age-washed mauve eyes moved to look at her husband as he grasped the hand that managed to combine strength with brittleness.

"How very—*alive* you always look, Ralph, you're like a dose of the very best tonic wine." The gaiety in Lady Doubleday's voice removed any possibility of offence from the words and the warmth with which she grasped his large hand was unmistakably sincere. Yet Monica couldn't help thinking, tonic wine, British wine, undrinkable, untouchable. Then took herself to task. After all these years, hadn't she trained herself not to be that sensitive?

She walked steadily in the wake of her hostess, sensing rather than hearing her husband following behind, for all his size he walked with the delicacy of a cat.

"Geoffrey, here are the Coxes."

"How nice to see you both, now have you met Jane and Henry Bryant? And Fiona and James Black? Ah, of course you already know each other. What can I get you to drink?"

Whilst her host busied himself at the drinks table, Monica gave her attention to the men, admiring the way James Black neatly stemmed Henry Bryant's mournful tale of the latest City bankruptcy he had the honour to handle as a leading receiver, then sighed inwardly as the barrister started a long-winded story of his own. If the rumour that he was seeking a safe seat at the next election was true, Fiona should tell him that though politicians could usually be relied on to hog any conversation, the successful ones were a great deal more entertaining. At this rate he would never make Attorney General let alone Prime Minister.

Her head at an attentive angle, the model of the perfect listener, Monica watched her husband charming both rabbit-toothed Jane Bryant, the most tenacious chaser of charity advertising in London, and Fiona

Black, a blonde bombshell who was their front line when it came to inviting the famous and influential to lend their names to functions. The days when she had had to coach and rehearse Ralph in how to behave were long gone. And, to be fair, he had not required much training. His charm, as potent to others as to herself, had nothing to do with public school manners or knowing which knife and fork to use.

Some auto pilot on the periphery of her attention registered that the barrister had made a joke. She smiled. "Tell me," she said, "what does it feel like to be a judge?"

"Dear lady, I have not aspired so high!"

"Come, James, you know it's only a matter of time, don't tell me you haven't thought about what it's like up there, handing out judgements from your seat set above all others. Will you really feel like God?"

Did he look slightly uncomfortable? Had she underestimated his self-esteem? No, his momentary unease gone, James was regaling her with stories of judges he had known and would no doubt one day emulate.

The door opened to admit more guests.

"Ah, my dears, you've managed it," the hostess moved across to greet the newcomers and Monica realised with astonishment they were that new girl Eve had working for her and the policeman who had acted as a waiter for her party. A moment later she was being introduced to Geoffrey's nephew, William Pigram, and his friend, Darina Lisle.

Well, she had thought him unusually presentable the other evening, no wonder. And the girl looked by no means out of place. Not nearly so obvious as Eve. How Ralph could be taken in by such meretricious glitter, she failed to understand. But there was nothing flashy about this girl. Pity she was so tall, but that pale gold hair was unusual and most attractive. Hidden the other evening, it was now swept into a glossy chignon that flattered her long neck. Her features were good, those grey eyes very direct. Figure a bit on the heavy side but with that height she could carry it off. And the loose fitting black dress she was wearing minimised her size. Monica eyed it more closely. A 1930s Chanel, unless she was mistaken. She wondered if it had been picked up at a local market or inherited from some relation. The girl certainly had unexpected style.

"William," said James Black, "it's years since we last met, what's your current posting?"

The tall young man shook the barrister's hand and nodded to Monica, showing no surprise at meeting her, "I left the Foreign Office some time ago, James. Had a go at the city and then joined the police force. I'm with the Somerset C.I.D., a lowly detective sergeant."

"So the future ambassador hopes to be Commissioner of Police instead, eh?" The barrister was jovial but clearly puzzled.

He got a cheerful grin in response, "Far too busy chasing minor crimi-
nals to worry about that sort of thing. How's the future Prime Minister?"

The summons to dinner saved Monica's companion from working out
an answer that was informative without being hopelessly self-confident.

The food was good without the flair The Wooden Spoon provided so
expensively and the meal unfolded pleasantly, the conversation civilised
and topical.

It was one of those houses that still separated the women from the men
when the port appeared. "I'm sorry," Honor said to Darina as she led her
female guests upstairs, "I've tried to wean Geoffrey off it but he says he's
too old to be taught new tricks. Now, there's one bathroom here and
another through here."

Monica sat in front of the dressing table and repaired her lipstick.
"Darling, where did you get that divine dress," asked the barrister's wife.
"You look such a sylph in it."

Monica's hand applied the fresh colour steadily whilst she gave her the
name of a new young designer thinking it would be a miracle if Fiona
went to anyone but Valentino.

"Not that I can buy a single thing more before next season, James has
absolutely put his foot down. Does Ralph ever threaten you, darling?"
The slim figure in its tight sheath with the breathtaking sequins sat on the
dressing stool beside Monica and drew a tiny brush through her cloud of
shoulder length blonde hair.

Monica smiled, "We have a joint account."

"A joint account!" Fiona sighed deliciously, "I don't know I could ever
trust myself with access to *that,* but then, you both trust each other over
everything, don't you, darling?"

"Everything? What are you getting at, Fiona?" Monica brought it out
abruptly, tired of playing games, tired of the pussycat purr, the sharp
scratching of kittenish claws.

The little brush was wielded more vigorously. "Nothing, darling, just
that I saw gorgeous Ralph and that catering girl you always use, what's
her name, Eve something or other, at lunch the other week, looking just
so friendly and I thought how trusting it was of you to let such a delicious
man play with such dangerous goods."

Monica turned to face her and saw that Eve's friend had come out of
the bathroom and was standing by the bed trying to look as though she
hadn't heard. "Come off it, Fiona," she said wearily, "You know as well
as I husbands have to have their little dates, it doesn't mean anything.
When the day comes I have to monitor Ralph's every move, I'll leave
home."

Fiona renewed her lipstick, "Brave words, darling," she murmured

and worked her lips together, smoothing out the colour, "Do make sure
you clear out the joint account first."

She replaced the gilt case in her evening bag, swung round on the stool
and addressed the tall girl examining a sampler hanging above the bed-
side table, "And where did you meet that divine William, my dear? We
all envy you, you know."

Monica was interested to note the girl almost blushed but recovered
quickly. "In Somerset," she said calmly, "my mother lives there."

"And you work in London? Or are you here for the weekend?"

"Darina is working with Eve," put in Monica, watching Fiona with
interest.

"How fascinating, all that delicious food. Are you a cook, too, or do
you waitress?" The voice was like cream.

Darina sat down on the bed, she appeared unconscious of anything but
genuine interest, "I am a cook, I'm helping Eve out. She's short handed
at the moment."

"Oh, I forgot," Fiona lifted a hand to her mouth, "Eve's just had that
terribly unfortunate tragedy, hasn't she? Jane," she called to the rabbit-
toothed woman who'd come in from the bathroom across the corridor,
"did you read that one of The Wooden Spoon's partners died of food
poisoning?"

"It was from eating a poisonous mushroom, actually," murmured
Darina.

Monica tensed herself for Fiona's next comment. After only the slightest of pauses she swivelled towards her and said, "Why, of course, wasn't
the mushroom gathered on one of Ralph's walks? How dreadful, does he
hold himself responsible?"

Not for the first time, Monica wondered how Fiona managed to ingra-
tiate herself so successfully with the powerful and influential. It surely
couldn't only be with her she was so incredibly bitchy? When they had
first met, she had found her attractive, fun, even witty. Then as she fought
to keep her temper and watched Fiona's mouth form a little moue of
distaste, light suddenly broke with the warmth and clarity of an equato-
rial dawn.

"No, he doesn't make mistakes like that, the mushroom was added by
somebody who didn't have it checked." She could sense Darina's interest
had sharpened, that she was looking at her quite intently but she didn't
care. Ralph had refused the invitation this whore in a loving wife's cloak
had at some stage offered and her heart did the sort of dance she thought
had been long forgotten.

Darina was asking her a question, "Where did your husband learn
about mushrooms?"

"He used to visit an uncle in Germany, his mother was half German. They're mad on wild mushrooms there, they have a mycologist in town halls during the season who will check whatever you gather. He made friends with one and used to go on his hunts. Now he must be the leading expert in England."

"Do you often go with him on these walks?"

Why was the girl so interested? Monica could feel tension flexing its tentacles round her intestines. "Sometimes and sometimes not, it depends what else is going on. I'm not the expert Ralph is, if that's what you mean. I could probably be sure enough of the very common ones but that's all. I couldn't even swear to identify the Death Cap that poor Claire ate."

Jane gave a quick shudder, "Thank heavens Honor didn't give us fungi tonight, I would be feeling quite ill."

"Have you met Lord and Lady Doubleday before?" asked Fiona in her purring voice.

"No," said Darina quietly.

"Such a lovely couple, they belong to the old school and Geoffrey's *so* fond of William. They had such high hopes for him." Just as though the poor boy had fallen from grace, thought Monica. One would not, of course, want the police in one's house generally and she could not say she would be pleased to find her daughter, Caroline, interested in him no matter how well connected he was, but there was no reason why a career in the force should mean becoming a social outcast. And Fiona had managed to make it sound as though Darina was responsible for his fall.

"I think being a policeman's fascinating." Now Jane was trying too hard to redress the balance and sounding quite gushing. "Don't you, Honor?"

Their hostess had reentered the bedroom, "Coffee's ready in the drawing room," she said, "What was that you were saying, Jane dear? Ah yes, the police. Geoffrey and I admire William very much for choosing to make a career with them. And he seems to be doing very well. But you know all about that, Darina my dear, don't you? Though it must have been such a wretched ordeal for you, that murder investigation, do you mind talking about it?"

Clever, thought Monica as the conversation now turned on the murder of Darina's cousin as the women returned to the drawing room. Quite brought her into the circle, though destroyed the nice impression she had given of meeting William socially. Then she grew thoughtful as it became clear that Darina had done more than a little detective work herself during the case. Indeed it seemed, however much she might disclaim any such matter, that she had caught the murderer.* Which did not say a great deal for young William's abilities, though Darina appeared to have greater respect for his qualities than those of his inspector. But then, in the immortal words of Mandy Rice Davies, she would, wouldn't she?

Honor offered Monica a cup of coffee, "It's so lucky I was able to get you both tonight, I know how booked up you are on Saturdays. Poor Ralph has to be at Covent Garden at some unearthly hour each morning," she said to the others, "so they hardly ever go out during the week."

"Really?" murmured Fiona, "Surely I saw you at the Beamishes last Wednesday, and didn't you go on afterwards?"

"I did but Ralph went home quite early," Monica said sharply.

"So nice to be trusted out on one's own," came sotto voce from Fiona. Monica refrained from pointing out the number of times she'd seen Fiona squired around town by other men whilst James was studying briefs.

"You must get wonderful fresh vegetables," Darina said to her.

Monica laughed, "It's one of the joys of Ralph's work, so much nicer now than when we first got married, then we seemed to exist solely on tired cabbage and bruised apples."

"How did you manage to meet?" Jane asked in innocent bewilderment.

Monica repressed a sigh. How had a nice girl like her, so well brought up, so nicely connected, managed to find an East End cockney lad and marry him? It was a question she was well used to answering.

What fun it had all been in those days. The men she had had running around her, the games they played. There had seemed all the time in the world, so many men to meet, to flirt with. And flirt she had, with any man, provided he was attractive. Even the barrow boy in Soho where she bought her fruit and vegetables. And when he asked her for a date, she had laughingly refused but in such a way he asked again, and then again. And finally she accepted. He had such laughing eyes, such zest for life, and what harm could it do? Such fun to go slumming for an evening, what a story it was going to make, it would enhance her reputation as a girl game for anything.

He said he would pick her up. And had arrived at her flat driving a Jag and wearing the smoothest of tailoring, a little flash in style maybe but excellent cloth. He took her to Chez Solange. He had offered Quaglino's but she said she was bored with Quag's. Had he known she had not wanted to risk meeting friends there? All right to tell them about him after the event, something else to be actually seen dining with a cockney. But the food at the French restaurant had been so good, he chose the best

* See *A Deepe Coffyn,* Doubleday, 1990.

wines and then paid the bill with as little fuss as though they were in the
Lyons Corner House she had expected. It was all much too exciting not
to say yes to another evening. And then another, and another. And then
he said he could not keep on taking her out like that and when she
offered to take him, he had laughed and said it was not the money, he
was exhausted from only having a couple of hours sleep so many nights.

There had been an excellent solution to that problem, not that he got
much more sleep. And the rest of her boyfriends began to seem anaemic
and life itself dull without Ralph. So she took him home and faced the
music. It had taken a little time to convince her parents he was a son-in-
law with a future. But who was it who helped them after Daddy's disastrous investment programme in the seventies? Who paid for Mummy to
have that operation privately and now supported them in a comfortable
retirement home? It was a long time since they had regretted she had not
chosen one of the well bred young men who had chased her round
London and the home counties.

Jane and Fiona were laughing at her barrow boy story. Darina was
smiling but looking thoughtful. An interesting girl. There was nothing to
Eve beyond food but this cook would seem to have a certain amount of
grey matter. Would it be wise to cultivate her?

The men came in, laughing also at some story of Ralph's. He was
smoking a cigar and looking relaxed. She caught his eye and knew they
were all right for another half hour or so. She had quickly learned to read
the look that said she must plead his incredible schedule and get them
gracefully away without further delay. Sometimes she wondered if he
really had to be up at such an ungodly hour still. But he was convinced
his empire would disintegrate if he did not keep a close watch on deliveries and sales and perhaps he was right.

She watched him seat himself beside Darina whilst the other men went
to a small alcove where Geoffrey kept his collection of political cartoons.
He engaged the tall blonde girl in conversation with his full panoply of
charm. Monica asked herself if she should be worried. But there was no
coquetry on the girl's part, she was asking him about exotic fruits with
every appearance of genuine interest.

"Ralph supplies my favourite restaurant, just down the King's Road,"
said their hostess.

"They were my first regular customers," he smiled at Honor. "When I
got their order, I knew I was on my way. No more barrows for me."

"You weren't still selling in Soho then, surely?" asked Jane in surprise.

"Ran a chain of barrows and how do you know the way the goods are
going if you're not in there as well?"

"Do you miss it?" That was Darina, watching him with interested eyes.

"Yeah, in some ways. The contact with customers, chatting up the regulars, making them feel they're getting that little bit extra."

"Whilst you're charging them that little bit extra," Fiona, of course.

"Any fool can sell over the top once, it takes quality to get them coming back. You know that, don't you?" he said to Darina.

She smiled at him but didn't say anything. It was Fiona who came back with, "Oh, The Wooden Spoon's food looks wonderful but does it really *taste* so much better than anyone else's? I mean, Monica, why do you keep going back to them? Surely it's because they've just got a name as the smartest outfit in town? Question is, will they manage to keep it after this debacle?"

Monica could sense rather than see Ralph tense.

"Surely it won't affect their business that much?" she said quickly.

"Well, I'd think twice before hiring a company with a reputation for food poisoning no matter if it was an accident. What about Tuesday's demonstration, Monica? Are you going ahead with that?"

"Of course," she said quickly before Ralph could intervene, "it's a sellout and it's going to be a first class event. Eve's a brilliant demonstrator and she's going to bring along knives and equipment to sell, ten percent going to the cause."

"And which one will it be this time?" The other men had finished examining Geoffrey's cartoons and joined the circle round the coffee table. Henry, Jane's husband, sat himself down beside Monica and included Fiona in his question. "I sometimes wish I could send some of my young chaps to do a bit of training with you ladies, the way you get money out of the rest of us." Monica allowed Fiona to develop the conversation and watched Ralph out of the corner of her eye.

William Pigram had joined him and Darina. The detective perched on the arm of the sofa and stretched his own along its back behind Darina. Monica couldn't catch what they were talking about but it seemed a relaxed group. She wondered just what sort of relationship existed between the two tall young people. They made a good couple. The girl was laughing at something William had said and the light in his eyes gave Monica a jolt uncomfortably like jealousy. But she sensed reserve in the girl, there was no answering spark, no sexual tension vibrating between the two of them.

Monica knew all about sexual tension.

"I'm sorry, I didn't catch that," she apologised to Henry as she realised he had turned and asked her something. Heavens, he was a boring man, how did Jane stand him? Except that she was as boring as he was. Monica decided people agreed to buy programme space merely to get rid of her. Or was that being too unkind? She had a tendency to become unkind these days. Is that what life did to you? Made you a bitch like Fiona, boring like Jane? What had it made herself? A tiny, icy shiver ran down her back, as though Jack Frost had drawn a finger down her spine. Monica looked across the room, would young Darina lose her sincerity and directness as life rubbed away at her vulnerable edges? Honor had not. Monica looked at her hostess with affection.

Ralph caught her eye. She rose immediately and gave their thanks for an enjoyable evening. In the car going home she sank back against the seat with a sigh. "Thanks for coming, darling, I hope it wasn't too boring for you."

Her husband glanced at her as he steered the Rolls up Sloane Street towards Hyde Park, "You know I like to help your charity efforts when I can. And I like Honor and Geoffrey. The others are a bit much though."

Monica sighed, "Good works are no guarantee of character or charm, I'm afraid. But you liked Darina and William, surely?"

"Oh, they're all right. Eve could do a lot worse than get that girl to take over from Claire in the business. She's got brains and knows her stuff."

"Perhaps she will," Monica said shortly. Ralph said nothing more and after a little she asked, "Is this poisonous mushroom business going to affect you?"

The large hands on the steering wheel tensed, "I don't see wild fungi making a great sale for a while and I certainly won't be doing mushroom walks until next season but it should all die down after a bit."

An unfortunate phrase. "What about The Wooden Spoon?"

"Depends on their finances. Probably be sticky for the next few months."

To her horror, Monica heard herself asking in a tight, expressionless voice, "You won't lend Eve money, will you, Ralph?"

The powerful car surged up Edgeware Road. "What are you afraid of?" He shot her a glance from eyes that betrayed nothing of what he was thinking.

"I don't know," she said after a moment. Nor did she.

CHAPTER TWELVE

The inquest on Claire's death opened on the Monday. Jo and Eve both attended so Darina was left in charge of that day's City buffet for thirty people.

By the time she got back to The Wooden Spoon, it was all over.

Eve was in the catering kitchen supervising Jo's preparation of the food for the next day's charity demonstration. Darina asked her how the inquest had gone.

"There wasn't a great deal to it," Eve said, watching her unload the remains of the meal and start to stack the large washing up machines with the dirty plates that had come back from the lunch. "Oh, good, enough leftovers to do us for supper tonight, put them in those plastic boxes. Claire's father identified her, Ralph was asked what happened on the mushroom walk and I had to give the lunch details. And they heard the medical evidence. Finally the judge, or coroner or whatever he is, said Claire could be buried but not cremated and adjourned the inquest whilst the police made further inquiries."

"Did they seem to think it was an accident?"

Jo slid chopped shallot into a small dish, wrapped it in cling film, wrote on a freezer label and stuck it on the top of the film. "It was difficult to tell. The medical evidence was given with a whole lot of other details about cases which had nothing to do with Claire and the police were awfully brief. I don't know about Eve but I got the impression they knew a great deal more than they were saying."

"I didn't get that impression at all," said Eve, picking at some remains of chicken in a lemon sauce. "I thought they just wanted to get it over as quickly as possible and move on to the next case. There was none of that business, 'administered by person or persons unknown.'"

"You've been watching too much television or reading too many crime novels." Jo turned over a page of her set of recipe sheets, fetched a pork tenderloin from the fridge and started stripping it of fat and membrane. Eve watched her for a moment then went back to the timetable she was drawing up for the demonstration.

"Jo," she said after a few minutes, "Did you go straight home after we'd finished clearing up last Wednesday night?"

Jo raised her head, the tenderloin now lay in neat, oblique slices about an inch thick on the chopping board. She thought for a moment, "That was the night of the Beamish do, wasn't it? Why do you ask?"

"Oh, I just wondered. I tried to ring you after I got home and there was no reply." Eve had gone back to noting down times and actions on her pad but she glanced at Jo through her lashes.

"That's odd," said Jo, "I thought Claire, well, that is, I didn't go straight back, I met a friend in a pub for a quick drink. Claire was there when I got home but I suppose she must have gone out earlier."

Darina finished stacking the dishwasher, added powder and switched it on. "How much are you going to need me this week?" she asked.

Eve sighed, "What events have we got left, Jo?"

The other girl laid a layer of cling film over slices of pork fillet arranged on more film then went and got a large diary from the desk in the corner. She opened it, displaying a whole week across two pages. Thick lines were slashed through various entries. Jo held it towards Eve.

"Not a pretty sight," Eve averted her head, "Thank heavens for the two day course on Wednesday and Thursday. At least that's still full. Darina, darling, if you could do the prep for both days, perhaps assist my demo tomorrow and maybe the course on Wednesday and help Jo with that lunch on Thursday, I think that'll be all that's necessary. You can cope with everything else that's left in the catering line, can't you, Jo?"

Jo nodded, she was using the flat edge of a meat cleaver to beat out the pork into small escalopes. "No problem," she removed the top layer of cling film, stacked the thin pieces of meat on some tin foil and lined up a new lot of pork for the same treatment. "We're not going to be exactly pushed, are we? It's a great pity you didn't adopt my suggestion of lower rates for established customers when we moved, maybe then we'd have kept a useful core of loyal clients." She wielded the cleaver with more force than Darina reckoned was necessary.

Eve flushed, "You know we decided we had to increase our prices."

"You mean you decided, Claire was putty in your hands."

Eve drew up her small frame and became immensely dignified, "The two partners decided." There was a note of finality in her voice.

Jo put down the cleaver, added the beaten escalopes to the piece of tin foil then arranged a last lot of pork pieces. She looked as though she was fighting back hasty words, her lips clamped together in a thin line.

Darina waited but she said nothing further. Silence gathered whilst Eve returned to working on her timetable, Jo flattened the remaining pork and Darina continued clearing up. Finally she asked, "When will Claire's funeral be, do you know?"

"I spoke to her family at the inquest," Jo said shortly, "They're going to try for Friday."

"Thank heavens," added Eve, "It would have been very tricky if they'd chosen Thursday."

Too right, thought Darina, if that would have meant her having to take over the demonstrating again.

"Be quite convenient for me, too, I could go straight onto the cottage from there. Joshua could get a lift back with Elizabeth or Monica and Ralph. He says he has to spend the whole weekend on that wretched book. I think it's a bit much but apparently he thinks he could finish it off."

Jo seemed about to say something then paused, studying the little collection of ingredients she had amassed. When she did speak it was without expression. "Do you want me to slice the apple now and toss it in lemon juice or will you do it tomorrow?"

"Tomorrow, Darina can handle it."

"What exactly are you demonstrating and where is it?"

"The theme's 'Thirty Minute Entertaining,' good quickies for the good ladies to use for their theatre suppers or bridge lunches. It's at some church hall in Hampstead. The pearls and gloves brigade will be out. Just hope there won't be too many hats."

"Why not?"

"Makes it even more impossible to see than usual. The travelling demo mirror isn't very large and there's always part of the audience that can't see anything in it, they keep whispering, asking their neighbours what's happening. And I know Monica's crammed in as many as possible."

Darina wondered if Eve was at all nervous at having to demonstrate after all the publicity over Claire's death. She did not seem worried by it at the moment.

"Grab two of those trays and let's sort out the equipment we want to sell," she was saying now.

Darina followed her to the small room on the ground floor that was both shop and store room. Shelves running from floor to ceiling held an assortment of cooking equipment: knives and gadgets, stainless steel saucepans, a range of earthenware casseroles, white porcelain ovenproof china and some attractive pottery dishes.

"Made for me in Ireland," said Eve as Darina commented on them, "Marvellous potter in Cork, he makes this design exclusively for The Wooden Spoon."

Darina looked at the price labels and blenched.

Eve had also brought two trays. She lined them up on the floor with the two Darina had brought and proceeded to load them with boxes of knives, a gelatière, an electric juicer, a couple of food processors, a range of gadgets, some gratin and ramekin dishes and several of the stainless steel pans.

"Make a note of everything we're taking then leave it all ready to be loaded on the van tomorrow morning, I'll be in the office when you've finished." Eve gave her a pad and pencil and whisked out.

Darina carefully worked through each tray, making a note of its exact contents, writing down sizes, stock numbers and prices. When she had finished, she made a rapid calculation. They were taking with them goods worth well over £2000 at retail prices. She looked at the shelves still heavily stocked with more goods. Even allowing for the retail mark up, there was a lot of money tied up here.

She took the list through to Eve's office. There was a diary open on her desk and she was going through a sheaf of messages and letters, marking up as she went. Darina could see her pen slashing through entries far more often than it added items. Her eyes were bleak as she looked up at the tall girl. "It's still going on, there seems to be some sort of jungle drum beating through Hampstead and Highgate, working its way down along Kensington and Mayfair. There's a bit about the inquest in this evening's paper, so there'll be more cancellations tomorrow."

"Can you do anything?"

"I'll try and say something at the demonstration but I doubt it will do much good."

Eve looked drained and tired, very different from her usual sparkling self. "Anyway, it should mean you can see more of your boyfriend."

"If you mean William, he's gone back to Somerset."

"Has he?" Eve rubbed her eyes and got up, arching her back as though it ached. "I don't know about you, but I'm going home, Joshua said he'd be early today, I'd like to be there when he gets back for once, have a meal ready." She opened the door of her little cloakroom and reached for a short leather jacket. "Not that I'll see much of him, he wants to work on his wretched book again tonight, he spent the whole of yesterday on it as well. God, I'll be glad when it's finished."

"Isn't it about time you were working on another one yourself?"

Eve shrugged her way into the jacket, flicking her curls out of the way of the collar. "The sales of my last haven't exactly encouraged my publisher to commission another and I'm damned if I'm going to get it all together before I have a contract and some money up front. No, I'm hoping the video will mean a book to accompany the series, I'm saving my ideas for that. What I shall have to do, and I suppose I might as well start on it this evening, is the first newsletter for our new club. Recipes, advice, special offers on equipment, it should be fun. That is, if we manage to get anyone to join. Well, Elizabeth ought to give us a good mention, she's responsible for our present state after all."

Poor Eve, nothing seemed to be going her way at the moment. Darina wondered what the chances were for the video. Then she asked, "Did you really ring Jo that evening when you got back after being nearly run down?"

Her friend looked a little smug, "That was just a shot in the dark."

"But you can't think Jo's trying to kill you, surely? She was safely in Yorkshire when you were all on the mushroom hunt."

Eve's face clouded over, "Ah, so she was. I'd better leave the detecting to you." She slung her handbag over her shoulder and picked up a carrier holding the leftover food, "Off early for once, how wonderful. See you by eight o'clock tomorrow morning, darling, I want to be there by nine to set everything up." Then she was off, leaving a faint aura of Opium hanging on the office air.

Darina went back to the kitchen. Jo had lined up a series of white trays and was just finishing arranging her prepared ingredients on the last of them. She started to wrap it in cling film. As well as a set of ingredients, each tray carried the bowls and pans needed to cook the dish. "The demo equipment is all in that cupboard there," she said, pointing to the back of the kitchen.

Darina went and opened the cupboard. Leaning against the wall were several pieces of wood and a mirror. On a shelf above was a large box holding a two-ring electric hob. Beside it was a small convection oven and several red checked plastic tablecloths.

"I'll put all these in the cold store until the morning," Jo picked up a couple of trays and walked over to the refrigerated room beside the cupboard. Darina closed the door and went over to help.

"What's your programme for tomorrow?" she asked as she handed over her trays and watched Jo slide them onto the shelves.

"Give this kitchen a really good turn out."

Darina glanced at the gleaming stainless steel, "It doesn't look as though it needs it."

"We manage to keep it ticking over pretty well but you know how things get after a while."

Darina thought Jo was just itching for some hard physical labour, something that would remove any necessity to think and make her so tired she would fall asleep immediately she got into bed. The cheerful looking Hammersmith flat no doubt seemed desperately lonely at the moment. "Would you like to come round to me for a meal this evening?" she offered.

Jo smiled briefly, "Thanks but I've arranged to see an old friend, we're going to try out a new restaurant that's just opened, might get some ideas for here, if we get any more business, that is. I must go or I'll be late. Are you coming?"

Darina picked up the running order Eve had been working on and the set of recipe sheets, "I think I'd better just look through this and check I know what I'm supposed to be doing tomorrow. I'll lock up, I know where the spare keys are."

The kitchen was eerily quiet as she compared the recipes with the time table and checked through the trays in the chill of the store room. Jo had done an efficient job of preparing everything. There seemed a lot to get through but no doubt Eve would make it all appear like magic. The Wooden Spoon was quite a concern to keep going, what with catering, cookery courses and a shop. Now she was starting this club and seemed to be breaking into television. Any one of those activities would be enough for most girls Darina knew. What was the relentless ambition that drove Eve on? And what did Joshua think of it all?

Darina remembered his comments whilst they had been clearing up the other night, he had not sounded too happy about all her involvements then. Was that just because he hadn't wanted to work for her that evening or was his discontent more deep rooted? Well, he could always walk out on her if it was. Whilst Darina could see Joshua wanting to throttle Eve at certain times, that was hardly the same as plotting to murder her in a particularly unpleasant way.

She stopped in mid-thought; was this theorising without facts? William's accusation the previous day came back to her. She had been avoiding thinking about the way they had parted, now she closed the store room doors, set the recipe sheets back on the table, rubbed her cold arms then put the kettle on and ground some beans to make a cup of coffee. Her actions were automatic, her mind had gone back to the previous day. Better to face it all here than at the house where the scene had taken place.

She had suggested he bring his aunt and uncle to lunch. They were far too nice to protest when, at the end of the evening, he asked her out for a farewell meal the following day but she felt they had every right to expect him to spend the time with them. And though she had enjoyed the evening, warning bells were ringing that William's air towards her was far too proprietorial. A joint invitation seemed a perfect solution to everyone's problem.

The lunch had gone well. Conversation had had a family feel, with no holds barred on political discussion or the position of women in public life, Honor and Darina banding together against none-too-serious male chauvinism, and the hostess was quite sorry when her guests said they had to leave.

Except that William insisted on staying behind to help with the clearing up and his uncle and aunt clearly expected she would want him to. Well, she was quite keen to discuss one or two things with him.

"What did you think of Monica and Ralph Cox?" she asked as he brought out the last tray of lunch things from the dining room and started to stack the dishwasher while she washed up the saucepans.

"Ah, yes, the suspects. How would you tag them? Black Forest gâteau and steak and kidney pudding?

"Not a bad effort."

William gave her a resigned look, "Go on, tell me yours."

"White chocolate mousse with Grand Marnier and carpet bagger steak."

"O.K., you win." She flashed him a quick grin then listened carefully as he went on, "They're an interesting couple. He's very intelligent, much more so than he appears at first meeting. Behind all that plain cockney lad front is a mind as sharp as one of your knives. His comments on the economic situation over the port were extremely interesting. If he ever went into politics, he would have a great future, you could see James filing away his comments for later use."

"And he's very attractive."

"James? You surprise me."

"No, you idiot, Ralph."

"Cave man appeal, is that it?" William carefully dried the Baccarat glasses they had used.

"Something like that. That sense of earthy appetite only just held in check. You feel he could say anything to you, that he wouldn't be constrained by convention, what you should or shouldn't do."

"And that's what females go for, is it?" He looked at her, an eyebrow lifted in a faintly derisive way that for some reason irritated her.

"Some do. Didn't you notice the way that Fiona looked at him? I thought she was going to eat him before dinner. And when we were upstairs she was more or less telling Monica he was having an affair with Eve."

"Was she? How did Monica react?"

"Very coolly but she practically admitted he had his little flings."

"And that Eve could be one of them? I'm surprised she uses her catering company in that case."

"I'm not. Much better to keep an eye on things and, after all, The

Wooden Spoon is one of the chicest companies in town. I don't see Monica settling for less than the best under any circumstances."

"No, a lady who doesn't do things by halves. Honor knows Monica's parents quite well. Apparently her family was shocked to the core when she brought Ralph back, her mother expected nothing less than the son of a duke, not necessarily the heir but at least a lord. And there was no lack of candidates with the right qualifications. Instead she insisted on marrying this cockney. Didn't even produce the first child until a respectable year had elapsed. Would you say she regretted her choice?"

Darina scrubbed away at the gravy saucepan and thought about it. "I'd say she was still very much in love with him. But even if she wasn't, that sort of woman doesn't admit mistakes very easily and he provides her with an enviable life style. She really enjoyed running that party the other night and Eve says they do a lot of entertaining, most of it business." Darina placed a gleaming saucepan on the draining rack. "If Ralph did fall for Eve, I bet Monica would fight every inch of the way to keep him." She glanced round the kitchen, "That's the last, thanks so much for helping." She hesitated a moment then said, "How about a cup of tea before you go?"

A few minutes later she carried a tray into the drawing room and put it down on a small table in front of the fire. William sat in the easy chair beside it, stretching out his legs as though quite at home.

"I still feel Eve was the intended victim," Darina said, handing him a cup of tea. "It makes sense. No-one could have known Claire was going to sit at that place. And there's another thing." Rapidly she told him how Eve had nearly been run over.

"Could just have been an accident, you only have her version of the event." He put down his cup and saucer and looked at Darina, "Don't you think you're getting just a little carried away over all this?"

The irritation she had felt in the kitchen escalated, "Don't start saying it's something only the police can deal with."

"At any rate they won't get emotional over it."

"I'm not getting emotional," Darina heard her voice rising, took a deep breath and said quietly, "You haven't seen Eve recently, she's had all the stuffing knocked out of her. She's an old friend, I can't just stand aside and let someone murder her."

"Don't be so melodramatic. I'm not saying it's impossible anyone could want to kill her, she strikes me as manipulative, over-ambitious and completely insensitive to others' needs, a prime candidate for murder in fact. But you've got to leave this to the professionals. Look," he came and sat on the sofa beside her, a mixture of exasperation and concern in his eyes, "What you're doing is theorising ahead of data. You can't possibly amass the breadth of background the police are building up, all you can do is barge around and possibly get in the way. And," his voice softened, his gaze fastening on her eyes and his hands reaching for her shoulders, "I don't want to spend the best part of the afternoon going into half-baked murder theories." He tried to draw her to him.

With a swift movement Darina avoided his grasp and stood up, "So that's all you want. I bet in another minute you'll be telling me not to bother my pretty little head with matters best left to chaps like yourself."

"Now don't go getting on your high horse just because you can't take a little criticism."

"That's unforgivable."

He had risen also and they stood glaring at each other, the easy camaraderie between them quite vanished. Darina lost sight of the attractive man who was fun to be with and saw a stranger who had an insulting way of putting things. Just because she was invading his precious territory, well, if that was how his mind worked, the sooner he went back to Somerset the better.

"I think I'd better go."

She said nothing, merely led the way out of the room.

In the hall he picked up his coat and stood looking at her for a moment then said, "I suppose you can't do much harm by continuing to speculate, you're hardly likely to get in the way of the proper investigation."

It was the last straw. Darina went and opened the front door. "I hope you have a good journey back."

The muscles round his mouth tightened, "Thank you for lunch, I'll ring you next week."

"Do." Her voice was not cordial. She closed the door behind him then went and did all the dirty washing that had accumulated over the last week, scrubbing out kitchen cupboards until it was ready to be ironed, finally dropping exhausted into bed, to a sleep disturbed by dreams in which mushrooms grew and grew until they towered over her and blotted out the light.

In The Wooden Spoon kitchen Darina dragged herself back to the present. She tried to look at William's criticisms dispassionately. Maybe she was theorising but she had precious few facts to work on, and there was no need for him to have been quite so rude. She washed up the mug and the little cafetière she had used for her coffee and looked around to make sure everything was straight for the morning. Consigning any further consideration of tall detective sergeants to the deepest reaches of her consciousness, she went through to the office, found the keys and set the alarm, then had to turn it off again as someone came through the front door. It was Kenneth, the photographer.

CHAPTER THIRTEEN

He looked dispirited, defeated. "Is Eve in her office?"

Darina shook her head, "I'm sorry, she's gone home for the evening. Is there anything I can do?" she added, not wanting to let one of her suspects disappear without talking to him.

"No, it was just about the vegetable video," he didn't so much finish his sentence as gradually stop speaking, his glance moving round the walls, resting for a moment on a still life of wine bottles and apples.

"Did you want to see when Eve had time to do some more filming?" suggested Darina.

"No." That word at least was definite, "It's more . . ." The hesitancy was back again.

"Come and have a drink and tell me about it. I'm just locking up here but there's a pub round the corner." Allowing him no time for thought, Darina reset the alarm, ushered him out of the building and hustled him into the nearest pub. He allowed himself to be organised, showed no surprise when he was asked what he wanted to drink and accepted the Campari and soda with the briefest of thanks. He sat on a bench by a small table nursing the drink, his eyes downcast, a small muscle working in the side of his jaw.

"What's the problem?" asked Darina gently.

He took a big gulp of the drink. "I don't know what to do about the video, now that Claire," he gripped the drink more tightly, "now that Claire can't be in it anymore. I'd really planned it round her, you see?"

Darina did not see. According to what she had heard from Eve, she and Claire were being featured in it equally, Kenneth had only finished one programme and it should not be at all difficult to reshoot the parts Claire had done. At least, that was what Eve had said.

"I can't explain," Kenneth said miserably, "You'd really have to see it to understand."

"Well, why don't you show it to me?" asked Darina, "I've nothing better to do this evening, how about you?"

For the first time since he had appeared on The Wooden Spoon's doorstep the photographer came to life. "Would you really come and see it? I'd be ever so grateful. You see, it means, has meant, so much to me. And now I can't really trust my judgement any more. I mean, it's so bound up with what I felt about Claire."

"Come on, then," Darina drank up her wine and rose.

They caught a cab to Kenneth's studio in Islington. It had once been a shop. A small office occupied the space behind the large window, now screened with a vertical slatted blind, and the space behind had been opened out and painted white. There were lights on tall stands backed with what looked like lurex umbrellas and long rolls of different coloured paper lay under a window framed with heavy black curtains. A couple of still cameras were placed on a long, free-standing cupboard. Two tables, a few chairs and a couch that would not have disgraced a bordello stood against one wall, a tall cupboard occupied another and a sink had been fitted in one corner underneath a flight of stairs. Kenneth led the way up these onto a small landing then into a living room furnished with several low seating units. Metal display shelves held rows and rows of tapes and a small collection of books. A large television set sat on a stand with a video machine underneath. Big colour photographs of food hung on the walls, their complex presentation giving Darina indigestion.

"Sit down, can I get you a drink, coffee, anything?"

She shook her head. Whilst Kenneth switched on the television set and rewound the tape in the video, she went and looked at the books.

Most seemed connected with food. Big books with glossy photographs of ingredients and dishes in various stages of preparation and presentation. Smaller books on fruit and vegetables, all with colour photographs. There was the book on mushrooms she had looked at the other night and another she hadn't seen before.

"Right, that's it. Now, this is the programme that I've been showing to people who could be interested."

She went and sat opposite the television. Kenneth pushed a button and the screen flickered briefly then showed a stunning array of glossy fruit and vegetables. After a moment the camera pulled back to reveal Eve and Claire behind the demonstration theatre's work counter.

The half hour programme concentrated on root vegetables used in a wide variety of ways, drawing on cuisines from around the world. Very quickly Darina realised why Kenneth was worried. He had used the girls as a foil for each other, focussing first on one, then on the other as they produced different dishes. Eve was all clever chat and complicated knife work. Claire concentrated on getting over the essential qualities of much simpler dishes.

The photography was stunning, the vegetables glowed with life and colour. But the greatest revelation was Claire. The camera discovered

planes to her face unseen in ordinary life, her eyes seemed larger than
Darina remembered and they glowed with enthusiasm for the food. Her
slightly breathy voice caught the viewer and held him eagerly awaiting
her next words, like a thriller reader desperate for the denouement. As
she talked about a parsnip purée with pine nuts, the viewer could almost
taste the subtle flavour of the simple dish. By contrast Eve was a distraction, all flashing eyes, tossing curls and witty phrases, the food took
second place.

After the tape had ended, Kenneth waited for Darina's comments.

"What were you going to do if Claire hadn't died?"

He brightened a little, "Reshoot that programme just using her. The
producer I first showed it to said Claire was a winner but that Eve ruined
the whole effect."

"Did you tell Eve this?"

He sat down and held his head in his hands, looking down at the cord
carpet as though it held the secret of life if only he could puzzle it out. "I
tried to about ten days ago. That's when we had our row. She didn't
understand at first, thought I wanted to feature each of them in alternate
programmes. When I said the series could be sold with Claire doing the
cooking but not her, she exploded." He looked at Darina, his eyes blink-
ing rapidly, clearly the encounter had shaken him badly. "She said I
didn't understand the television business, I should stick to still photography. That I hadn't been in touch with the right people, she was making a
name for herself on TV and she was the one who would sell the programmes, the producer I'd been talking to was obviously a nincompoop."
He took out a large silk handkerchief and passed it across his forehead,
wiping away the beads of sweat that had sprung out.

"She talked as though the video was entirely for her benefit. She
doesn't seem to realise how much it matters to me, it could make my
name. Once you've sold one production to these people, it's so much
easier to interest them in something else. And I'd had such a good initial
response, they seemed really enthusiastic, until I showed that pilot." He
hesitated, when he continued the excited note had drained out of his
voice. "But then I thought perhaps she was right. I get confused talking to
Eve, she's such a strong personality, whilst Claire . . ." Again his voice
drifted to a stop but the pause this time was momentary. He looked at
Darina and there was a light in his eyes as though someone had lit a tiny
candle. "I loved her so much," he said simply. "She was like my mother,
so warm, so loving, she really cared about her friends. Normally I find
women a tiny bit frightening. Eve, for instance." The candle was snuffed
out, he put the handkerchief back in his pocket.

Darina waited.

"It was such a relief when she was so pleasant on Sunday. I even agreed to have another try at using her in the video. But it's just been a waste of time and tape, her approach hasn't changed at all. I came round tonight to tell her I couldn't take it any further. I was so nervous, I knew she'd be as angry as she was before. She hardly spoke to me on the mushroom walk. And there was one moment, when I was taking some pictures of the mushrooms and asked her if she'd move a little, that her eyes flashed at me and I felt seared—it was like being caught in a rocket's exhaust, you know? I tell you, I hadn't looked forward to the lunch at all. But then I saw I was to sit next to Claire."

"You checked the seating, then?" Darina interposed quickly.

"Oh, everyone was doing it, Eve had said we had to find our own places."

"Were you all doing it at the same time?"

"Oh, no. It was such a lovely day, most of us were drinking in the garden, just popping in to have a look at the tables and everything—Eve can really organise a party, I'll say that for her—then going out again. It was the first time they'd entertained since doing up the house and we were all fascinated to see what had been done."

"Which was?"

Kenneth became animated, "Oh, you should have seen it before, such a gloomy house. Some William Morris freak had lived there and it was all dark wall paper and brown woodwork. The basement had been a warren of little rooms and cupboards but they'd knocked all those into one when they moved in, Eve used to run the catering company from there. But now she's taken out all the stripped pine units they first put in, added that big patio window and redone the terrace. Then they took down the wall between the living room and the study, made it all one, and completely redecorated."

"Must have cost a lot of money," said Darina slowly.

"The earth," agreed Ken. "But Joshua's last book did terribly well and he's got a terrific advance for his next, or so Claire said, everyone wants to know about food production nowadays, he's such a gift for being controversial, comes of his journalist's training I suppose. And The Wooden Spoon must be bringing in a lot too, they charge such outrageous prices."

"Where did Eve get the money for the Marylebone building?" Darina asked, not really expecting Kenneth to know but thinking how much the beautifully appointed demonstration theatre and catering kitchen and the stylish offices must have cost, quite apart from the lease itself. But Ken could provide an answer and it was completely unexpected.

"Claire invested the trust fund money she came into on her twenty-fifth birthday."

Darina took a moment to take it in. "How much was that?"

"I don't know exactly, something around fifty thousand pounds, I think."

"What happens to her investment now?"

But Kenneth had no idea and wasn't interested. He went and rewound the video tape. "This is all I've got left of her," he took it out and held it in his hand. "And I don't suppose it's worth anything to anybody but me."

"If you want to go on with the idea, I think what you need is to bring in an experienced producer who can direct Eve, get her to simplify her approach. I don't know much about television but she has a lot of talent and her food presentation is superb."

"Do you think so?"

Darina remembered something he'd said earlier, "Have you got the photographs you took on Saturday?"

He picked up a folder sitting on a low table, took out a sheaf of glossy prints and handed them to her.

Darina looked carefully at each one then went through the set again, sorting them into two piles. In the first she put the shots of people. There were a number of Claire, some of her looking directly at the camera, some taken whilst she was talking to others. There was a lovely one of Joshua and her looking at some mushrooms, Eve in the background and out of focus; one with Ralph, his eyebrow raised quizzically, she laughing, and one with herself, helping to lay out the food for the picnic, Joshua and Monica assisting.

The second pile of photographs were of mushrooms. Some were growing, peeking through piles of leaves, in a clump at the roots of a tree, or layered on fallen logs, but there were a number of the hunt's haul. There were baskets loaded with fungi and several shots of what seemed the whole collection spread out. Darina showed them to Kenneth, "Were these taken at lunchtime or at the end of the day?"

He studied the photographs, "Both. I liked all the different shapes and colours. After Ralph had finished going through them after each session, I spread them all out and took these shots."

He must have done that whilst she was packing up the car after lunch, before she had been handed the basket to take back.

"Can I borrow these?" she asked, "I'd like to show them to Ralph."

"Have them, I was going to print some more anyway, I thought the police would like copies. They're coming to see me tomorrow."

Darina supposed the police would get round to her in time. As someone who had been on the mushroom walk but not at the lunch, she would not be very high on their list of interviewees but she would be there all right. Well, there was not a lot she could tell them. She had seen nothing particularly significant during the picnic. Groups of friends chatting together and eating, that was all. Or was it? She glanced at the other pile of photographs.

"Could I possibly take these as well?"

"Sure, it's no problem to run the whole lot off again." He showed no curiosity as to why she might want them. He sat sunk in his chair, still holding the video, encompassed by gloom. Then, to Darina's embarrassment, two large tears slowly slid down his cheeks. He made no attempt to wipe them away but said, "I don't know how I'm going to manage without her. She was the only one I could really talk to since Mother died. I knew she'd maybe get married or something some day. That I couldn't hope for anything more than friendship but at least then I'd have been able to talk to her sometimes. This way . . ." He fished in his pocket for his handkerchief.

Darina watched him mopping his now overflowing eyes. "Did she confide in you at all?" she asked but her words were lost in a trumpeting blow of his nose. She repeated the question.

"Oh, she used to tell me lots of things," he said proudly. "What sort of things do you mean?"

"I wondered whether, well, whether she was involved with a man?" Darina could not think of another way to put it that might be less wounding to his self-esteem.

Kenneth gave a last snort into his handkerchief and put it away. He seemed pleased to be able to give proof of how close a friend Claire had thought him. "There was someone she was in love with. She didn't tell me much about him, just that she was very unhappy about the situation."

"Why, didn't he love her?"

"No, he did but he was married and I think Claire didn't know whether she meant enough to him for him to leave his wife. Or she didn't want him to leave his wife, or something." Kenneth wrestled with the words. Darina thought he would have been happier photographing the situation.

"And you don't know who it was?"

He shook his head, "I didn't want to. Claire only talked about it once. She was so unhappy. She cried and I held her and stroked her hair." He broke off and used the handkerchief for more mopping.

Darina gathered up the photographs as quickly as she could without damaging them, placed them back into the folder and fitted it into her satchel-like bag. She wanted to get out of here, away from this tortured man. She had learned things from him, important things, and she needed to think about them on her own. But could she leave him like this?

"Can I get you a drink?" she ventured.

He shook his head and gave a last blow to his nose before putting away the now sodden handkerchief. "I'll be all right. It's done me good, getting it all off my chest. My trouble is, Mother always said, I can't talk to people. Nobody should have to bottle everything up inside. Poisons you, she said. That's why Claire was so good for me. I could tell her anything."

Darina waited for the waterworks to start again but he seemed to have spent his emotion for the time being.

"You have the same sort of softness," he went on, "But you're stronger, I can tell." Just like the best sort of loo paper, thought Darina.

"If you're sure you'll be all right, I must go," she said hastily.

"And I'll think about the producer idea. You might have something there. Claire wouldn't want me to give up on the programmes, she believed in them."

CHAPTER FOURTEEN

Darina closed the door of Kenneth's studio and stood on the pavement. It was just after 7:00 P.M. and pedestrians were not plentiful. She wondered which direction the tube was in or if it would be better to find a bus. The night was fine, a little chilly but with a clear sky; tiny stars pierced the dark, competing with the lights of the street and the busy traffic. For a brief moment Darina wished she was in the country where little interrupted the dark velvet of night. Then she made a quick decision and started walking in the direction of Piccadilly Circus.

She passed the Angel underground station without giving it a second thought, turned into Rosebery Avenue, crossed over Gray's Inn Road into Theobald's Road. She passed old houses converted long ago into offices, purpose-built blocks of undistinguished style, the Mount Pleasant main postal sorting office, no doubt there was activity behind its blank windows but no sign of it showed. It was a route that knew little night life, its pulse stopped early evening when office workers flooded out and only started again next morning when they arrived back, refreshed or tired after a night spent elsewhere. Darina's heels clicked on deserted pavements, only the swish of traffic kept her company. But she hardly noticed her surroundings, her mind was busy on the problem of Claire's death. The broad picture she had formed now had added brush strokes bringing new detail into focus.

Kenneth had revealed two facts that must be important. Claire had been involved in an affair with a married man and she had invested some £50,000 in The Wooden Spoon. Love and money, both powerful incentives to murder, opening up the possibility that she could have been the intended victim after all.

Who had she been in love with? Not to have told Kenneth the name of her lover suggested it was someone he knew. Joshua or Ralph? One the husband of her partner, the wife of the other a valued client. Either choice would have presented Claire with divided loyalties, quite apart from the fact that Darina felt she was the sort of girl who would never have wanted to become involved with a married man.

It could only have happened, she felt sure, through either overwhelm-

ing physical attraction or a determined assault by the man in the case.
Darina thought about Joshua. She was sure his and Eve's marriage,
though certainly rocky, was not dead. She remembered the way Eve had
fallen into her husband's arms the night of Monica's party. A chicken
coming home to roost, a diamond nestling into its setting, a tongue of
wood slotting into its groove could not have looked more natural. And
there had been no hesitation in the way his arms had come round her.
That there was genuine feeling there, Darina had no doubt. But he had
spoken of the instant chemistry between them both when they first met.
If it had happened once, could it happen again and, if so, could quiet
Claire spark off such a response?

Darina could imagine Ralph laying siege. And could see that he might
find a girl like Claire an irresistible challenge. But what about Eve?
Wasn't he supposed to be having an affair with her? How accurate was
that malicious piece of gossip from an envious woman? Eve flirted with
every man she met, it was part of her make-up. Look at the way she had
behaved with William.

Darina wished William had been more willing to discuss her theories
and the details surrounding Claire's death. The more she found out, the
murkier the picture became. Take the matter of Claire's partnership in
The Wooden Spoon. How relevant was that?

Fifty thousand pounds was quite a lot of money. Would it give control
of the business? How had Claire left her shares? And how many shares
did she have? Were they split fifty-fifty between her and Eve? Was there
another partner? Was Joshua one? It hadn't sounded as though Jo had
that sort of interest in the company. Darina thought of her little outburst
that afternoon, it had been that of an aggrieved employee rather than
shareholder. Just how well was the business doing anyway?

Darina's conviction that Eve had been the intended victim was gradually evaporating. Now she was considering seriously the possibility that
Claire had been deliberately killed, that the intended victim had, after all,
eaten the poisonous mushroom. But in that case, what about the business
of the changed places?

Darina reached Shaftesbury Avenue. Round her now were lights, people, noise and action. As she walked down to Piccadilly Circus, the
crowds grew thicker, people were out on the town, hurrying to bars,
restaurants, night clubs, thronging into theatres and cinemas. There was
bustle, activity. She brought again before her mind's eye the picture of
that luncheon. Another scene of bustle and activity. Could the poisoned
mushroom have been kept hidden until the last minute? It would have
made sense not to place it until the murderer was absolutely sure where
his victim was sitting. But how could it have been done? Had Claire sat

down early, or when everyone else had been seated? Could the deadly toxins have been extracted and just squeezed over the dish? If so, how? A syringe, a small bottle?

Difficult, surely? Others would have been bound to notice. It would be possible to distract one person, maybe, but a whole table?

Darina walked along Piccadilly then through Belgrave and Eaton Squares towards the King's Road thinking of the various characters involved in this horrible crime. Thinking who could have been cold blooded enough to add that poisonous mushroom to Eve's chic starter. Did the heart of the mystery lie in The Wooden Spoon, that temple of gastronomy? How well had the three girls actually got along? Such disparate characters. Eve, scintillating, full of energy, a communicator. Yet with the sort of character who could stimulate envy and dislike as easily as affection and admiration. Claire, quiet, lovely, gentle. Could anyone really be driven to murder her?

Then there was Jo, sensible, efficient and down to earth. The little she had said about her background suggested it was very different from that of the other two. And there was definitely friction between her and Eve. But she had obviously got on well with Claire and she had a cast iron alibi for the whole weekend, hadn't she? Well, if it was not quite as cast iron as it appeared on the surface, that was something the police would undoubtedly discover.

Which brought William back into the picture. Reluctantly, Darina conceded that Detective Sergeant Pigram might have had a point about amateurs. Had she imagined clues would pop up in front of her just because she was there? But she was still angry at the dismissive way he had treated her. As though all she was was a sex object! Darina's long legs moved a little more quickly.

By the time she reached home, Darina was very tired but her mind was clearer. Now she felt she had a better picture of what had to be done, the questions that should be asked. And she would start first thing tomorrow morning.

CHAPTER FIFTEEN

Eve was edgy, nervous. As soon as Darina arrived the following morning, she told her to check all the ingredients prepared by Jo. When Darina mentioned she'd looked through them all the previous evening, she snapped that she wanted them checked again.

"Jo seems very efficient," Darina laid the trays from the cold store in rows on the white Formica working surface.

"She'd better be, she's nothing else." Eve was hauling the demonstration unit and mirror out of the cupboard.

"You mean she isn't capable of taking over from Claire?"

"Can't or won't. Says she's a cook not a demonstrator or a PR girl. If she had her way, we'd still be doing nothing but catering." The tiny figure struggled with the heavy wood.

"Let me do that, you check the ingredients," Darina came over and lifted the folded wood with ease. "Shall I put it in the van?" Eve looked as though she would protest, then nodded with resignation and suddenly collapsed onto a stool.

"Oh God, I'm tired, put the kettle on, will you? I don't know how I'm going to face all those women, all wondering if my recipes are going to poison them." Darina leant the wood against the sink for a moment and turned on the tap. A few minutes later the unit was in the van and Eve had been furnished with one of her herbal teas.

"Bliss," she said, sipping the steaming liquid.

Darina lifted down the little oven from the cupboard shelf and took it out, then the two-ring hob. She came back into the kitchen to find Eve still sitting on her stool drinking tea. She had made no attempt to check the ingredients.

"Did you manage to get an early night?"

"No, dammit. Josh and I were arguing about The Wooden Spoon. He wants me to close down," she rubbed her forehead with the back of her hand. There was no trace of the animation that usually lit her face.

"Close down! Why?"

"The difficulty of replacing Claire, of keeping going until people forget about her death, he says it's all too much for me and why don't I sell up and try staying at home for a bit." Her fingers pinched the bridge of her little, tip-tilted nose. Her eyes were closed.

"What do you feel about it?" asked Darina curiously, wondering what Eve would find to do with her time if The Wooden Spoon no longer existed.

"I *can't* give up now. I'm so near breakthrough point, I can feel it." Eve's eyes opened wide, the blue blazing through as she switched on the energy button.

"Breakthrough point?"

"Becoming a name, getting known on television, publishing lots of books, making loads-a-money."

"If you weren't running this place," Darina gave the sparkling kitchen a quick glance, "You'd have more time for writing books and getting TV ideas together."

"You don't understand, it's this place that gives me my contacts, keeps my name before the press, known. Without it, everyone would forget about me in five minutes. And it provides the money. Well, should provide the money." Eve was once again fully energised. She finished her mug of tea. "Come on, we'll be late, I hate getting to a demo without time to organise myself properly." She picked up one of the trays and took it outside.

As they were driving towards Hampstead, the trays and equipment safely installed in the back of the van, Eve suddenly said, "Would you consider joining us, taking over from Claire?"

Darina put the gears into neutral and pulled on the hand brake as they stopped at some traffic lights on a slight hill. She had seen the question coming for several days and she knew what her answer was going to be. It was not only the questions surrounding Claire's death, she knew she wanted to get out of the catering business. She was tired of the pressures of turning out food in one place to be finished and served in another, tired of juggling customers' demands, tired of stretching resources to cope with the maximum amount of work, of dealing with orders that always seemed to come together instead of being nicely spaced out. Tired of finding and keeping part-time staff. It was time for a change.

And there was something else. She did not think she could work with Eve on a permanent basis. Her friend had a volatility that would be very wearing after a little, and her ideas on food were not Darina's. No, it was not a position she could even consider. But just as she opened her mouth to say so, another thought took over.

"You'd really like me to come in with you?"

"Darling, you'd be ideal! You know as much about the catering side as Jo, you'll be fine demonstrating as soon as you've had a little more practice and you can talk to people, communicate, all the things Jo's so bad at. Of course," Eve glanced back into the van's interior, checking the contents, "Of course, you'd have to invest some money, buy out Claire's share."

"What sort of money are we talking about?" Darina let in the clutch and the van moved smoothly away.

"I'm not sure, Claire had fifty percent of the shares when we set up the company about eighteen months ago. And they must be worth much more than her original investment, now that we've started the courses and are getting the club going. I should think about a hundred thousand pounds."

Darina just stopped herself jamming her foot down on the brake. "That's a lot of money."

"But you must have it, didn't your cousin leave you everything?"

"It might be possible to find it," Darina said slowly, "But I'd have to get my accountant to go through the books, make a valuation of just what the business is worth."

There was the tiniest of hesitations then Eve said quickly, "Of course, tell him to contact mine, Jackie will give you the number."

Darina refrained from saying her accountant was female, little point when she had no intention of taking the matter any further. "Perhaps I could have a quick look through the books first myself?"

"Sure, ask Jackie to let you see her accounts, she does the day-to-day book-keeping." Eve swivelled slightly in her seat so she could look at Darina, "Does this mean you could really be interested?"

She sounded so thrilled, so enthusiastic, Darina felt horribly guilty. What was she going to say after everything had been sorted out? How was she going to explain? Would Eve accept that it had been necessary for her to check out every possibility, even the state of her friend's business?

"It's quite tempting," she said mendaciously.

They crossed some more traffic lights then Darina asked, "What happens to Claire's shares now, do you know? Did she tell you if she'd made a will or anything?"

Eve sighed. It was a little sigh but it seemed to express bewilderment, doubt and frustration equally intermingled. "I don't really know. We spoke at one stage of leaving our shares to each other but there was Joshua."

"Is he part of the business?"

"Not really but he does have a sort of interest in my share."

"A sort of interest?" Darina repeated, slightly foxed by this description. Eve fidgeted with her seat belt. "Well, I suppose it isn't really an interest but he is my husband and I couldn't just leave my business to someone else." She suddenly leaned forward in her seat, "You turn down here, right by this newsagent's."

Darina hit the brakes, indicated a left turn, rapidly changed down and swung into the side road, leaving honking horns behind them. A moment later they had arrived at the hall and there was no more opportunity for talk about The Wooden Spoon and shares.

Eve seemed to have conquered her nerves. She opened the demonstration with great aplomb by going straight to the heart of the matter and talking of Claire's death with touching simplicity. "It was a tragic, unforeseen accident. You have probably read my friend Elizabeth Chesney's wonderful description of our mushroom hunt and her warning. This morning I'm going to go further. During the demonstration I am going to give you some advice on avoiding food poisoning. Not the deadly mushroom sort but the more everyday variety that probably won't do more than give you a severe stomach upset, unless you are old, pregnant, very young or already ill. But why take risks with your or your family's health? If you are unlucky or frail it could even be fatal."

Assisting Eve by stirring, sautéing, stuffing chicken breasts or wrapping slices of goat's cheese in filo pastry, Darina listened in admiration as Eve cleverly interspersed her explanatory chat on the cooking she was doing with advice on elementary kitchen hygiene.

"Now that we've finished with these pieces of chicken, Darina is going to scrub down the board I've been using and I shall use another for putting together the smoked meat salad. This avoids any possibility of cross contamination if the chicken was infected with salmonella. Watch the defrosting of a frozen chicken in the fridge. If you allow it to drip over other food, you could be spreading infection."

She ran through the importance of cooling food quickly, reheating cooked meats really thoroughly, not leaving food in the warm or vulnerable to flies. She never remained on any point long enough to be boring, each piece of advice was mixed with cooking hints, alternative suggestions for the dishes she was preparing, addresses for where to get certain ingredients, little anecdotes. It was a tour de force that kept her audience enthralled.

Darina hardly had a moment to study the rows of women in front of them. She was aware of those at the sides and back craning in an effort to see what Eve was up to, of the rustle of recipe sheets as they were turned over at certain stages, and of Monica sitting right at the back.

She had been at the hall when they arrived, as calm and composed as at her party, soothing Eve, organising her helpers into putting up an extra table at the back of the demonstration area to hold all the trays, not allowing Eve to get in a state because it wasn't already there. She'd even got a little box of the special herbal teas that were Eve's favourite and produced two steaming mugs as soon as all the equipment and food had been brought in. Darina could understand why she was such a successful raiser of charity funds. She would have made a brilliant business woman.

The demonstration ended at 12:30 with Monica giving a graceful little speech of thanks and inviting the audience to view the equipment that had been brought along for sale. "Mrs. Tarrant has generously offered to donate ten percent of her takings to our most worthy cause. I know it's all excellent quality and is being offered at very good prices so come along, ladies. And if you have any queries on cookery, either on the wonderful dishes we've seen demonstrated this morning or on anything else, Eve has said she is very willing to deal with them."

Darina started clearing away the demonstration equipment, then had to abandon that as it became clear someone had to take money whilst Eve dealt with the ladies who crowded round her. Then she became involved herself in explaining which knives were used for what and the uses of various dishes and pans. And the money poured in. Her pockets became stuffed with bank notes and cheques and the little bag of 5p pieces Eve had supplied—every price ended in 95p—was almost exhausted by the time Monica announced that her ladies had lunch laid out at the back of the hall. Finally the crowd melted away and they could finish the packing up, refusing the plates of game pie salad that were offered.

The hall was humming with happy chat as they returned from loading up the van to say goodbye. Darina wondered how many of these women would go home and actually make any of Eve's fantastical recipes. And if any of them realised that they would take a good deal longer to do than had appeared? They had, in fact, been subjected to a giant con trick. All the preparatory work and Eve's deftness had produced dish after dish in no time at all. Each of the recipes in theory could be done from start to finish in under thirty minutes but only by a very experienced cook. Ah well, it had been good entertainment. And the hygiene advice alone had been worth their morning's attention.

"Why don't you suggest to Elizabeth you do an article for her on how to avoid food poisoning in the home kitchen?" she suggested as they drove back to Marylebone. "Put together all the advice you gave this morning?"

"That's a wonderful idea," Eve turned a beaming face towards Darina. "It's the least Elizabeth can do for me and it could do us no end of good. Why didn't I think of that? I'll ring her as soon as we get back."

She disappeared into her office the moment they returned. Darina, too, left unloading the equipment and went to consult the demonstration kitchen's telephone directory.

There was an entry for Cox's Fruit and Vegetables at Nine Elms. Darina dialled the number and asked for Ralph.

"I'm sorry to trouble you," she said when his voice, vibrant as ever but sounding more cockney than usual, came down the line, "I've got some queries I'd love to run through with you, would it be possible to see you sometime?"

She could feel his surprise coming through the telephone. Was she ultra sensitive or was there something else as well? For the first time she wondered whether she might not be laying herself open to misinterpretation.

"Of course, be delighted. When were you thinking of? How about a drink this evening?"

"I'm sorry," Darina said hastily, "I've got a date, what about sometime tomorrow?"

"Have you ever seen the market in action?" Damn the man, he sounded amused, as though he knew she had been free. "No? Well, if you're an early bird, come along about seven-thirty and I'll show you around. We can have a chat at the same time and end up with a cup of coffee. O.K.?"

Darina agreed with relief and a sense of anticipation. She had always wanted to visit the market but in her busy life the right occasion had never before presented itself.

She went down and took the first load of demonstration equipment into the kitchen. Jo was there, surrounded by chickens, plump and gleaming, their flesh not golden from a maize diet but softly flushed. Free range and organic, diagnosed Darina, dumping her box of utensils and dirty containers by the side of a sink.

"How did the demo go?" Jo reached for a fresh bird, expertly sliced through a leg joint, neatly flipping the knife under the oyster so the tender little nugget of meat remained with the thigh instead of being left on the carcass. A couple of quick cuts revealed the wishbone for Jo's long fingers to detach and discard. Then the wings were removed. A moment later the skin had been stripped from the breast, the slim boning knife was stroked along the ribs and the supremes lay in neat pillows on the working surface. Finally Jo removed the opaque muscle from underneath each breast fillet, then added the fillets and legs to a tray of more at her side, the joints carefully placed so that no one touched another. The stripped carcass received a couple of mighty blows from a cleaver with the pieces being thrown into a large stockpot to join the remains of some half dozen other birds. The whole process took no more than a few minutes. Already simmering on one of the stoves were two stock pots of more carcasses.

Darina brought in the rest of the equipment, giving Jo a somewhat breathless account of the morning as she trotted in and out of the kitchen.

"I hope Elizabeth is interested in the hygiene article," she finished, emerging from the cupboard where she had replaced the demonstration equipment and going over to the sink to start the washing up.

Jo snorted, her hands never ceasing their activity but her head jerking back like a horse's. "She'll go for it. Elizabeth not only knows a good idea when it presents itself, she'd do anything to keep in with Joshua and he won't be too pleased at seeing his wife's business go down the plug hole." She threw more pieces of carcass in the stock pot and reached for another chicken. "I just wonder if he'll have time to write the article."

"Write the article? Can't Eve do that?"

"Never has." The knife flashed and a severed leg lay beside the chicken.

"But she's written a book, and what about the Newsletter for The Wooden Spoon Club? She was working on that over the weekend."

Jo dropped her knife, wiped her hands on a towel hanging at her waist and went over to a small set of book shelves. She looked along the second shelf, took out a glossy volume and handed it to Darina without comment.

Darina hastily wiped her own hands and opened the book. Beautiful photographs of complicated dishes arranged on smart porcelain plates filled half the pages. The recipes themselves were a typographer's dream, laid out as skilfully as the food. Each introduction was hardly more than a sentence or two, sometimes not even that. Darina turned to the title page, noted that Kenneth had done the photography and that Eve had scrawled a dedication to Claire, "Without whom I could not have produced this book."

"The number of times those bloody recipes were cooked," said Jo, back at her task of dismembering. "Claire even used to prepare them back at the flat. 'Who ever's going to use them?' I used to ask her. Talk about coffee table cookery. Anyway, you can see how much writing she had to do and even that was polished by Joshua. I don't suppose the Newsletters will be much more than recipes and suggestions strung together with an odd word or two, unless she can cajole Joshua into working on them. And I suppose she just might do that, she never seems to realise he has important work of his own to do when his regular day is finished." She gave the current carcass a particularly savage blow with her cleaver and reached for the last bird. "Nearly there, thank God. I just hope they'll actually get used, the way business is going at the moment they may end up sitting in the freezer for ever."

Darina put the book back on the shelf and finished her washing up, watching Jo take the tray of chicken joints to the big upright freezer and slip it onto a shelf. Arranged on other shelves were more trays of chicken pieces. When frozen, they would be piled into plastic bags and kept until needed for any one of a host of different dishes. Jo shut the door and started to clear her equipment.

Eve came into the kitchen, smiling brilliantly. "Oh, Jo, you've done all those chickens, that's marvellous."

Jo, scrubbing down her work surface, said nothing.

"Darina, darling, Elizabeth thinks it's a splendid idea."

Jo raised her head, "I gather all that hygiene information you asked me for went down well."

Eve gave her another flashing smile, "It was wonderful, quite made the morning, didn't it, Darina? And now we can put it all into an article. Darling," she laid her hand on Darina's arm, a cajoling note in her voice, "You couldn't try your hand at writing it, could you? I'm so tied up with the demos and everything, I don't think I have time."

Darina heard Jo give an exasperated snort. She felt an urge to laugh, Eve was so transparent, just like a child. "I'll try if you like, but I've never written anything before and I'm not sure I can."

"Ring Joshua, he'll tell you what to do."

"Eve, you're the bloody limit." Jo emptied a bowl of scalding soapy water into the sink and stood facing her, the skin drawn tight across her prominent bone structure, her mouth pressed into a thin, angry line. "Don't you think Darina's got other things to do with her time, not to mention your poor husband whose services you volunteer so readily? When are you going to face up to your responsibilities? All you ever want is the glamour and the glory, everyone else has to do the hard work. It's not even as though you're the greatest cook in the world, take away the tricks and trimmings and what's left? You haven't even cottoned on to the new flavours that today's food is all about. Without Claire and me you'd have been dead long ago." With that she strode out of the kitchen, banging the door behind her.

Eve gave a helpless cry, her hands fluttered towards Darina and tears welled in the big eyes.

"Don't take it to heart, she didn't mean all that, she's on edge, worried about the business and missing Claire." Darina gently sat Eve down on a stool then put the kettle on and opened the cupboard where the tea bags were kept.

"It's not fair," wailed Eve on a long note of distress, "I was the one who started The Wooden Spoon, she only came along after we were doing so well and needed more help. I *am* a good cook, I *am.*" She gulped, found a paper handkerchief in her pocket and wiped at her eyes, smudging the mascara.

"Of course you are," soothed Darina. "Would everyone have kept coming back for your food otherwise?"

Eve took the mug of tea she offered and sipped at the hot liquid. "Of course Claire was a wonderful help, she was so good at making everything taste really good. We were such a happy team, Claire and me. You say Jo's missing her, what about me? I really don't know how I'm going to manage without her. That's why I want you to join us so much. Oh, do say you will?" She looked at Darina with real entreaty in eyes that were comically ringed with black.

"Look, I'll have a go at this article and keep on helping you for a little, then we'll see how things work out." Darina remembered the suggested visit to New Covent Garden market the next morning, "Which reminds me, if I do the prep now for your demo tomorrow morning, would it matter if I came in a little late?"

Eve rubbed at her eyes again, smudging the mascara some more, "Of course," she said eagerly, "That'll be quite all right, in fact, Emily could help with the demo, you don't need to come in at all, perhaps you could write the article instead."

The phone on the wall beside her rang, she picked up the receiver, "Yes, Jackie, what? . . . Really? That's great, of course we can do it, tell Mrs. Burns I'll drop suggested menus in the post to her tomorrow. Cocktail party for sixty? Right. And, Jackie, you did send that certificate to the insurance company, didn't you? O.K. then." She replaced the receiver and turned to Darina with one of her old smiles. "A new booking, maybe our luck's turning."

CHAPTER SIXTEEN

Ralph Cox's company inhabited anonymous premises in Nine Elms. By the time Darina presented herself at 7:30 A.M. most of the business seemed to have been done. Odd crates of fruit and vegetables lurked in corners and by the side of loading bays. Many of the units had their roller doors firmly closed. There were fork lift trucks zipping about carrying crates to lorries, their burdens being loaded by men dressed in sweaters and jeans but the party appeared almost over.

Darina found Ralph's unit and parked between a sleek dark green Rolls-Royce, the numberplate bearing the letters COX, and a white estate van, then walked towards the open unit where Ralph was standing talking to a young man in a leather jacket. On the floor around them were crates and cartons of fruit and vegetables. There were boxes of the largest pineapples Darina had ever seen, melons, avocados, passion fruit, mange tout, she couldn't take in the full range on offer.

"O.K. then, I'll phone through our order each day. And you can bet I'll be on the telephone pretty damn quick if the goods aren't up to snuff."

Ralph smiled, "I can guarantee you'll have more complaints about your food than I will about my produce."

The young man looked at him sharply then turned on his heel and left.

"Darina, my dear, how nice to see you. Would you like a look round?" Was this the smile given little Red Riding Hood, the lips drawn back a little too wide, the teeth gleaming a little too white?

"I'd love to see anything you care to show me," she said—and wished she had chosen her words with a little more care. But he just gave another wolfish smile and took her through to the wide corridor that ran down the middle of the units. It was lined with displays of fruit and vegetables and filled with a colour and life hardly hinted at by the utilitarian exterior. Here was a specialist in exotic fruits, there boxes displayed wild mushrooms, chanterelle, pleurotte, pied de mouton and Japanese shitake, here twelve different varieties of potatoes. "Isn't it nice," said Ralph, "to see so many different kinds of spud? Such a pity your average punter knows so little about them. In most shops they'll just be labelled 'reds' and 'whites.' "

Darina noticed a vegetable that could have been designed by a renaissance architect; a cross between broccoli and cabbage, each pale green curd was a spiralling collection of points, the curds themselves forming a pattern of yet more complex spirals. Far too decorative to be cooked, perhaps a triumphant centrepiece for a display of fresh vegetables? And here was a box of what looked like lamb's lettuce with bronzed edges.

"I've never seen that before," exclaimed Darina, pausing by the stand.

Ralph took out a small head and pulled the little leaves apart, rubbing his thumb over them. He showed Darina the fine earth or growing medium that had stuck to his flesh. "Someone will have to wash all that off or the customer will complain. Most restaurants can't afford the time, yet it'll sell, everybody's looking for something new. The question is, does it taste any good?"

They munched on a couple of leaves and agreed the flavour was non-existent. "The fashion today," said Ralph, "is for salad that looks French but without the bitter flavour that's so popular in France."

They moved on. Ralph pointed out a box of superb looking grapefruit. "Something tells me they aren't really juicy," he said. Darina lifted one, it felt far too light. She put it back. A little further on, Ralph picked up a melon, rubbed the stalk end and pressed his nose onto the fruit, he offered it to her. A waft of irresistibly sweet perfume seduced her nostrils. "That's nice," he said, "but the flesh will be woolly. Just O.K. if you refrigerate it well and serve it today."

"How do you know?" asked Darina, who reckoned herself no bad judge of fruit and vegetables.

"You get an instinct," he replied.

Everywhere they went, he was greeted. Everyone seemed to know him and he knew everyone. As they went around, he plundered boxes of various specimens; a small bunch of seedless grapes, a huge radish which was, he said, a cross between a Chinese white and the ordinary English red, a piece of green ginger, so fresh the skin rubbed free from the flesh like a new potato, a star fruit, some mange tout, a few lychees. Soon his pockets were bulging. There was no furtiveness and no-one objected, it seemed accepted behaviour.

At Honor and Geoffrey's dinner party, Darina had seen a contained, urbane man, not hiding his origins but not flaunting them either. He had had the confidence of the successful man who has no need to impress. She remembered their talk after dinner, when she had asked him about his children and listened with interest to details of their talents and activities. Would either of them be following him into the fruit and vegetable business, she had asked?

"Christ, no. Only fools go into this line. You live your life when most others are fast asleep, sleeping when others are out enjoying themselves. I wouldn't want it for either of them."

"Yet you seem to have done well out it?"

He had grinned at her, "Yup, it's meant I can give the family everything they want. The kids can choose whatever it is they want to be. They won't have to scratch and claw their way to the top as I've had to."

"Was it really a great struggle?" Darina had asked then felt very foolish as he looked at her in silence.

"I'm sorry," she had apologised, "that was a stupid question."

"When we know each other a little better, I'll tell you about my early days," his eyes had glittered at her.

William had come and joined them. She had felt his arm reaching behind her along the settee, not touching but offering a sense of moral support. Or was it staking a claim? She felt herself retreat, concentrate on Ralph, refusing to admit the other man had any rights to her attention.

"You chose the right wife, anyway," she had said, ignoring any possible innuendo in Ralph's remark and looking across at Monica, chatting to Honor. "She's one of the best hostesses I've ever met." He'd followed her gaze, his heavy face softening as he looked at the poised woman talking rapidly with great verve to an audience that now included the barrister and accountant. There came a gust of laughter as she finished her story, her head tilted back like an actress who knows the line she has just delivered always gets a laugh.

"Yes," he said slowly, "I never made a better move, she's one in a million." Monica had looked across and they had exchanged a tiny, intimate moment, two people who understood each other perfectly.

Here in the market, Ralph was somehow larger, coarser, relaxed and totally at ease. But even whilst he joked and steered her around, his eyes flicked everywhere, noting everything. Under his relaxation, Darina sensed a core of tension. Deep inside his engines were idling, waiting for the moment when he would engage gear and bring them throbbing to life.

Or was that her being fanciful? No one else seemed aware of anything more than an amiable but acute businessman, one they knew well, liked and respected. There was a sense of deep camaraderie, the market seemed to be a giant club. A male club. The only women were a few nuns and one or two customers making late purchases.

"This is when the bargains are available," said Ralph, watching a pretty young girl trying to beat down a beaming wholesaler for a crate of ripe tomatoes. "Come and have a coffee, you've seen enough now."

He took her back to his unit and through a general office. A bank of answering machines was plugged into several telephones, battered

wooden desks were mostly unoccupied. Credit notes and invoices hung
in wads from butterfly clips. Metal trolleys carried computer terminals,
there was a fax machine and a photocopier. Beside them on a cupboard
stood a microwave oven. The sounds of Capital Radio drifted in from a
ghetto blaster stationed in the sales area outside, where pineapples and
melons were being sorted into ripe and over-ripe.

Ralph led the way into a further office, a small room furnished with a
slightly smarter desk and chair, a computer and two telephones. On the
walls were photographs of the old Covent Garden and charts of vegetables and herbs.

In a corner sat a coffee machine keeping warm a jug of already prepared coffee. Ralph half filled two large mugs then opened one of the
drawers of his desk and removed two bottles. "Whisky or brandy?" he
asked Darina.

She laughed, "Neither, thanks very much. It's much too early for me."

"Well it's after the middle of the day for me," he poured a generous
measure of brandy into one of the mugs, added more coffee to the other
and gave it to her. "Milk?"

She shook her head, took a sip of the hot liquid and sat down in the
uncomfortable chair beside the desk, finding room for the mug by moving a pile of computer printouts. She looked back through a glass partition to the other office where the desks now seemed to be filling up with
people. "Is this the day shift arriving?"

Ralph had remained standing, leaning against a filing cabinet, his
bulky figure looming large in the small, overcrowded office. "Accounts,
administration. They'll work through the day and when they go home,
the answering machines come on. Many customers ring in during the
evening with what they need for the next day. The messages get attended
to in the late evening when the orders are finally sorted out."

"When do you have to start work?"

"Oh, I turn up in the early morning, see how the goods are moving,
what the position is, then go round on my sales calls during the rest of
the day."

"So you still keep in touch with your customers? I thought you'd be the
big wheel behind the scenes now."

"Can't afford that. Need to keep in touch with what the market wants,
the way it's moving. And the punters like to talk to the boss but I have to
admit I choose who I see these days, treat myself as back-up to the main
sales force. I'm even back-up to the delivery chaps as well. Many's the
urgent order I've delivered from the back of the Roller on the way to
some do, handing out a crate of melons in my best bib and tucker." He

looked through the partition, beyond the sales area towards the sleek car with an obvious pride in its possession.

"And is that your delivery vehicle?" Darina pointed to the estate van parked beside the Rolls.

He nodded, "We've several of those, that one's waiting to be painted with our logo." He switched his attention back to her, "I have other parts of the business to see to as well. We have a warehouse and a preparation centre in Whitechapel, frozen vegetables, fresh fruit salad, that sort of thing, it's all added value."

"It sounds quite a little empire," said Darina slowly.

Ralph waved a large, negligent hand, "Surprising how it all builds up from individual decisions that just seemed common sense at the time. All at once you find you've got property that's leapt in value, assets your accountant says are ripe for stripping. We went public a few years ago, found ourselves paper rich but now he says we've got to watch out for predators. All I want to do is run my fruit and veg outfit. Sometimes I wish I was back with the barrows." He gave her a broad grin that openly acknowledged what a con that was.

"It must be a bore having to get to bed early. Monica was talking about it on Saturday," said Darina artlessly, opening her eyes wide. "Fiona was saying what a pity it was you had to leave so early from some cocktail party she saw you at, I think she said it was the Beamishes'?"

"Ah, yes, the Beamishes and Fiona." His grin turned into a saturnine smile, "My lifestyle provides some convenient excuses."

"You mean you don't always go straight home?" Darina gave him what she hoped was a conspiratorial smile. "I suppose you sometimes come down here and see how things are?"

"Shall we say my services are needed in various directions, eh?" The saturnine look became more of a leer.

Hastily Darina hauled her large handbag onto her lap and opened it. "What I wanted to see you about was these." She brought out the envelope with Kenneth's photographs, fished out the ones showing the mushrooms and handed them to him.

Ralph sat himself in the swivel chair, put down his mug and took the prints. He riffled through them rapidly then moved the mug and placed them carefully on the desk. He looked up at her curiously, his eyes dark and wary. "Where did you get these?"

"Kenneth showed them to me on Monday evening. He took them during the mushroom walk. I thought if you had a look at them you could check and see if . . ." She paused, suddenly aware exactly what she was suggesting.

"See if maybe I wasn't mistaken and a specimen of Amanita phalloides did slip through the net?'' His voice was wry and bitter. He sat and looked at her, his lids heavy, giving his eyes a hooded, reptilian quality. Then he dropped his gaze to the photographs, picked up the first and held it slightly above the surface of the desk, tilting it so it caught the light. He studied it for several minutes, laid it aside and picked up the next one.

Darina sipped her coffee and waited, watching the total concentration on his face as he looked at each photograph. There were no more than half a dozen but it must have taken him nearly twenty minutes to work his way through. Once the telephone rang. He picked it up, scribbled on a scrap of paper, said, "Right, one box of ready-to-use avocados by this afternoon. Sure, they'll be as ripe as your first girlfriend," then put down the phone and gave his attention back to the photographs.

She found herself fascinated by his hands. These were large, a black fuzz covered their backs and the first joint of the thick fingers. The nails were broad, heavily ridged and neatly cut. The warmth of the office after the chill morning air outside made her feel drowsy, she looked at those black hairs and wondered what it would be like to run her fingers lightly across them, then went on to wonder if his chest was similarly covered. Matted, she thought, with hairs that would feel coarse and springy, covering a well muscled body. With skin that would be smooth and fine, not leathery like his hands. Her eyes caught his and she felt hot colour surge through her body, flooding up her neck and into her face.

One dark eyebrow raised itself very slightly then he looked back at the last of the photographs. He placed it on top of the others and laid his hands either side of the little pile, "There is no Amanita phalloides in any of these photographs," he said. Then he looked full at her. "Will the police be given copies of these?" He picked up the photographs and weighed them in his hands.

"Kenneth is going to let them have a set, plus the others he took."
"Others?"

Darina opened her bag and took out the remaining prints.

Ralph let the first lot fall back on his desk. He spent less time on each of the second set but he paused at the one with him and Claire, a reminiscent smile lighting his eyes.

"Did you know her well?" Darina asked, drinking the last of her coffee, making the question casual, remembering the way he had demanded to know where she was the night of the party at his house.

"Claire?" He turned the word over reflectively, his manner changing, the macho challenge of his body softening. "We see a good deal of Eve and Joshua. They have this cottage in Sussex and we get together on Sundays. Eve loves partying," there was an odd, ironic twist to his voice, "she's always having people over. Claire was often there." His eyes dropped to the photograph again then, with a sudden, violent movement, he dropped the prints, swivelled his chair round and looked at a chart of wild mushrooms pinned to the wall behind his desk.

"Of all the people in all the world, to die of eating Amanita phalloides! And after one of *my* mushroom walks." The muscles of his back moved convulsively under the smooth cloth of his navy blue coat and his hands clutched at the arms of the chair.

There was a moment's silence, then he swivelled himself back again, once more fully in control. "She was a very special person. I think we'd all have rather eaten that mushroom ourselves than have her suffer such a fate."

He picked up the photographs again. None of the other shots raised either comment or change of expression.

When he had finished, he placed them on top of the first lot.

"Do you think they could be relevant?" He sat back in his chair and the question was offhand, he seemed more interested in looking at Darina; she felt herself growing hot again, felt as though he was mentally stripping the clothes from her body.

"I don't know," she heard herself say and held out her hand for the prints.

He gathered the photographs together and handed the little pile across the desk, watching her place them back in her bag. "You've got problems, you know that?"

"Problems?"

"You're far too uptight. You need to relax. Look at you, sitting on the edge of that chair, clutching your bag, as though you're some aged virgin expecting to be assaulted. You don't imagine I'm going to leap across the desk and rape you, do you?" His voice was lazy and amused, velvety soft, his body relaxed in the swivel chair, but it swayed from side to side as he gently shifted weight from one foot to the other.

Darina heard herself give a little gasp. There must be a witty riposte but it did not leap to mind.

"You're very attractive, you know that? All that long fair hair. And you've got a body, not like so many women today, twiggy bones, nothing to get hold of. You, my dear, could be an armful. But not holding yourself like that. Too rigid, nothing yielding, nothing soft." He tilted back the chair, looking at her out of half closed eyes, assessing her qualities, amused at her loss for words. "But your mouth is almost irresistible. That's soft all right, full and soft," his voice was caressing, "One of these days I'd like to release your hair from that stupid clasp, let it fall either side of your face, run my fingers through it and then kiss that mouth until it's swollen with wanting."

Darina forced herself to stand up and her hands to stop their stupid trembling. "What an instructive morning it's been," she said pleasantly, "I can't thank you enough for taking so much trouble to show me so many interesting things. And for checking these photographs so carefully." She rested the bag on the desk and held out her hand, she had regained total control of herself and was now amazed to find a pleasurable excitement surged through her, "You are a very interesting man, Ralph Cox, one I could wish I'd met in entirely different circumstances."

He looked at her, his eyes dark and calculating, then his face crinkled in a beguiling way as he laughed and took the outstretched hand, "So do I, my dear, so do I."

His large hand continued to grasp Darina's and his eyes to hold her gaze. She felt each understood the other perfectly.

"Let me know if you ever want choice fruit and veg. I can supply to order, it will be an experience you won't regret."

"I thought Eve liked to keep her supplier exclusive."

There was a flash of something in the ophidian eyes. Anger? Distaste? Then he said, "Eve does not have exclusive rights in this market."

Darina started to laugh then checked herself as she saw his eyes narrow slightly. This was no pussycat, this was a tiger at home in his jungle. "Life is full of might have beens," she made her tone regretful, found she didn't have to try very hard, he really could be a devastatingly attractive man, one with an unsettling ability to rip away conventional approaches and stir unsuspected emotions into life. It was time she left.

She turned to go but he asked her to wait a moment, scrabbled in a drawer, found a paper bag and fished in his pockets for the harvest he had gathered that morning. By the time he'd finished, the bag was bulging with fruit and vegetables. "A few samples," he said as he handed it over, "I hope you will enjoy them."

Darina eyed the bag as though a tarantula spider might crawl out from beneath its contents. "How extremely kind," she said, "What a feast." She looked him straight in the eye as she spoke, her tone sincere and innocent. A reluctant smile came into his eyes.

"Good hunting, I look forward to our next meeting."

At the door Darina swung round, "Are you a good cook?"

"A cook? Good heavens, no. A fry up is my limit. Mind you, I'm a dab hand at sausages." He didn't ask why she enquired but she had a shrewd idea he knew exactly what she was getting at. The only doubt was how truthful his answer had been. By now she felt he was most devious when he appeared most open and frank. She gave the briefest of goodbyes and left. It had been an interesting morning.

CHAPTER SEVENTEEN

The supermarket was busy. Mid-week shoppers thronged the aisles filling their baskets. Darina worked her way slowly along the shelves, consulting her list. There had been little opportunity for shopping over the past ten days or so. Or for housework. She had got back from Nine Elms and plunged into an orgy of vacuum cleaning and dusting, then checked her supply situation. Whilst she worked, she allowed her mind to absorb the nuances and undercurrents of her meeting with Ralph Cox before grappling with its implications.

As she was standing in the checkout queue, Darina became aware the woman in front of her was Honor. At the same time, Lady Doubleday turned and saw her.

"My dear, what a pleasant surprise. We did so enjoy our lunch with you on Sunday, there's a note in the post but the service is so bad these days even when it's just round the corner you never know when it will arrive. Have you got the day off?"

Darina said yes, more or less, and helped Honor take her purchases out of the trolley.

"This is nice," said the older woman as she paid for her shopping and started piling it in plastic bags, "It's just about lunch time, why don't we have a bite to eat? Geoffrey's in the city today, some board meeting, so I'm on my own, would you be free?"

Darina mentally consigned starting on Eve's article to later and suggested they caught a taxi to her place.

"No, you mustn't cook. I thought we'd go somewhere." Honor gave the idea illicit overtones.

"Well, why don't we still take a taxi and dump our stuff at the house then walk round the corner to The Front Page, it's such a nice pub and the food's usually very good."

"A splendid idea."

It was not long before they were sitting in a wooden booth sipping glasses of white wine and waiting for their lunch.

"Isn't this nice?" Honor was looking around her, "All this beautifully polished wood! I must get Geoffrey to bring me." She leaned towards

Darina conspiratorially, "I love having him retired and at home so much
but lunch time does sometimes seem a remorseless institution, I run out
of ideas for quick and inexpensive snacks. Now if we came here sometimes it would be a real treat. Look at this wonderful rack of lamb, and
what a lovely mint sauce, so creamy, so unusual! What have you chosen?"

She peered at Darina's salmon fishcakes with hollandaise. "Far too
fattening, I'm afraid," said the tall girl, tucking in with relish, "But I just
can't resist them, I salve my conscience with the salad."

"Ah but with your height you don't have to worry about weight, you
look marvellous. Now, how's your investigation going? Don't look so
surprised, William told us you were going to try and repeat your success
in finding your cousin's murderer."

Darina made a wry face, "I'm surprised he even mentioned it, he
seemed to ridicule the whole idea."

"Ah," Honor's fork paused a moment between plate and mouth as she
looked at Darina, then she continued eating, gently touching her lips with
the paper napkin after finishing the mouthful. "You mustn't take him too
seriously. He still tends to react first and think afterwards." She broke off
and helped herself to a roll and butter. Darina watched her mobile face,
its fine bones and lined skin framed in curly white hair, the faded eyes
still a remarkable shade of pale violet. She must have been a great beauty
in her day, or was it just age and character that gave her that quiet
loveliness? How old was she? Around seventy probably, Darina decided.

"We're so fond of William," Honor continued, "Geoffrey and his
brother are very close, despite John being so much younger, and we've
always looked on William as the son we've never had. It was so exciting
when he became a diplomat, we were sure he was going to end up an
ambassador, if only he could learn to keep his mouth shut at the right
time." She looked at Darina with a comical twinkle in her eye, "We
should have known he'd find it all too constricting, not enough action."

"He must have had that in the city," remarked Darina.

"Yes, but he's not really interested in money. When he told us he was
joining the police force we felt he'd really found his niche. He could
employ his intelligence and his concern for people. I think, though,
much of it is as routine as the Foreign Office and as impersonal as the
City."

"He seems to be happy with the life."

Honor eyed her lunch companion. "He looked so depressed when he
came back on Sunday. Wouldn't say anything, just picked up his bag and
left for Somerset. Geoffrey said he'd been laying down the law to you and
you wouldn't take it."

"That's one way of putting it."

"Well you stick to your guns," William's aunt said unexpectedly. "He's a dear lad but all that family have a tendency to think they know what's best for everyone. His mother and father have had some right dust ups over the years."

"Have they?" Darina eyed her curiously, Honor didn't seem the gossiping type.

"They're absolutely devoted to each other but Joyce has a mind of her own and doesn't mind telling John exactly what she thinks. And insists on leading her life her own way so they've had some royal battles."

"William told me she was very active in the county."

"Oh, runs it, my dear. If John makes High Sheriff, which is very likely in a year or so, it'll be more than half thanks to her."

"Perhaps she'll get the job instead?"

"What a delicious thought and not impossible. Now, I'm going to get us another glass of wine and what about a pudding? No? What a sensible girl you are. I shall emulate your example. You sit there, it's my turn."

Darina watched the slight figure work her way gently but inexorably to the front of the bar and obtain two glasses of wine. "When did William tell you I was trying to find out who killed Claire?" she asked as Honor sat down opposite her again.

"Let me see, I think it must have been on Saturday sometime, when we were discussing the dinner party. He said you were going to be particularly interested to meet Monica and Ralph outside business, so to speak, and then he explained the whole dreadful affair. I'm so sorry to hear of Eve's difficulties, we were appalled when we read that article."

"Do you know Eve?"

"Her mother and I grew up together in Norfolk. We didn't see much of each other after I married and she went to Cambridge but we kept in touch and I had Eve round once or twice when she first came to London. She quickly found lots of friends her own age, though, and then she got involved in her catering business. I haven't seen much of her these last few years but it was I who introduced her to Monica. I've sent her several people over the years, though I don't think any of the others has turned into a friend the way Monica has." Not to mention Ralph, Darina thought.

"I suppose you met Monica through your charity works," she suggested.

"Funnily enough, her mother is another old chum, she was married to Geoffrey's first chairman and was very kind to me, we spent a lot of time together when our husbands were abroad. It was just after Walter retired that Monica brought Ralph home and announced they were going to be married."

"Was it a great shock?"

"My dear, a cockney barrow boy to marry the daughter of a family that could trace its ancestry back to 1208? No title but they always looked on that as a matter for pride. Showed the family had never been into politicking. But Monica has always had a will of her own. I remember her as a small child throwing the tantrum of all time because she wasn't allowed to have a puppy she'd set her heart on. I regret to say she ended up with it. But the argument had been she wasn't old enough to look after it properly and she proved them wrong on that count. It was the light of her life, went everywhere with her. Everyone, including her, was afraid it would pine away when she went to boarding school."

"And did it?"

"Attached itself to her younger sister instead. Monica was very upset. I really think it made her dislike poor Mary, who wasn't responsible at all. But they were always rowing after that. Her parents thought the marriage couldn't last. But it was just like the puppy, she'd set her heart on it and made sure it worked. Of course, Ralph has been very successful, which has helped, I don't like to think what the outcome might have been if he'd continued selling from his barrow."

"She's probably had something to do with that."

"Yes indeed, he's been the driving force but she's provided him with the most marvellous backing, always entertaining the right people and running his home on the strictest of budgets in the early days. Whatever she says now about his picking her up in a Jaguar and taking her to the best restaurants, there wasn't enough money when they first married to live the sort of life she thought should be theirs and she made every pound do the work of two or three. That's why she's so good at fund raising, she watches the accounts like a hawk and knows exactly how to extract the maximum from everybody else, doesn't matter whether it's work or money."

The coffee Honor had ordered at the same time as the wine was brought to their table and she added a little sugar to her cup, stirring it in thoughtfully. "So how is your investigation going?"

"Slowly. I'm afraid William was probably right, I don't really have the qualifications for the job."

Honor gave her a steady look, "What do you think you lack?"

"Well," said Darina slowly, thinking as she sipped her coffee, "I haven't approached this problem systematically enough, I haven't been asking the right questions and I'm beginning to think I've been wrong about almost everything surrounding Claire's death. I drew a number of conclusions based on what I thought I knew about the situation. William warned me against 'theorising ahead of data,' as he put it, and, much as I hate to admit it, I am now beginning to feel he was right. What is worrying me is that I now have nothing to put in place of my original theory.''

"Which was what?"

Darina told Honor the full story of the mushroom walk, the lunch and the tragic details of Claire's death. ''I was sure that Eve must have been the intended victim and it was sheer bad luck Claire ended up with the poisonous mushroom–laden plate. But now it's beginning to look as though someone may very well have wanted Claire out of the way. But I'm not going to repeat my mistake, I'm going to keep firmly in mind the possibility that the plate could well have been meant for Eve after all."

Honor looked doubtful, "Maybe she's changed, I certainly hope so, but when I knew her, poisoned food was the last murder method I'd have chosen to get rid of her."

"What do you mean?"

"She hardly ate a thing, she was anorexic. The hours her mother spent trying to get her to eat. And I finally gave up asking her to dinner, she just pushed the food around on her plate, swore she'd managed more than half of it and then said that really she only ate health foods. Absolute nonsense. I made her a whole meal with ingredients from the leading health store in London, I even kept the labels to show her exactly what had gone into it, just the same result. She wasn't hungry, she said, and anyway she had to watch her weight. Like a sparrow she was. I know that twice she ended up in hospital being fattened up."

A number of things fell into place. Darina remembered Eve on their cookery course always pairing up with a girl who could be relied on to taste and eat everything they cooked. Much of the time it was Darina herself. "You try it, your palate is so good," Eve would say. And Darina, who was fascinated by the subtle changes ingredients underwent as you added more salt or spices, and loved getting the balance of a sauce exactly right, would dip in the tasting spoon again and again. Eve would only try a tiny bit of the finished dish. "Delicious!" she would say, "You've got that absolutely right." Giving her partner a wonderful sense of accomplishment.

Had she changed all that much? What had Darina seen her eat over the last ten days or so? Almost nothing. At The Wooden Spoon she made a great thing of going round picking at food but she took infinitesimally tiny portions. Hardly enough to keep a bird alive. Darina wondered what she actually subsisted on, it must be more than cups of herbal tea.

"She was always taking vitamin supplements and mineral supplements and heaven only knows what other supplements," Honor might have read her mind.

"Do you know what triggered it off?"

"I wasn't closely involved, I only know because I rang her mother after the second time she dined with us, I was so worried. And Rachel told me what a battle they were having. I think myself it was all to do with the fact that the rest of the family are highly intellectual, her parents are both philosophers and her elder brother and sister mathematicians. Eve was a late baby and it seemed as though all the brains had been used up, her only talent was cooking and none of the others thought that was worth much beyond keeping body and soul together."

Darina was appalled, "But she's brilliant, a real artist. Didn't they realise?"

"My dear, all far too cerebral to need more than bread and cheese to keep going. No, it was always, 'Poor Eve, we don't know what's to become of her.' What I could never understand was how she could be so interested in food in one way and yet deny it in another. But I gather from a psychiatrist friend of mine that the whole thing is bound up in a very complicated relationship with eating and an inability to deal with the world, particularly personal relationships. It must be very difficult to be the stupid one in a very bright family, very easy to believe you are unlovable as well. It was one of the reasons I made such an effort to send her clients when she set up, I thought she needed as much support as she could get.

"You mustn't blame them too much," she added as Darina sat sunk in incomprehension, "they really did worry about her and her mother tried everything to get her to eat when it seemed she was starving. Didn't do any good, they finally got professional help and found a psychotherapist who got through to her and gradually her weight crept up from under six stone to a more respectable seven and a half."

"I should think that's about what it is at the moment. Does Joshua know about all this?"

"Her husband? No idea, we've never met him. They married in a great rush with a very small wedding. We all thought the obvious, I'm afraid, with no justification as it turned out. But she could hardly keep going in the way she does without feeding herself properly, could she?"

"I wouldn't have thought so, it's very tough work."

"What makes you all do it?" Honor looked genuinely interested.

"For some of us, like Eve, it's the only real talent we have and, if you run an efficient business, the returns are quite good these days."

Honor eyed her affectionately, "But you've got so much intelligence, it's surely not the only thing you can do?"

Darina blushed and said, "It's what I'm most interested in. I love food, I love thinking about it, cooking it, serving it. I love watching people eat, enjoying a meal I've prepared." She stopped herself, she had to be careful not to get carried away talking about food. People either understood the fascination of all its different aspects, the fact that you were dealing with an essential element of life that behaved according to scientific principles but could also allow a cook to be as artistic and creative as a musician or painter, or they were bored by it. In her experience, there was no halfway house.

It appeared Honor was one of the latter, "I really appreciated that lovely lunch you gave us on Sunday but food isn't an essential in my life. I could quite happily subsist on scrambled eggs and sardines for whatever period it is I have left on this earth. Geoffrey, alas, has higher standards so I make the effort but I have to confess it is a struggle." She looked comically shamefaced, then brightened up when Darina laughed and said it was just as well there were people like her to keep the balance right.

"So, my dear, where do you go from here in your investigation?"

Darina hesitated, "I'm not at all sure," she said finally. "I need to spend some time reviewing all the information I have."

"I'm sure William would be delighted to help if you wanted someone to talk to about it," suggested the older woman hesitantly. As Darina looked doubtful she added, "The nice thing about the men in that family is that they never mind admitting they are wrong and they never say 'I told you so.' "

"I don't think talking to him would really help," Darina said decisively, thinking she was damned if she was going to ring him after all he'd said on Sunday.

Honor looked conscience stricken, "I'm an interfering old woman, pay me no attention. You have to do what you have to do, as they say in films. But I hope you will come and see Geoffrey and me again one of these days, I won't ask you if William is likely to be around."

"I'd love to," said Darina warmly. She liked this gentle, intelligent and civilised woman. She thought that this was the sort of mother she would like to have had, someone it was possible to talk to, who understood how necessary it was sometimes to stand back from relationships. "Now let's go back and collect your parcels and then I'll run you home, it won't take a moment."

Honor demurred but didn't need much persuading.

Afterwards, Darina went into the study and tried to write an article on home hygiene.

Two hours later she had a couple of pages of notes, a pile of screwed up efforts and one she felt was only marginally better than those already discarded. She got up and stretched herself. The thing was hopeless, she had no idea how to write and she did not even know what sort of article it was Elizabeth wanted.

Perhaps it would be best to ring and discuss it with her. She looked up the *Recorder*'s telephone number. Then she had second thoughts, if Elizabeth knew it wasn't Eve writing the piece, perhaps she would refuse to print it. Darina thought some more and then dialled the number.

CHAPTER EIGHTEEN

"It's awfully kind of you," Darina said to Joshua Tarrant at the Putney house an hour or so later.

He led the way upstairs, "Nonsense, I was dying for a good excuse to leave the office and it sounds as though you are the one doing a good turn."

She followed his solid back into a first floor room at the rear of the house. Once a sizable bedroom, it now appeared to be his office. Ordinary shelving covered most of the walls and held rows of books and filing boxes and stacks of magazines and cardboard folders bulging with papers. Only the walls on either side of the window were left clear and they were covered with framed photographs. Darina went and studied them. Some were of Eve, including a couple of posed shots in the basement kitchen in its stripped pine days, but pride of place was given to a photograph of an enormous bull with tight blond curls all over his head, sporting a rosette and leering at a very young Joshua. The rosette itself was attached to the photograph frame with a number of others.

"That was my bull," Joshua came and stood behind her, looking at the picture. "Father gave him to me when he was born. He was a champion in every way. His progeny have gone all over the world."

"Your father was a farmer?" Darina looked at the strong face intent on the photograph. It was still lit by that aura of youthful enthusiasm.

He nodded, "Farming was my first love but the family land had to go to my elder brother, there wasn't enough for two and my father said I'd be better off using my brains than trying to get a tenancy somewhere."

"So that's why you became an agricultural journalist?"

"It wasn't a conscious decision but I had the background and I gradually got channelled into it. Not that I'm complaining, I enjoy every minute. But I miss the land." He looked out of the window at the trees and shrubs crowding the little back garden. "I put all the profits from that bull into a savings account and finally managed to buy a cottage in Sussex, not far from Petersfield, near the family farm. I love it and so does Eve. We go down most weekends. You should see my vegetable garden."

His pride was unabashed, that of a schoolboy offering the first fruits of his garden patch. Something about its total innocence jarred on Darina. She wondered why, then remembered his remorseless nosying around that night at the Thompsons', his compulsive need to find out what was going on.

She looked round the rest of the room. Sideways on to the window was a desk bearing a computer video screen with keyboard, printer and a box of data discs.

"Is that a word processor?"

Joshua laid a gentle hand on the video screen, "Best friend a writer ever had, saves me endless time. Though I shall be trading it in shortly for one with a daisy wheel printer." He picked up the top sheet from the pile on the desk and handed it to Darina. It looked exactly like the printout she'd seen in Ralph's office, the type face lacking the clarity and sharpness of a typewriter.

"That's a dot matrix printer," Joshua said as he saw her studying the paper, "fine for giving a variety of type faces, but I really need better reproduction. Now you've heard enough about word processors, let's see what you've done."

Darina handed over her scruffy notes and the handwritten effort she'd made at the article.

Joshua waved her to an easy chair and sat himself down in front of the desk, reading the pages swiftly with concentrated attention.

"Right," he said when he reached the end, "Is this a way of asking me to do the article or do you really want to write it yourself?" The eagle-yellow eyes gave her a direct look.

"I'd like to do it myself, if I can. I just don't know how to begin, or finish for that matter."

"You've made a good start with your list of points. At least you know what you want to say. Did Elizabeth tell Eve how many words she wanted?"

"She didn't say anything about that."

"I expect it will be about seven hundred and fifty. Aim for that anyway. If it's too long she can probably cut it. Just write it as simply as you can. Remember you're talking to a reasonably intelligent housewife who's concerned about her family's health. She's also likely to be very busy; if she's not interested in your first sentence, she'll move on to another article, so make that punchy. Don't try and wrap up what you've got to say in clever phrases and don't use long words. A lively style helps but don't worry about it. Does that sound too difficult?"

Darina smiled at him, "You've made it sound so simple I think it must be extremely difficult."

"If you've got the sense to realise that, you'll do well. It'll have to be

typed, in double space. Have you got a typewriter?" Darina nodded.
"O.K., then. Don't have sleepless nights over it, what Elizabeth wants is
information, she can supply any lively writing that's needed." He glanced
again at the pages of notes, "These are good points, all you need is to
string them together."

"Jo supplied most of them."

Joshua handed back the pieces of paper and sighed, "Eve has a genius
for getting other people to do her work. How are she and Jo getting on
without Claire there to act as buffer?"

"I think both of them are under a lot of pressure at the moment."

"You mean not at all well. I hope Jo doesn't walk out, I don't think Eve
realises just how much she relies on her. Jo's a strange girl in some ways,
a bit prickly, but she's a first class worker and a wonderful cook." He
fiddled with a pencil for a moment, then said, "Claire thought Jo's background had a lot to do with her attitude, something to do with her
parents. She was endlessly patient with her."

"It's not very easy at the moment with so much business being cancelled. I'm sure Elizabeth didn't mean to harm The Wooden Spoon but
her article is having quite an effect."

Joshua threw the pencil onto the table at his side and placed his hands
behind his head. "It's the very devil. She was so helpful to me when I
first joined the *Recorder* I owe her a great deal, but at the moment I could
cheerfully kill her. I've asked if she can't do something on the catering
company to compensate but she says not at the moment. Apparently a
by-line for Eve on a hygiene article is as much as the editor will wear. If
you need any more help with it, don't hesitate to ring. Come on," he got
up and gave Darina a smile of devastating charm, "let's go and have a
cup of coffee and you can tell me what else is happening in Marylebone,
it's difficult to know exactly how seriously to take my dear wife."

She followed him down to the basement feeling she could quite understand how Eve had found him so irresistible at their first meeting. Joshua
put the kettle on then found a jar of instant coffee.

"Do you mind this stuff?" Darina shook her head and he spooned the
granules into two mugs then stood looking round the stylish kitchen and
living area. "Can't think why Eve wanted to change all this, it looked so
homely before and it must have been reasonably efficient, they turned out
any amount of food. They should have stayed here."

"But isn't it more peaceful now, an easier house for you to work in?"

Joshua gave a wry grimace and ran a hand through his thick hair, "It's
funny but I preferred it when all the activity was going on. At least one
could always find something to eat then, now half the time the fridge is
empty and we have to go out. That is, I have to go out, Eve is either

working or says she's eaten already. At least there's a good takeaway down the road." He looked moodily at his mug. "I suppose it's being used to working in a busy newspaper office but all this quiet is not what I need to finish that bloody book. I find it unnerving knowing I'm the only one in the house."

"Is it nearly finished?"

"Another week and it'll be there. Just as well, something tells me we're going to need the rest of the advance I'll get when it's delivered."

"When what's delivered, my darling?" Eve came in looking tired, her face drawn and without animation. She seemed unsurprised to see Darina, gave her a brief nod and went to the kettle.

Joshua leant on the counter dividing the two parts of the room, "My book."

"You mean it really is nearly finished?"

"Yup, if I have that uninterrupted weekend you promised, I should be able to deliver next week."

"Well, you know I shall be at the cottage, I have no intention of disturbing you, you're unlivable with when you're in the last stages of a book."

"What's it about?" asked Darina hastily, sipping her tea and leaning on the counter opposite Joshua.

"The possible perils of genetic engineering in agricultural bio-technology."

"Don't get him going on that, you'll be here all night, and you won't understand more than one word in twenty." Eve was petulant.

"It doesn't sound a very accessible subject."

"You'd be amazed at how accessible the book will be, the publishers are expecting massive sales. It's highly topical and the public nerve is going to respond with agitated twitchings that will mean a merry ring of cash tills." Joshua was cheerfully imperturbable.

"He's so clever, it's just a pity he never has time to share his intelligence with his stupid little wife." Eve poured boiling water into her mug, her voice bitter and ugly, "Always locked in his room with his books and word processor."

"You find the money useful enough." Bitterness was catching, Joshua's tone was equally sour and pointed.

Eve drooped, "We had more cancellations today."

"Why don't you move out of those ridiculously expensive premises and come back here?"

"Don't start on that again. I'm not going to give up all I've fought for and achieved, just as I'm getting somewhere."

"Just where are you getting, exactly?"

"You know how much publicity there was when we opened, if I move back here, everyone will think we've failed. And when Kenneth sells the video, we'll be all right. We've just got to get through this patch, that's all." Husband and wife faced each other. Eve's colour was high, her voice shaking slightly. Joshua's mouth was set hard, there was no suggestion of innocent enthusiasm about his face now.

"How are you going to manage without Claire even if you do get the business coming back in? And what about me, isn't it time you remembered you're my wife and gave me a bit of support?"

"You, what do you need from me?" Underneath the wildness there was scorn, "You're always at the paper or locked away in your study writing your damn books or out investigating some story or attending a press do. Are you suggesting I just sit around here producing the odd meal and waiting for you to take a bit of notice of me?" Her head made a curious motion, like a turtle indulging in calisthenics, the movement brought Darina into her sight line. "And you're going to work with us, aren't you, darling?" The pleading was unmistakable.

Darina placed her mug on the counter. "I can't make a decision on that yet," she said quietly. "And now I must go back and have another go at that article. Thanks for all your help, Joshua."

Eve's face lightened, "Oh, are you working on it? That's great, it could do us a lot of good. I said Josh would help. And I'm sure you'll come and join us in the end." She led the way out of the kitchen up to the hall, "Don't worry about the money angle, we can work something out." She seemed to have recovered her equilibrium and some of her old bounce. Darina said a quick good night and left.

She spent the rest of the evening working on the article but went to bed far from satisfied with her efforts.

CHAPTER NINETEEN

Thursday brought another early start.

Darina worked swiftly at weighing and chopping ingredients for the demonstrations that day, placing them in order on trays, one for each recipe, and listening with half an ear to Eve and Jo bickering in the background.

It seemed Eve had promised to prepare new menus to offer clients and these had not been forthcoming.

"We can't go on suggesting the same dishes," Jo complained, counting out duck breasts.

"It's not as though clients are queueing up for quotations," protested Eve. "But if you're so damned worried, why don't *you* come up with some new ideas. Use some of those new flavours you say I know nothing about."

"I would if I thought there was a chance in hell that you'd use them. The last ones I did never even got offered to clients. You claim to be the one who knows what they want." Jo poured peach brandy into a large dish and added the duck breasts.

Eve flushed. She pushed her hand up into her mass of hair, lifting it away from her neck. "O.K. I'll work on them this weekend at the cottage."

"Oh, yes, you're leaving Joshua to finish his book on his own, aren't you? Much better if you cooked him some meals and spent some time here," Jo's voice dripped acid. "You could get together a list of clients you should be talking to about confidence in our services and enthusing about the new menus. If this business is going to survive, it needs attention."

Eve gave her a withering glance, picked up two of the prepared trays and left the kitchen.

Darina finished wrapping the last little dish of chopped onion with cling film, labelled it, took the remaining trays upstairs then turned her attention to the meal Jo was preparing.

Producing a gourmet lunch for thirty people in two and a half hours is not a relaxing business and the two cooks worked in almost total silence.

Nor was there much chat on the way to the City location where they finished off and served the meal. Once they had cleared away, however, Jo relaxed.

"At least that's gone well," she said as they started loading up the van. "Thanks for your help. Has Eve asked you to join us?"

"Yes," said Darina, wondering how Jo was going to react.

"And will you?" Jo stacked the last of the equipment inside the van, closed the doors and stood looking at her.

"I'm not sure yet, it would mean totally changing my plans," Darina was deliberately evasive. "Would you like me to?"

Jo's face broke into a wide smile and Darina thought how attractive she could look. "I'd say! You're almost as good a cook as Claire and you work faster. We could really build the business into something, if you can only control Eve." She walked to the driving seat and got in. Darina opened the door on the passenger side.

"How do you mean?"

"Get her to stop firing off in so many directions, messing around with this video idea when she should be out reassuring people we really do know our business. And she should be watching costs more closely. Look at her paying you to do her prep when business is being cancelled every day, she should be coming in early to do that herself. And what she wants to run these courses for, I can't imagine."

"They seem to be going very well. Don't they make money?"

Jo started the van, "Just about cover their costs, I should think, when you take into account the capital tied up in the kitchen equipment that's on sale and the returns on that never seem worth the trouble. Well, now that I'm a shareholder, I'm going to have some say in things."

"A shareholder?"

"Yes, Claire left me her shares in The Wooden Spoon. Her father made her write a will after she came into her trust fund money and decided to invest it with Eve. Bloody silly that was. We were doing so well at Putney but Eve had big ideas, wanted to expand, start the cookery courses, have a prestige base. She talked Claire into it and the two of them went out and found the Marylebone premises. Which had to be totally redone. The kitchen's marvellous, of course, I have to give Eve that. And she's full of ideas but she doesn't seem to realise that the catering side needs proper attention. It could be a real little gold mine despite the overheads she's saddled it with. Even the cookery courses could be made to bring in extra business but is Eve pushing that? Like hell she is! She's not really interested in that side of things anymore. She wants to be a name, get away from the hard work. I tried to get Claire to reason with her but she, poor darling, had absolutely no head for business. Said Eve was brilliant and it would all work out in the end." There was a despairing note in Jo's voice.

"I'd have thought Claire would have been more likely to leave the shares to Eve than to you," said Darina provocatively.

"Aye, well, she did think about it but then she said Eve had so much anyway and it would be nice for me to have a proper stake in the company. But we didn't think it would ever actually happen, it was all pie in the sky." Jo rubbed her hand over her face.

"So now you own part of The Wooden Spoon," Darina brought out the words slowly, "Does Eve know yet?"

Jo grinned, "She hasn't said anything so I reckon not."

"Claire had fifty percent, didn't she?"

"Yes, they were supposed to be equal partners but Eve always made the decisions, Claire just followed along." Once again there was that despairing note.

"I was talking to Ken the other night, he said she was involved with a married man, did you know anything about that?

Jo blew a long horn blast at a taxi cutting in front of their van then said, "I knew she was seeing someone, someone she didn't want me to meet. If I was working or meeting a friend, she'd ask if I would stay out until a certain time. I didn't really mind, the flat's so small it was impossible for one of us to have any privacy unless the other one was out."

"You didn't wonder who it could be?"

Jo made a hopeless little gesture, "What was the point? She didn't want me to know and I accepted she was entitled to a life of her own."

"Do you think it could have been Joshua or Ralph?"

"Joshua?" Jo gave Darina a quick glance, "What makes you think of him?"

"Just that I think it must have been somebody you knew otherwise she wouldn't have been so secretive and he and Ralph seemed to me the obvious candidates."

"Well, Ralph could certainly have been making a play for her. But I'm sure she wouldn't have looked at him." Was there an uncertain note in her voice? If so it disappeared as she continued, "How Monica puts up with his goings on I can't imagine, she must know which side her bread is buttered."

"You mean?"

"Haven't you noticed the way he leers at any halfway good-looking female? And more than leer, some men just can't keep their hands to themselves. He seemed pretty interested in Eve at one stage."

"At one stage? You mean it's over now?"

"Who knows? He just doesn't come round to The Wooden Spoon so much these days."

That could mean any one of a number of things. "Did he try anything with you?" Darina eyed the handsome girl beside her.

Jo gave the equine snort with which she greeted any particularly fatuous remark. "Didn't get a chance." She shot a quick glance at her companion, "But I don't think he would have anyway." Darina waited but nothing more was forthcoming.

"What about Joshua? His and Eve's marriage doesn't seem all that satisfactory."

"Satisfactory! He's highly intelligent, overworked and in need of some looking after: she's got the sense of a three year old child and is completely self-centred. How on earth could it be satisfactory?"

"So he may well be looking at someone else. Why not Claire?"

Jo's foot pressed harder on the accelerator and the van whizzed through the traffic until it came to a halt at the rear end of a long jam. She sighed with frustration and put the engine into neutral. "I suppose if you want to think that way it could have been possible. I'll tell you one thing, whoever it was, Claire was determined to get him."

"Are you sure? She didn't strike me as that sort of girl at all."

"She wasn't. There was a period when they didn't see each other. She wouldn't tell me if it was his decision or hers but I watched her get paler and quieter and finally told her for once in her life to fight for something she wanted. And about a week before she died she told me she'd decided to follow my advice."

"What happened?"

"I'm not sure, I think he told her he'd try and work something out. It sounded like a stay of execution to me but Claire seemed happy enough about it. I think you must have got it all wrong, it couldn't have been Joshua."

"Why not?"

But Jo just shook her head.

Darina turned to another of the tangled relationships circling round The Wooden Spoon, "What about Elizabeth? Do you think her affair with Joshua could have started up again? It seems to me he would have been happier with her."

Jo gave another of her snorts, "Elizabeth! Ten years older than he if she's a day, and another one that's wrapped up in her career. But she's dotty enough about him still. If Eve wasn't around, maybe it would work for a bit, until he found himself looking at someone younger."

"You sound pretty cynical. Don't you know any happy marriages?"

The traffic moved a few feet, Jo followed the car in front, brought the van to a stop once again then turned towards Darina. She'd lost her usual composure, her eyes were bright with some tightly controlled emotion, her fingers thrummed on the steering wheel. "There are no happy marriages in my family, that's for certain. My sister tied the knot in much too much of a hurry. I told her to have the baby and be damned, bring it up on her own if she really wanted the brat but not to land herself with that goon for a husband. Did she listen? Now she's grateful if he just spends the evenings at the pub, drinking with his mates, and doesn't give her a black eye at the end of it. You'd have thought after watching Dad beat up Mum all those years she'd have learned something. Not her."

"How is your mother?"

"O.K., I think. If business does dry up for a while I might get to spend some time with her. Try and make up for not getting there before that bastard died."

"You mean your father? I thought you said you were with him at the end."

Jo looked at Darina in silence for a moment, then averted her gaze to stare at the unmoving traffic ahead of them.

"That was pretty stupid of me, I wasn't thinking and it just slipped out." Darina had to strain to hear the mumbled words over the traffic and street noises clogging the surrounding air.

"I couldn't face it. I did set off on the Thursday but I'd told Mum I mightn't be able to get away. She wanted me there, had visions of a death bed reconciliation, I suppose. I got somewhere beyond Stevenage, I hate motorways so I never take the M1, and I just ground to a halt. It was like," she paused, "like driving to a battle front. You knew when you got there you were going to be shit scared, your stomach gone to liquid and your hands trembling like milk coming to the boil. I couldn't believe the bastard was actually dying. I thought when I got there, he'd be out of bed and—and it would all start again."

"All what start again?"

Jo was silent again for several minutes. Then, "Oh, things," she said with a little whip in her voice.

"So what did you do?"

Jo turned towards Darina, her voice got stronger. "Found a B and B place and rang Mum. Pretended I was still in London, might be able to get away next day. I could hear she was crying, if she'd been round the corner, I'd have gone straight there. But she was hours away and I knew as soon as I started driving again, it'd all be back with me." She swallowed hard and stared grimly at the unmoving traffic. Darina said nothing. "I stayed at that revoltingly uncomfortable guest house and rang Mum every few hours. I went for walks, to the cinema, read, anything to stop me thinking, until he died on Sunday morning. Then I started off again and got there that evening." She paused once more. "I went upstairs and looked at him and waited for the relief to come. The realisation he could never again . . . that I'd never again have to look at Mum and wonder if she knew and why she didn't do something. But there was nothing. It wasn't him. It was a shell. I couldn't even feel hate anymore. And Mum couldn't stop crying. When I tried to tell her how I felt, why I hadn't come sooner, she said, 'As far as I'm concerned, you arrived on Friday.' And that was that, she had convinced herself it was the truth. She even told the police I was there. I think she has a nice little picture now of me holding my dying father's hand, like something out a Victorian picture. It's easier than facing reality. She's always been like that."

Darina could think of nothing to say and both girls stared at the unmoving traffic.

After a bit Jo shot her a sideways glance, "So I have no alibi for Saturday and Sunday."

"You mean?"

"Don't pretend you aren't trying to find out how Claire died. And if I could help you, I would. But I was nowhere near that lunch party, I just wish I had been."

Behind them hooters set up a cacophony of sound. Jo hastily put the van into gear and closed the gap that had opened between them and the cars in front. This time the jam seemed to have cleared and they made slow but continuous progress.

"I daresay the police will solve it all long before I do," Darina said calmly.

"Yes, it's rather like a housewife setting out to do one of our contracts without any of the right techniques or equipment."

Darina thought it was an apt, if unkind, analogy. "Have the police talked to you yet?"

"Oh, aye, came round the kitchen yesterday, wanted to know how we all got on, all about the business and everything. Plodding little man with a notebook and blunt pencil. I don't see him making much progress."

"How do you think Claire died?"

"I think bloody Ralph made a bloody mistake, that's what I think. He won't ever admit it, though, it would dent his macho image. The sod should be struck off, or whatever it is they do to stop food sellers purveying eatables."

"You think a poisonous mushroom can be cooked with others without contaminating them?"

Jo fell silent and said nothing more.

"I think," said Darina as they drew up outside The Wooden Spoon, "you should tell the police exactly how long you took to get home."

"Or you'll tell them for me, is that it?"

"If it matters, they should be able to check out exactly how you spent the time," said Darina calmly. "But if you are right and Claire did die accidentally, it won't mean anything and you will have got it off your chest."

Jo swung herself out of the van without comment and started unloading their equipment.

Once the dirty dishes had been cleaned up, Darina went along to Jackie's office. Claire's funeral was to be held the next day. The secretary wanted to attend and Darina had said she would come in and look after the telephones and mail whilst everyone else went down to Surrey.

As she crossed the entrance hall, Darina could hear Eve's voice. "And they said they didn't know when the claim could be paid?" She sounded exasperated. "They've got the certificate, haven't they? So what's the delay."

"I'm sorry," Jackie sounded tearful, "They said it wasn't a proper death certificate and there would be a delay in making payment until enquiries had been carried out. I spoke to the Manager of the Claims Department himself," she added.

"It's typical," the intensity level of Eve's voice rose from exasperation to real anger, "they take your premiums quickly enough but when it's a question of paying out, it's delays all the way."

She came out of the office and almost bumped into Darina. "Hi!" she said. "How'd it go? We've had a new enquiry today, things may be looking up." She seemed to have thrown off her anger at the insurance company. It was as though it had been a gadfly's ire, quickly aroused, quickly dissipated. She disappeared into her office.

"The police have rung," said Jackie as Darina entered her office, "They want to know when they can interview you about the mushroom walk."

CHAPTER TWENTY

The Wooden Spoon was silent as Darina let herself in the next morning.

She hung up her jacket then stood for a moment, absorbing the atmosphere. It was as though the spirit of the building held its breath, was lying still, guarding its secrets. She gave herself a small shake. It was not as though it was her first time alone in the building, not as though it was here that Claire had died. She was not even sure that it was here the answer lay to the mystery of how she had died but she was sure the office contained the answers to certain questions.

The post yielded a new enquiry, two urgent requests for bills to be paid, a couple of queries about what to serve for special occasions from women who had been on courses, and the usual junk mail. Darina threw the last into the waste paper bin and took the remainder into Eve's office.

The stylish little room held a faint evocation of the Opium scent Eve always wore, its heady notes invading the quiet air. The desk was clean and tidy, its wicker baskets empty. Darina laid the mail neatly on the pale wood and returned to Jackie's office.

She opened the drawers of the secretary's desk and found some large index cards, sat herself down behind the typewriter and inserted one in the machine. She found out how to switch it on and started pecking at the keys with two fingers. Steadily, with much use of the correction key, she made notes on Claire's death, on the mushroom walk, the celebration lunch, and on all the suspects.

As she did so, she couldn't help thinking of her police interview late the previous afternoon.

A detective sergeant had taken her through her account of the picnic that Saturday, making careful notes. There was none of William's quick intelligence, or charm, but he had been thorough. She realised with a sinking heart just what advantages the police had. No one questioned their right to ask for details, probe motives. They could contact anyone, ask any questions, had resources for checking facts. She supposed the sergeant must know, for instance, about her involvement in a previous murder. When he asked her what she had done on the Sunday, she took great satisfaction in telling him the greater part had been spent with a member of the C.I.D.

It did not appear to impress him greatly. He merely asked what she did before her "friend," he gave it a delicate emphasis as though a member of the C.I.D. with a private life was a rare specimen only occasionally seen outside captivity, before Mr. Pigram had arrived.

Did he think she could have dashed over to Putney, slipped the mushroom into place, then dashed back again, all without being seen? His manner indicated every possibility had to be considered. Darina mentioned two telephone calls taken during the morning and gave him the names and telephone numbers of the callers. He asked if she minded if they checked out the details but it was obvious that her name was not high on the list of suspects.

She was as co-operative as she could be, offered tea and home made biscuits, tried to open him up and discuss the case. He would not play. He drank the tea, ate the biscuits, made his notes and stonewalled all her questions. Made her feel a cross between an amateur Mata Hari and a scandal seeker. No information was to be gained from that source.

Now she rattled the keys of the typewriter with unnecessary force as she filled cards with notes. The telephone rang twice whilst she worked. Two cancellations for courses sometime in the future by ladies who were immensely regretful. Both excuses sounded genuine but Darina wondered as she made a note of each on the message pad if the blight that had struck The Wooden Spoon's catering side was spreading to its other activities.

When she had finished her typing, she pushed aside the machine, laid out the cards and looked at them like a patience player, studying them as though to decide which should be moved where. This, she said to herself, should have been done earlier. How many little details had she forgotten, things that seemed irrelevant at the time so had not lodged in her memory?

She separated out the cards that dealt with each of her suspects and read them again, searching her memory for any further detail that might be helpful, then assessing the interplay of the various relationships. How far had they been responsible for Claire's death?

After a little thought, she took another card and drew a circular diagram, with Claire in the centre and each of the other characters in the drama round the outside. Then she drew a series of lines connecting Eve to Joshua, Joshua to Elizabeth, Monica to Ralph, Ralph to Eve, Kenneth to Claire and one out from Claire that ended in a question mark. She looked at the card for a long time, finally adding a question mark over the

Eve/Ralph line and two question marks over the Joshua/Elizabeth line. Then she put more question marks beside Jo's name.

After a moment she took another card and redrew her diagram with Eve's name in the middle. The results were interesting.

She assembled the cards into a neat pile, made a mental note to buy some replacements, sat back in the chair and looked round the office. It was time to take advantage of having the place to herself. She started opening drawers. In the third she found Jackie's account book. At first glance, The Wooden Spoon's financial position looked astonishingly healthy. Then she studied the figures a little more closely.

The book was merely a record of cheques paid out and monies received. The cheques were mainly to suppliers and part-time staff plus the odd refund of fees for cookery courses. They were heavily outweighed by the receipts from clients of both sides of the business plus what seemed an astonishingly small sum for a television spot. But there were no entries for rent, rates, services, salaries or bank charges nor any mention, either by receipts or payments, of the kitchen equipment that was sold on courses and demonstrations.

Darina left the account book open on Jackie's desk and started looking at the filing system. It seemed to be reasonably well organised. Each client, each supplier, each course, had its own file. She picked out the one marked *Cox* and raised an eyebrow as she noted the frequency with which Monica and Ralph entertained. Valued clients indeed. She opened a few others at random. The files were in two parts, letters on one side and invoices on the other. The system seemed to be that when an invoice had been paid, Jackie gave the copy a giant tick and wrote a date beside it, presumably when the money had been received. Darina checked with the account book and matched some dates with credit entries. Two of the files she looked at had invoices clear of ticks, one had been outstanding a few weeks, one more than two months.

Darina found Jackie's diary, went back to the start of the year and started looking up each client for whom a function had been logged, making a note as she went of the invoice amounts and dates, adding the date when each had been paid, or an asterisk if it was still outstanding. Then she made some rough calculations. It appeared Eve's catering business had some 25 percent of its outstanding bills more than two months overdue and that this was no new phenomenon. A few files with sizable unpaid bills had copies of polite letters requesting settlement.

Darina knew from running her own business how vital cash flow was. Most of your supplies had to be paid for on purchase and any accounts had to be settled promptly. You also had to pay staff promptly. Good workers are hard to find and need looking after. Part-timers particularly resent no wages at the end of the day.

Darina looked again at the list of outstanding bills. If this was the way Eve was running her business, she was in trouble. She wondered by how much. Where were the other accounting records? In Eve's desk?

Hadn't there been a couple of ledgers in there when she'd been looking for the whisky for Elizabeth the previous week? Darina went and tried the bottom drawer she remembered as holding the books. It was locked.

She sat and pondered for a moment. Real detectives would whip out a hairpin or a skeleton key and open it in a twinkling. She eyed it with misgiving then remembered reading a dodge in detective novels. She fetched her handbag, extracted a credit card and tried inserting a corner of the plastic between the edge of the drawer and the desk. Nothing happened. Perhaps it only worked on Yale locks. She put the card back and picked up a paper knife from the top of the desk, pushed it into the lock and fiddled. Once again nothing happened. She wondered if she could use the end of the knife to force the drawer open but couldn't see how she was to explain the inevitable broken wood to Eve.

She put the problem aside for a moment and tried opening the other drawers. No problem.

The long middle drawer held paper clips, pencils, a tape measure, vitamin pills and the odd desk detritus, including a couple of keys. Darina tried them, neither would open the locked drawer.

She investigated the rest of the desk. There was not much of interest. Notes on future courses, suggestions for dishes, trial recipes, cuttings from cookery columns of various newspapers, personal letters. Darina had a moment of hope here but they turned out to be from an old school friend with news of another's marriage and an aunt expressing regret she was not going to see Claire at a family reunion, with full details of various relations. There was a collection of health food fruit bars and packets of trail mix. All the date stamps were long expired. Darina sampled one of the mixes, the nuts were rancid and the coconut stale. She put them carefully back, trying to ensure the packets looked more or less as she had found them.

The other bottom drawer, twin of the locked one, still held the whisky bottle, its level now considerably lower. Beside the bottle were piles of glossy literature on The Wooden Spoon, the courses, the catering and the photographic possibilities of the demonstration theatre. No expense seemed to have been spared in their production.

Darina started to shut the drawer, then looked at it more closely. It had runners to hold hanging files. These had not been fitted and there was a large gap between the solid part of the drawer's sides and the bottom of the drawer on top. It also looked as though the drawer was shorter than the desk. Darina crawled underneath and tried to reach inside the locked drawer by stretching her arm up into the gap between the end of the drawer and the back of the desk. She could just feel the edge of what could be an account book, or some other type of office book, when her shoulder seized up with an agonising pain. She crawled out and massaged the joint, leaning against the desk and looking down at it in frustration. There must be some way to open the drawer.

The pain receded. Gingerly she tried moving the shoulder and found it sore but seemingly in working order. As a last hope, she went back to Jackie's office and looked at her desk. It seemed very similar to Eve's. And in the middle drawer was another collection of small keys.

The third one she tried was sticky but seemed possible. After a couple of minutes patient lifting and pressing, it turned and the drawer came open. Darina felt triumphant.

In it were cash books and bank statements and a file of unpaid bills.

Darina spent a long time studying them, trying to disentangle the full story of The Wooden Spoon's financial situation.

When she had finished she knew without any doubt that she would not be investing in this company. She wondered if even Jo's hard work and limitless energy could turn the situation around. Perhaps if it was allied to some smart marketing and an injection of cash. But not hers. Perhaps a bank? Or someone like Ralph?

She started to replace the books then saw there was a small one she hadn't noticed before. It recorded purchases and sales of the cooking equipment. Considering the level of investment the goods represented, Darina agreed with Jo's opinion of the sales. Then she came to the last entry, which was for Monica's charity demonstration. She looked at it and then went through the figures again. Whichever way she added them, the total still came to some £300 less than the amount she remembered handing over. And according to the book, most of the money taken had been by cheque. Darina thought of the pile of crumpled notes she had given her friend. She sighed, how did Eve think she would get away with it? One good audit and a stock taking would reveal all.

A fragment of remembered conversation drifted into her mind. She rummaged around in the desk drawer again without finding what she wanted. The filing cabinets in the other office were more productive. In one of them she found a copy of a policy insuring Eve's life for Claire's benefit and Claire's for Eve's, both for £100,000. There was a carbon of a letter on the file sent to the company enclosing a copy of the certificate issued by the court authorising Claire's burial. The covering letter re-

ferred to previous notification and asked for payment under the policy to
be made to Eve. And Eve had been chasing the cheque yesterday.

Had she really expected to receive settlement of the claim before the
police finished investigating Claire's death? It was unrealistic, to say the
least. Was it sinister? Darina closed the filing drawer slowly. Eve never
had been a very realistic person. She always expected instantaneous results, was a cook who would rather stir fry than casserole.

Was Joshua aware of The Wooden Spoon's financial state? How much
did Jo know? And had Claire been aware of their difficulties?

Darina restored both offices to the state she had found them in, finally
managing to relock Eve's desk drawer after a titanic struggle with the key,
which she then replaced in Jackie's desk.

She stood looking around her for a moment. Nothing else struck her as
worthy of investigation. She went up to the demonstration theatre. All the
cupboards contained equipment except the one with the alcohol. The
fridges were clear. The collection of books still lacked the one on mushrooms Elizabeth had borrowed for her article.

Darina went down to the catering kitchen. Like the demonstration
theatre, it was sparkling clean and immaculately tidy. There seemed
nothing here, either, that could yield a clue. Fridges, chill room, cupboards, all contained the most ordinary of contents. Darina carefully
inspected the stores and kitchen necessaries stacked on one of the cupboard shelves, some in use and more waiting to take their place. Everything was in order, squared away, beautifully organised.

Finally she looked at the small set of shelves where Jo had found Eve's
book the previous Tuesday. Each row contained a number of cookery
books, many well thumbed, some falling apart. Darina recognised many
of her own favourites amongst them, plus some newer volumes and
several notebooks. Each was labelled with one of the girls' names. Darina
picked out the one marked "Jo."

Neatly arranged inside was a collection of recipes, many written in a
clear but unformed hand, some typed, a few were cuttings stuck on a
piece of A4 paper with various notations added, changes in ingredients
and method, scaled-up quantities for larger numbers, alternative suggestions for presentation. It was all as efficient as everything else about Jo.

Darina replaced the book and took out Claire's, on the next shelf
down. This was bulkier and not nearly so well organised. It was so fat the
rings strained to keep closed. Loose cuttings were slipped in between
pages of hastily scrawled recipes. Typed sheets were stuck together with
unidentifiable scraps of some food or other. Every now and then Claire
had noted "V.G." beside a recipe, or slashed a red felt-tipped pen
through another. "Don't bother to do again" was written beside a tempt-

ing looking dish ripped from some magazine. Then, as Darina flipped through the pages, the rings gave up the unequal struggle to hold everything in place and a whole section slipped to the floor.

She stooped and picked up the collection of typed sheets, cuttings and scrawled pages, put the ring book down, opened it out and tried to fit the sheets back in place. Then she realised that sticking to one of the pages was a sheet of paper that didn't look like a recipe.

Gingerly she detached it, flicking away whatever it was that had glued the pieces of paper together. She found she was holding a typed letter.

There was no address or date. "Darling" it began. Darina pulled out a stool from under the counter, sat down and read it slowly.

Darling,
You know I love you. Everything I've said to you is true. You mean more than I can ever put in words but we can't go on this way. I know you want a proper home, children. I wish I could give them to you. But I can't ask for a divorce, it would destroy her. You must understand. I shan't contact you again and you mustn't get in touch with me.

Goodbye, my darling, I shall always remember our hours together.

The letter was signed with a roughly sketched broken heart.

Darina leant back and looked at the sheet of paper. It had been folded in four and bore signs of having been much handled. There were several marks on it that could have been tearstains. The paper itself was flimsy and the type face was fainter and less sharp than the effect she had been getting from Jackie's machine. She tried to cast her mind back and remember where she had seen a similar print. After a little, she carefully fitted the loose pages onto the rings of the open book, slipped the letter into the middle, and replaced the file on the shelf.

Eve's notebook was much slimmer and composed almost entirely of typewritten recipes. But beside it was a notebook, its grease-stained pages filled with rough outlines of recipes, the ingredients noted in a sort of speed writing, the methods no more than an occasional instruction or order of working. Some of the recipes had been ticked, others crossed through. Darina looked through both the file and the notebook but found nothing that seemed significant. She replaced them and left the kitchen, closing the door carefully behind her.

Back in the office Darina realised with surprise it was long past lunchtime. She had no desire for food but needed to get out of the building. Switching on the answering machine, she went out. As she walked towards Wigmore Street, she thought of Claire's funeral, of the mourners gathering round the grave: Eve, Jo, Monica, Ralph, Joshua and Elizabeth. No Kenneth, he had said he couldn't face the occasion. She gave a little shiver as she turned the corner and met a biting wind.

CHAPTER TWENTY-ONE

The north wind brought its chill to a small Surrey churchyard. Mink jackets and cloth coats were pulled tight round the bodies huddling beside the grave as dry leaves were whipped around legs and into the open earth lined with artificial grass. But when the mourners regrouped in the Montagues' large hall to eat sandwiches and drink white wine, there was little of the relaxation that comes so often at a funeral after the rites are completed, when friends and colleagues relax in the warmth, meet seldom seen relations and swap memories of the departed. Such occasions are for when a long life has ended or death has come as a friend. Claire had been too young, too full of life and love to be remembered with anything but anger at the way her promise had been cut short.

Ralph Cox found himself beside Eve, standing next to a long, highly polished table displaying a collection of antique games. She fiddled with a bowl of mother of pearl fish, running her fingers through the little shapes, lifting and letting them fall back with a gentle shimmer into the wide Chinese bowl. "How amazing it would be," she said, her eyes wide and expressionless, "to use some of these to decorate a salmon."

Ralph looked at her. He was bored with Eve. The time had passed when she could excite him with a look, when her tiny body, so alive, so full of movement, had seemed to offer unique delights. They had had fun, no doubt of that, but fun never lasted. He looked around the room. Monica was by the huge, carved wood fireplace, talking quietly to Claire's mother. She met his glance but did not cease her conversation. He looked round the rest of the room, seeking distraction. In a corner Elizabeth was standing close to Joshua. As he finished whatever it was he had been saying to her, she put out a hand and gently laid it against his cheek in an intimate, comforting gesture. Ralph watched Joshua close his eyes for a brief moment then take the hand and press it lightly to his lips. The little scene was over almost before he had had time to register it.

"Eve, I've hardly said hello. How are you?" Monica had arrived by his side and proceeded to engage the tiny girl in pleasant inconsequentialities.

Looking back at the corner, Ralph saw Elizabeth had disappeared and

Joshua was making his way towards them, pausing to say a few words to Claire's brother, something in the City, Ralph remembered. He watched the journalist detach himself from the younger man and move on through the crowded room, wrapped in his own world. When he reached them, he made no attempt to say anything but stood nursing a glass of wine and gazing abstractedly at an oil painting so layered in varnish it was impossible to make out the subject. Ralph wondered what the little scene he'd just witnessed actually meant. Was there still a spark amongst the old ashes?

Ralph studied Joshua. He was a cold fish, really. Had no understanding of his wife. Too concerned with his own doings. Clever, of course. His books always made an impact. Did he realise how jealous Eve was of his success? That book of hers had really bombed. Pity, Ralph thought, that she had not shown it to him before it was published, he could have told her it was far too clever. The food was way over the top. It might, perhaps, become a bit of a cult book in time, after the returns had been pulped and too late to do her much good.

Ralph allowed his glass to be refilled, Monica would drive back. The wine was not worthy of Claire, an unassuming Riesling. He wondered briefly what he would have chosen. An Italian Chardonnay, perhaps, not quite so full bodied as the Australian but full of flavour and with a subtle depth, not bone dry but with none of this pedestrian touch of sweetness. A sudden vision of Claire filled his mind. What a special girl she had been, goodness had shone out of her like phosphorescence in a tropical sea, refreshing in this day and age. Not a girl it was easy to love and leave. Not like Eve.

Ralph sighed, Eve was proving unexpectedly difficult to detach himself from. He wondered, as he had so often recently, how to get rid of her, he did not want to provoke another hysterical scene. She was not as street wise as he had thought.

"I don't think I can take much more of this."

Jo appeared on his other side, her eyes hollow under the prominent brow line, her handsome features stripped of emotion. For once she was in a dress, a plain black wool that hung from her broad shoulders with little suggestion of feminine form.

Behind her was Elizabeth. "Eve and I wanted to leave after the burial but Joshua insisted we come on, said it would be unforgivably rude not to." She engaged Jo in conversation, saving Ralph from having to make any effort himself. He raised his glass in a silent toast to the journalist, thinking how attractive she looked in a well cut black suit softened by a stone silk blouse with a ruffled neck that framed her face.

He wondered idly why it was he found it so difficult to like Jo. Her legs were good and lack of curves had failed to put him off any number of other less attractive women. Was it her bluntness, lack of sophistication and social graces? Perhaps he demanded a certain subtlety in his women?

Now that other girl Eve had found, who had so unexpectedly contacted him earlier that week, she was quite something. The body of a Valkyrie with the freshness and fragrance of a newly picked peach. He spent a happy couple of moments imagining her stripped of the uninspiring clothes she wore. He could clearly see the shape of her full breasts and the long line of her thighs. Then he abruptly wiped the image clear from his mind. He had a feeling danger lay in that direction.

The decibel level in the high hall was rising as mourners began to talk more generally and alcohol loosened inhibitions. Snatches of conversation reached him:

"Of course Marjorie and Peter didn't like her cooking for a living, not what they'd wanted for their only daughter even though it does seem so smart these days."

"Give me a ring on Monday, I've got a couple of really hot tips, I've done awfully well for Ma and Pa recently, only wish Claire had let me handle her money."

"Have you tried Brittany, my dear? It's marvellous, like England was fifty years ago."

"All this emphasis on food, most unhealthy."

"Well, they did Robert's twenty-first and I have to say the food was too chic for words and the whole operation went like clockwork."

"Clive and I went to their celebration lunch, he sat next to her, thought it was going to be Eve but wasn't sorry to find Claire, he always had a soft spot for her. I had a lovely time chatting to the most interesting man who's something in the fashion world. Of course, I went to my doctor immediately I heard about the food poisoning but he said if I hadn't suffered anything by now, not to worry. Well, you can't help but worry, can you, especially these days when it hardly seems safe to eat a thing. Sometimes I wonder if we'll all end up popping protein pills."

"I thought we'd have a look at the Dordogne, the weather's so much better and there are so many English there; the French are all right but you don't want them all the time, do you?"

"I don't know about all this switching of investments, isn't it a very chancy business? We've got the boys' schooling to pay for, after all."

"I wish they'd let that girl who redid our Eaton Square flat do something with this place, it has such potential."

Ralph looked round the hall, lined with oak panelling, a gallery supported by handsome oak pillars running across one end. Huge flagstones lined the floor, deep window bays were at the other end of the room, the mullioned embrasures filled with diamond shaped leaded panes. Two enormous dogs lay in front of the blazing logs that filled the huge fireplace. It was, he supposed, redolent of an England that was passing. Nothing much could have changed here in the last couple of hundred years. He liked its lack of pretension, it had a take it or leave it air. When Monica had redone the Highgate house, he knew exactly what he wanted. A background that reeked success, style and money but nothing brash or too obvious. The house had needed a complete overhaul, it had been falling apart when they bought it. If they had found something like this, he thought, he would have left it exactly as it was.

He looked at his watch, they had spent long enough here. He tried to catch Monica's eye. But she seemed deep in conversation with Eve. That was the second time today she had failed to pick up his signal. Which was unlike Monica. Now he came to think about it, she had not been at all herself lately, her usual ability to take whatever life handed out had crumpled on more than one occasion. What was it she had on her mind? His large hand came up and grasped his wife's upper arm, forcing her to take notice. Monica gave him a quick glance then turned to Eve.

"We must go, my dear, are you coming back to London or going to the cottage?"

Eve glanced round the room, "Back to London. I've got so much to do I cancelled plans for my country weekend. Elizabeth's going instead, she wants one of her detoxification weekends. Where has she disappeared to, she was here a moment ago, I must give her the keys."

"Isn't that her over there, talking with the chap in the double breasted suit and the old Etonian tie?"

"Clive Thompson," said Joshua, his attention caught. "I wonder what she's talking to *him* about?" As he spoke, Elizabeth finished her conversation and came and joined them. She looked very pleased with herself.

"Well, that was fascinating." She glanced round the little group, "And it's no use asking me what he said, that's my secret, at least until after the weekend, then it will be official."

"Official?" said Monica, "Reminds me of that policeman who came round the other day, I don't think I want to be involved in anything more official."

"Ah," said Elizabeth pleasantly, "Sometimes we don't have a choice, do we?"

"Oh, stop being so mysterious, I can't think it was anything we could be interested in." Jo was at her most caustic.

"Oh no? Well, I must be going. All I need are the cottage keys, it really is very good of you to lend it to me."

"You're doing us a favour, Joshua won't leave his precious word processor, I've decided to see he eats properly and I've got any number of things to do in town so you'll give it an airing. The spare bed is all made up but there's very little food there."

"Food is the one thing I can do without this weekend. Lemon and hot water and herbal teas are what I shall exist on."

Elizabeth slipped the small bunch of keys Eve handed her into her bag and with a brief wave of farewell she melted out of the room.

Joshua looked after her, his face puzzled. "She's found something out, I can't imagine what but wait till I get hold of her on Monday, I'll make her sorry she didn't share whatever it is. Come on, darling, let's make our goodbyes, it's time to go." He nodded to Jo and the Coxes and placed his hand in the small of his wife's back, forcing her to move.

Ralph watched Eve look back with a little moue of apology to him and Monica. Claire's death had undoubtedly hit her hard, her face was pale, her lips thin, her big eyes tired under a forehead knotted in a worried frown.

"I must find Jackie and Emily and get them on the road home," said Jo abruptly and she set off through the thinning crowd to where the secretary and assistant were chatting to another client.

Ralph started to steer Monica in the direction of Claire's mother, the sooner they got out of here the better. He approached the drawn looking but dry eyed woman who seemed to be comforting her friends rather than receiving their support and for one blinding moment wondered how he would be coping if it had been his daughter Caroline that had suddenly died.

CHAPTER TWENTY-TWO

Darina looked at the badly typed pages in front of her. Writing an article had to be one of the most difficult tasks she had ever attempted. Well, at least this effort made some sense, unlike some of her earlier drafts, but it was ridiculous how difficult it was to put together a few simple points. The question now was, would Elizabeth like it?

She looked at her watch, 10:30 on a Saturday morning. She wondered if she dared ring Joshua again and ask him if he'd give her the benefit of his advice. Well, he had told her to get in touch if she needed any more help. She looked up the number.

An answering machine offered to take a message. Darina did not take advantage of the invitation. Perhaps after all he'd gone down to the cottage with Eve?

After a moment's thought, Darina got on to directory enquiries and asked if there was a number for Tarrant near Petersfield. There was. If she rang, she wondered, would he mind listening to the article on the telephone? It was worth a try, she really didn't want to spend any more time on this if he thought it would do.

Darina was so surprised to hear it was Elizabeth Chesney on the other end of the line, she forgot why she was ringing. Then she pulled herself together, decided this was fate, consigned Eve's sensibilities to hell and explained why she had been trying to get hold of Joshua. "Perhaps I could read it to you?" she finished.

"Much better if you left it until Monday, I'm very bad at taking in that sort of thing over the telephone."

Darina looked at the article she was holding, if Elizabeth said on Monday it was no use, when would she find the time and energy to rewrite it? "Could I come down and show it to you?" she asked. "I've nothing much else to do this weekend."

"Oh God," came a sigh from the other end of the telephone. Then, "All right, dear, but not today, today is just for me, total relaxation. Tomorrow morning I could just about take it, as long as you promise to go as soon as I've given it a quick once-over."

Darina promised, asked for directions on how to find the cottage and rang off. She refused to feel guilty. Half an hour was not going to ruin Elizabeth's peace and quiet and it was a small price to pay for the havoc she'd brought to The Wooden Spoon's business.

She reached for a clean piece of paper and wound it in to the typewriter ready to start the laborious business of making a fair copy of what she had written. And when she had finished that, she was going to sit down and look again at all the notes she had made yesterday, both those typed in the office and the additions she had made at home in the evening. It was time to make a cool assessment of how far she had got in the matter of Claire Montague's death.

What she was not going to do was wait for the telephone to ring. It had shown remarkable stubbornness in that respect. There had, it was true, been odd calls during the week but none of them was from the person she hoped would call. Well, if he wasn't going to get in touch with her, she certainly wasn't going to ring him. She smoothed out the somewhat crumpled pages of her article and applied her fingers to the typewriter keys.

Whilst Darina slowly and painfully typed her 750 words, Detective Sergeant William Pigram was driving up the M3. He longed to let his classic Chevette show its paces. Longed to press his foot down until the speedometer needle hovered around the 120 mph mark. Now that he'd finally made the decision to go to London, he wanted the journey over and done with. But he was mindful of his position as a member of Her Majesty's Police Force. Getting done up for speeding would not be a sensible move.

He had lost count of the number of times he'd reached for the telephone and then drawn back. Twice he had actually rung the number, only to find there was no reply. Was she working or had she gone out? If so, with whom? He cursed himself for his stupidity the previous Sunday. How could he have made such a crass fool of himself? Of course she would resent his patronising approach to her concern over that girl's death. And why had it taken so long for him to realise that he had been patronising?

By Friday he'd realised it was too difficult to try to make things right on the telephone. Sunday he was on duty so a weekend in London was out but what if he suggested coming to see her on the Saturday? And what if she said "no"? Much better just to turn up. And if she wasn't in? he asked himself as the car ate up the miles between Somerset and London. Then he'd just park at her door and wait until she came back, whenever that was.

It was half past eleven by the time he'd worked his way to Chelsea through the Saturday morning traffic. He rang Darina's door bell with his heart thumping, feeling an awkward teenager again.

There was a long pause, then just as he was about to give up, the door opened and there she was, dressed in old trousers and a sweat shirt, no make-up on her face, a smudge on her nose and her blond hair wild, as though she'd pulled at it in frequent desperation. She looked gorgeous.

"William!" It was as though floodlights had been switched on, her smile was so bright.

"I'm sorry, I apologise, I should never have said what I did. I've brought you these," he held out the enormous bouquet of flowers he'd stopped in the King's Road to buy.

She took them shyly, sniffing at their fragrance and trying to look at him at the same time. Then she stepped aside, "Come in, what am I doing keeping you here on the doorstep? And I should apologise, too. I was pretty rude."

He stepped inside, wanting to sweep her into his arms, gather up that incredible hair and use it to bind her to him. But she was taking him into the drawing room, then saying something about putting the flowers into water and did he want coffee or a drink? He opted for coffee and followed her into the kitchen, watching her put on the kettle, find a vase, fill it with water, add the flowers, seeming with a few gentle movements of her hands to make a perfect arrangement without effort. Then she ground beans and made coffee.

All the time his eyes followed her, drinking in the way her long legs moved, the thrust of her breasts against the sweat shirt, the shimmer of her hair, the way her grey eyes had gone almost green, shining with pleasure at seeing him. He hardly took in what she was saying.

It wasn't until they were sitting down with the coffee he realised she was back on that wretched mushroom poisoning. What had she been saying? Something about a multiplicity of motives, that someone might have wanted to get rid of a lover, or a rival, or it could have been for financial gain. But he hadn't been following the details and he was afraid that if they started discussing all that it would end in another argument.

He cut in on a rambling account of a van ride after some luncheon do with references to frustrated passions and a broken alibi: "Look, if I tell you I came to take you out to lunch, not to go into the details of a possible murder case, will you throw me out again?"

For a moment the shutters came down over her face and he held his breath, not daring to say anything more. Then a faint smile appeared, "You're a pig, you know that? You could be giving me the benefit of your experience, helping to solve a crime instead of which you are just after a bit of socialising."

"You see I get the other every day," he said apologetically.

She got up in a single graceful movement, "And this is your day off and you've come all the way to see me. The least I can do is go and make myself respectable. I should offer to cook you lunch but that is what I do every day." She laughed at him and left the room, leaving him sighing with relief. Everything seemed to be all right.

It was a delightful day. They had lunch at Alastair Little's in Soho, one of Darina's favourite restaurants, managed to get tickets for a matinee performance of a play they discovered both wanted to see, spent a happy hour over tea at the Savoy discussing the contentious issues it had raised without discovering any serious divergence of opinion between them, then ended up eating scrambled eggs back in the Chelsea house.

Yet though it had all gone so smoothly and enjoyably, William had not been able to get closer to Darina. Every time he made a tentative move, she retreated. Perfectly charming, with great friendliness but, nonetheless, retreated. She made it quite clear that, much as she was pleased to see him, much as she enjoyed his company, she was not ready for anything more. William made himself as agreeable as he could and fought down his frustration. Almost he succumbed and brought up the mushroom poisoning he knew she was dying to discuss. If that was the route to her heart, why not take it? But he resisted the impulse, he knew with deadly certainty that it could only end in another disastrous argument as her amateurish bumblings and half-baked theorising irritated him beyond measure. Better to keep to neutral ground and maintain this pleasant relationship, given time it must surely deepen.

"I must go," he said reluctantly as a bracket clock chimed ten o'clock.

"But we haven't finished the wine," she said, picking up the bottle. "You've only had one glass."

"I don't like more when I'm driving," he apologised, placing his hand over the top of his crystal goblet.

"You mean you're going back to Somerset tonight? You're not staying with your uncle and aunt?"

He shook his head, "I'm on duty tomorrow, so I really shouldn't be too late."

She sat and looked at him, "You drove all that way just for today?" Did something stir in the depths of her eyes? He held his breath, said nothing.

She dropped her gaze and rose. "Come on, let's set you on your way. I don't want to be responsible for the Somerset and Avon constabulary falling down on the job, particularly on a Sunday."

At the door she looked at him slightly shyly and said, "I am glad you came."

"So am I," he bent and kissed her lightly on the mouth. She stood still and returned the kiss as lightly. He sighed inwardly but produced a cheerful grin and said, "I'll give you a call tomorrow."

"Do, I'd like to know you got back safely." She opened the door and watched him get into his car, waving as he drove down the road, a fine drizzle calling for the windscreen wipers. He hoped it was not going to develop into a real downpour.

By the following morning the rain was falling in an impenetrable curtain making a drive down to Sussex a less than attractive prospect. Darina tried to ring Elizabeth and say the article could wait until Monday but all she could get for the cottage number was an unobtainable signal. So she got in her car and made her way down the A3.

It was nearly midday by the time she located the little backwater where Eve and Joshua spent their weekends, grateful that she had been given such clear instructions for the cottage was tucked away. Only the telegraph wires looping alongside the long lane indicated there could be any habitation before she turned a sharp bend and saw a picture-book thatched cottage.

Tiny windows were tucked under overhanging eaves, a few late roses still decorated the rambler trained over a studded wood front door and a little path ran down between two patches of lawn edged with borders filled with the autumn remnants of herbaceous plants. A high, evergreen hedge divided the garden proper from a stream, and a wide verge thick with wild plants ran between that and the lane. It was an illustration from a book of fairy tales.

A little bridge straddled the stream in front of the gate and another, much wider, led to a cleared area beside the cottage that ran up to a car port. In it was a car.

Darina drove in and stopped behind the small BMW. She got out, glad that the rain had eased off into a light drizzle, and stood for a moment drinking in the quiet. There was no traffic, no bird song, no sound of a tractor, nothing. A tall hedge hid the parking area from the house, it had a little gate that opened onto a side path leading to the front door. She walked through and rang the bell. There was no answer.

After a little she rang again. The rain was not as light as she'd thought. She wished she had an umbrella and that Elizabeth would answer the door quickly. Where could she be? The car was there, the cottage was sufficiently isolated for it to be impossible she had gone anywhere without it, it wasn't a day for a walk. Surely someone couldn't have called and picked her up when she was expecting Darina?

There was a heavy knob on an iron ring in the middle of the door,

Darina grabbed it and the door rattled with the force with which she rapped out the fact that she was there. Still no one came.

She stepped back, moved round to one of the windows and peered in. The interior was so dark she couldn't see more than the shapes of chairs and tables. A portable typewriter and papers littered the surface of a table in the window, it looked as though Elizabeth had been working on some article of her own.

Darina returned to the front door and tried the handle. The door wasn't locked. She pushed it open and went inside, calling out, "Elizabeth? It's Darina." The front hall was little more than a corridor. A door led off either side. Facing the entrance was a steep staircase. A narrow passage ran beside it to the back of the house. The floor was tiled in squares of black and red. Prints of old cookery illustrations lined the whitewashed walls, cord carpet ran up the stairs, an old, converted oil lamp hung from the ceiling. It was all very simple but very stylish, very Eve.

Darina called again. Again there was no response. The silence hung and infected the air with unease. She opened the right hand door, revealing a dining room with a round oak table, a dresser, ladder back chairs. The room on the other side of the front door was the sitting room she had peered into earlier, with an ingle-nook fireplace in which there were the dead ashes of a fire. Two wing chairs sat either side, a small settee faced it on a slant, a table in front of the window complete with windsor chair did service as a desk, more prints filled the walls.

She went across to the fireplace. An empty tea mug sat on the hearth and the ashes were cold. Darina went back to the hall and explored the passage. At the back of the cottage, obviously built at a later date than the main part, was the kitchen. Done in stripped pine, with old pieces reworked to make fitted units, it was hung with bunches of dried flowers, herbs and grasses.

Darina went back to the hall and started climbing the stairs. She had not taken more than a few steps before she stopped and sniffed, her nose wrinkling distastefully. Then she moved up again at a faster pace. There were four doors leading off the tiny landing. The first led into a large bedroom with a double bed, two side tables, a chest of drawers furnished with a swing mirror, and a wardrobe, all in polished pine. A patchwork quilt covered the bed. More food prints hung on the walls. Darina closed the door and opened the next. Then stopped short on the threshold, overwhelmed by the smell that had halted her on the stairs, a foetid, rancid, sour odour.

Clamping a handkerchief over her nose, she came closer to the bed. Elizabeth was in the middle of a tangle of sheets and blankets, her body arched and stiff, her eyes wide open and staring, her dark hair in sticky hanks. Vomit and bodily fluids were everywhere. Darina wanted to retreat but her feet seemed anchored to the floor. Her stomach churned dangerously. She closed her eyes and thought of the clean rain outside. After a few moments she opened them and, avoiding the figure on the bed, glanced quickly round the room. It was sparsely furnished much as the first, except that here was a single bed and the chest of drawers that did double duty as a dressing table was scattered with make-up, hair brush and jewellery, and clothes were thrown over an upright chair.

Then Darina delicately walked backwards out of the room, carefully closed the door and stood, still holding the handkerchief to her nose, breathing slowly and deeply. She tried one of the so far unopened doors and found the bathroom. That, too, bore signs of violent illness. She hastily shut the door and went down to the kitchen, throwing open a window and drinking in the fresh air that came flooding in, grateful now for its rainy dampness. She ran the tap and filled a glass of water then leant against the sink sipping it, allowing her body to regain control.

She finished the water, rinsed the glass, dried and replaced it in the cupboard. Then she went looking for the telephone, locating an old black instrument in the sitting room. It was dead. No matter how she jiggled the receiver, there was no dialling tone, the instrument was useless. She went outside, closing the front door behind her. She wondered if she should lock it, then decided there was little point in searching for a key.

A small village a mile or so away offered a pub with a public telephone. Darina dialled 999 and specified she wanted the police, an ambulance seemed redundant. She gave a brief description of what she had found then said she would return and wait for someone to arrive.

She drove back down the long lane. The cottage had changed since she had first caught sight of it. Sleeping Beauty had metamorphosed into a more sinister tale. Even the thatch had lost its picturesque quality and the dark of the reeds merged with the dark of the sky to lower over the scene like an ominous twilight invading the middle of the day.

Darina sat in her car, her mind grappling with what she had found. Elizabeth must have been poisoned, surely nothing else could account for that terrible scene. But poisoned by what? She quickly checked her watch, the police could not possibly be here for at least another ten minutes. She slipped on her gloves, got out of the car and retraced her steps to the cottage.

She had to force herself to open the front door again. The smell was now floating more noticeably down the stairs. She went through to the kitchen. The only food she could see was a bowl of fruit on a dresser behind the door. Darina looked at it then went and checked inside the fridge. There was a tub of vegetarian margarine, unopened, an intact carton of six eggs and a tin of anchovies.

She moved onto the cupboards. These yielded half a packet of oat cakes, sugarless, a box of Eve's special herbal tea bags, almost empty, several packets of pasta in various shapes, some opened, some intact, brown rice, a variety of pulses, some upmarket tins of soup, beans, tuna fish and sardines, and a collection of home made pickles. The jars and tins were all unopened. Darina tried to remember what she knew about botulism, that most virulent of food poisons. Wasn't damaged canned food susceptible? Had Elizabeth eaten the contents of a contaminated tin?

She opened the cupboard underneath the sink. There was the waste bucket, neatly lined with a plastic bag. Darina investigated its contents. Several tea bags, a quantity of grape stalks and pips, a few banana skins and some apple cores. That seemed to be it. No empty tins, corroded or otherwise.

After a moment's thought she opened the back door, like the front, it was unlocked. Outside was the dust bin. She lifted the lid and found it was empty. In the whole of the kitchen there was no sign that anything had been consumed beyond several oat cakes, some fruit, and half a dozen mugs of herbal tea. Could Elizabeth have eaten out? If so where? And with whom?

Darina glanced at her watch and hurried back to the car. The rain had now stopped. She walked round the little parking area. Perhaps forensic science could provide a clue as to any other vehicle driving up to the cottage but to her untrained eye any such evidence had been completely washed away. She got back in her car and started the engine to produce some heat. Chill had seeped into her and she found she was shivering. But that was due to more than the weather.

Unless a meal outside the cottage could be implicated, accidental food poisoning looked unlikely, which meant that there was now a second mysterious death. Two murders?

But who would want to kill Elizabeth? Darina had thought at one time that maybe the journalist had wanted Eve dead. Then when it seemed more likely that Claire had been the intended victim all along, she had more or less discarded Elizabeth as a potential murderer. Now she wondered if her original theory hadn't been right after all. That it was Eve who had been the intended victim and what she had found now was a second attack that had misfired.

After all, who had known Elizabeth was to be here this weekend? Eve had announced her intention of spending the weekend here alone. Darina had expected she would be there, the change of plan must have been made at the last minute.

Darina thought again about the cream coloured car Eve had said nearly ran her down. If that had been the first attempt on her life, she had now escaped death three times.

Cramp attacked her legs, she tried to stretch them out then got out of the car, sighing with relief as the crippling pains eased. The air was fresh after the rain. She walked up the lane a little way. Lush green vegetation still grew in the shade of the hedgerows though autumn was rapidly advancing into winter and leaves were falling from the trees. The lane became narrower and started climbing. Darina turned and retraced her steps, looking around her with interest, resting her eyes on the sweep of hills, the recently tilled earth. How restful it all seemed after the pressures and bustle of London, no wonder Eve liked coming down here, to her rural retreat. What was the phrase she used, "Getting back to nature"?

As the words echoed through her mind, it was as though a projector started up, replaying the scene in the demonstration theatre after Claire's death. Once again Darina heard Ralph's impassioned speech on the inimical qualities of nature, detailing the toxic traps laid for the unwary.

She almost ran back to the cottage. The strip of ground running alongside the stream in front of the hedge was wild and uncultivated, no tidy verge. The grass was long and thick and amongst it grew the remnants of what looked like large cow parsley. Darina walked its length, carefully examining the ground. She went to the end of the garden hedge. Here the border strip almost vanished as the lane came up to the edge of the stream, which now ran beside a hawthorn hedge and assumed a more ditch-like character. She walked back and studied one spot in particular, crouching on her haunches to take a closer look, parting the vegetation to inspect the earth. Could someone have dug up one of the plants then covered the traces?

The hoot of a horn alerted her. She looked up to see a small police patrol car.

CHAPTER TWENTY-THREE

A young constable got out of the car. Darina took him into the house and warned what waited upstairs. He gave her an uncertain look but climbed the stairs steadily. After a brief moment he came down and went straight outside. Darina waited in the hall until he returned, looking slightly pale but otherwise composed, and then offered him a cup of coffee.

"I'd like that, miss, but I don't think we should touch anything yet. I've radioed through for the inspector, he shouldn't be long. Now," he pulled out a notebook and pencil, "just tell me exactly how you found the body."

Darina suggested they go and sit in the little sitting room where the odour from upstairs hardly penetrated, she felt her nostrils would never be free of the taint. She went through all her movements, the only omission was her investigation of the kitchen. But she told him she had gone in there after discovering Elizabeth's body and that she had opened the window and taken a glass from the cupboard. "I'm sorry, I probably shouldn't have done that but I wasn't really thinking and I needed . . ." She hesitated and the constable chipped in,

"Quite, miss, I quite understand." Then he suddenly got up.

A burly man in his mid-forties stood in the doorway. A dark blue anorak hung open over cord trousers and he wore a dark grey sweater over a black crew neck jumper. Darina bet herself he had just been preparing to sit down to Sunday lunch. Then regretted she had thought about food. He, too, went upstairs but spent rather longer than the constable.

As she waited with the young policeman, Darina realised she had not heard the second car approach, the high hedge had blotted out the engine noise as well as hidden any vehicle from sight.

When the superior officer came down, the constable started to repeat Darina's description of her movements but the burly inspector stopped him, "Let's hear it from the horse's mouth, shall we?"

So Darina retold her story but this time when she reached the end she added, "I think Elizabeth's death could be connected with another," and gave an account of the way Claire had died from food poisoning.

The constable took down everything she said. Half way through, a doctor arrived and was shown upstairs. When Darina had finished the inspector looked puzzled, "You say this other girl, Claire, was that her name? Right, Claire died of eating a poisonous mushroom. Do you think your friend upstairs," he gestured towards the ceiling, "also died of eating a poisonous mushroom?"

"No, at least, I don't think so. I think she has been poisoned in some other way, it could be hemlock."

He sat and looked at her. Darina thought how unlikely the whole story must seem to him. How very garbled and difficult to understand.

"Right, let me get this straight. One girl has died from eating a poisonous mushroom, we now have another death from some other poisonous substance, you think hemlock and perhaps in a moment you will tell me why you think that; both the dead women were at some lunch together when the poisonous mushroom was served and they were both friends of another girl whose cottage this is. And that's why you think their deaths are linked?" He gave a heavy sigh and exchanged a look with the young constable.

"The metropolitan police are investigating Claire's death, they seem to think it was probable that she was murdered," said Darina patiently.

Somehow she had pressed the right button. "Are they, by God!" The inspector rose. "Right, I'm afraid I have to ask you to leave this house, Miss Lisle. Constable, secure the premises. I'll contact C.I.D. and the police surgeon. Has that doctor finished?" The constable reluctantly went upstairs, Darina and the inspector moved outside. He suggested she sit in his car whilst he got onto headquarters.

The doctor came out a few minutes later, followed by the constable, who took up a position by the side of the front door. Darina wondered who on earth they were denying access to.

"She's been dead about twelve to fourteen hours. Most probably from some form of poisoning, there is considerable dilation of the pupils and signs of convulsions before death. I would suggest you look for the remains of anything that could have been ingested in the recent past." The doctor was a bouncy young man who looked at Darina curiously.

"Thanks, we won't keep you from your lunch any longer," the inspector dismissed him without ceremony.

There followed a period of waiting until two more cars drew up outside the cottage. A thin man with a balding head and a younger chap of unremarkable appearance came over to the inspector's car.

"Afternoon, Dick," said the thin man, "remind me to ruin your Sunday afternoon next month, will you? The doc's on his way and so are the forensic boys. Come over here and fill me in."

The little group of men stood by the corner of the parking area, the inspector talking, the newcomers listening intently. Then the older man spoke briefly before coming back to Darina. "Now, Miss Lisle, I'd like you to go with Detective Sergeant Pearce here to the station and give him your statement. Jim, when you get back there, get in touch with the Met and see what you can find out about this other death. O.K.?"

"O.K., sir."

Darina followed the sergeant's car to the local station, where she was taken to a featureless interview room and grilled, there was no other word for it, about her arrival at the cottage, the circumstances that had led to her visit, and everything she knew about Elizabeth and her connection with Claire and Eve. By the end she knew what overdone steak felt like, dried and frizzled. The sergeant was perfectly pleasant, he didn't act as though she was under any suspicion. His first action on arrival had been to order tea for them both. It came scalding hot and Darina was grateful. She had had no lunch but the last thing she wanted was food, it was the tea she craved, its warmth, its unaccustomed sweetness comforting and sustaining, she even felt grateful for its strength.

The interview dragged on and on. The same points were covered again and again from every conceivable angle. At one point the sergeant leant back in his chair and looked at her as though he was genuinely puzzled,

"What I don't understand yet is why you are so convinced this woman died from hemlock poisoning."

Darina gave him an account of the conversation in the demonstration theatre. He looked unconvinced.

"Bit far fetched, isn't it? An unlikely murder weapon?"

"Amanita phalloides—the Death Cap mushroom—is a natural poison, it would make sense for the murderer to use the same method, it's probably someone who understands these things very well. A deadly mushroom wasn't on hand but an equally deadly alternative was." It seemed obvious to her.

"But you say you don't think this woman was the intended victim?"

Once again Darina tried to explain the events of the past few weeks and the background to The Wooden Spoon. It was a relief to be able to talk so freely.

The hours stretched on and as she was taken over and over the same ground, odd details began to rattle around Darina's tired brain, motive, opportunity, means; pieces began to form a pattern and she began to wonder if she hadn't found the answer to both deaths. A certain amount of luck would have been needed when placing the poisonous mushroom on the plate that Sunday. But, given that, maybe everything else made a certain sense. It was a theory that seemed to tie the facts together. Darina looked at the sergeant, would it be worth offering it to him? Then she decided more thought was needed. She was exhausted, it could all be an hallucination. Part of her hoped it was.

Finally the sergeant must have decided he had pulled the last relevant detail he could from her tired mind. He prepared a statement and offered it for her signature.

She scrawled her name and staggered out of the station. After a few minutes sitting in her car wondering whether she had the strength to drive back to London, she started the engine and moved slowly towards the main road.

The weather had cleared and the traffic was light, Darina supposed most weekenders had already reached home. She made good progress. As she approached Putney her watch showed almost nine o'clock. It seemed not too late to call on Eve and Joshua.

They had already heard about Elizabeth. A sergeant had been that afternoon, given them the details and taken a brief statement.

"Joshua has agreed to carry out a formal identification tomorrow," Eve said, "Her only family is a brother she never sees, I think he's abroad." She put her hand on her husband's arm, "It's a rotten thing for you to have to do, I wish I could go with you tomorrow but we've got Tuesday's wedding to prepare."

Husband and wife were sitting together on a sofa in the large living room. Joshua looked drained, shadows under his eyes emphasised the craggy features, the beak of his nose. But Eve was full of energy. She seemed unable to stop talking.

"If only I'd been down there as well. If only I'd left Joshua to his own devices and spent the weekend with her, I could have done something, got her to hospital. What on earth could it have been?"

"What food was there?" asked Darina.

"Only odd tins of things. I told her there wasn't much but she said she wasn't going to eat anything, it was to be one of her 'detoxification weekends.' Every now and then she used to starve herself for a couple of days, to get rid of all the toxins, stabilise her weight."

"I rang here in the morning, wanted to ask Joshua if he'd have a look at that wretched article. But a machine answered so I thought you had both gone to the country. I was so surprised when I got Elizabeth on the phone there."

"I decided on Friday I shouldn't desert Joshua and I really needed to spend some time in the office, check up on the mail, work on some new menus and that client list Jo talked about. When Elizabeth heard the cottage would be empty, she asked if she could borrow it for the week-end. But Joshua was here the whole day."

At the sound of his name, her husband retrieved his attention from the corner of the fireplace where it seemed to have been riveted, "I put the answering machine on because I didn't want to be disturbed."

"When did Elizabeth ask if she could borrow the cottage?"

Eve thought for a moment, "It was Friday morning. I rang to ask if she wanted to come down to the funeral with us, she only lives just round the corner, and she said weren't we going on to the cottage and then it all came out and she asked if she could use it for the weekend."

"So as far as anyone else knew, you were planning to stay there as usual?"

Eve looked slightly mystified, "I suppose so." Then light dawned, "You're thinking someone poisoned her instead of me? Just like Claire? Oh, no, that's awful!" She looked horrified.

"Yes," said Darina.

"And I gave her the keys at Claire's funeral, just before we left, as we were saying goodbye to everybody."

Darina's thoughts were diverted for a moment, "Claire's funeral, how did it go?"

"Pretty grisly, wasn't it, darling? I can understand why Ken refused to attend." Her breath caught on a sudden thought, "To think that that was the last time we saw Elizabeth. Isn't that terrible? And you were saying you'd make her sorry on Monday. Oh," she put her hand to her mouth, "perhaps I shouldn't have said that, Darina may think she should tell the police."

Joshua made an impatient gesture, "Not the sort of remark that gets taken seriously, is it?"

"What was it all about?" Darina asked curiously.

"Nothing at all," said Eve hastily, "Just a silly joke."

Joshua sighed, "Such a little thing, I saw Elizabeth talking to Clive Thompson and when I asked her what it had been about she wouldn't tell me. I thought she might have got a line on his takeover plans. As Eve says, it was a joke, really, Elizabeth was making such a mystery of it, even Jo told her it couldn't be that important."

"You won't have to mention it to anyone else, will you, darling?" Eve reached across and laid an imploring hand on her friend's arm.

"I hardly think the police will be asking me any more questions, at least for the moment," Darina said, "I've told them everything I know about Elizabeth and Claire and The Wooden Spoon."

There was a little silence.

"What have you told them about The Wooden Spoon? How does that come into it?" asked Eve sharply.

"It seems highly possible that Claire and Elizabeth's deaths are linked.

They could both be failed attempts at your life so the state of the company could be important. I had to tell the police," she hesitated for a moment then continued, "I had to say that The Wooden Spoon's finances are rocky."

Eve drew her breath in with a quick gasp, "What do you mean? How can you know what sort of state the company is in?"

Darina looked at her, meeting the brilliant eyes calmly, "I examined your books on Friday, you remember we said I would have to do so before I could decide whether to join you or not."

"But Jackie's account books show the business is going extremely well," Eve's voice rose in an excited curve.

Joshua laid a hand on her arm, "Don't get overwrought, darling."

She shook it off with an impatient gesture, "This is my business we're discussing, I want to know what Darina thinks she knows."

"The account books in your desk tell a different story."

"My desk, but that drawer was locked."

Darina said nothing.

Joshua's attention had now been fully brought to bear on what was being said, "Are you telling us the company is in real financial trouble?"

Eve tossed her head, "It's only something temporary, a little cash problem, that's all. As soon as we get some more business coming in and the insurance company comes up with the payment for Claire's death, or Darina decides to join us, we'll be fine."

"You mean you need an insurance handout to remain liquid?"

"No!" Eve got up from the sofa and walked across the room to the window, then back again, tension vibrating through her fragile body, she stood poised between the sofa and Darina's chair, looking from her to Joshua and back again, hands on nonexistent hips, "It's just that the conversion costs were a bit more than we expected. I can always get some more investment money; if Darina won't come in, I'm sure there'll be someone else. If only bloody Ralph would help, it would all be simple."

Joshua's mouth thinned, "You've asked him for money?"

"It would only be a business arrangement. You can't help, you've made that clear as Perrier."

His frown deepened, "You know I can't. You got every possible extra penny out of this place when you bought Marylebone and then we mortgaged the cottage to do the renovations here. You can't seem to realise there's a limit to everything. But to go to Ralph."

Eve gave another little toss of her head, the wiry curls quivered like grasses in a wind-blown meadow. "You needn't worry, he wouldn't help."

Darina wondered why not.

For a moment Eve remained poised, balanced on the balls of her feet, her mouth curving down, "Anyway, if Darina has told everyone all about it, we're finished. The vultures will descend." With a strangled hiccup she flung herself into her husband's arms and spoke through a torrent of tears, "Oh, darling, I'm so frightened, you've got to help."

He held her abstractedly, "Ssh, ssh, don't, darling, we'll work out something, it'll be all right."

Darina rose, "I'm sorry," she said, "I had to tell them but I'm sure you don't have to worry about anyone else knowing. Do you still want me at The Wooden Spoon tomorrow morning?"

Eve turned a tear stained face towards her, looked at her in silence for a moment, then said, "Of course, we can't manage without you."

"Right, I'll be there. Don't move, I'll let myself out."

As Darina opened her front door, the phone was ringing.

It was William, "Where have you been?" he asked, "I rang you this morning and again at lunchtime and when I got back this evening." He sounded worried rather than aggrieved.

Darina gave him a brief account of her day.

"You poor thing," his voice was warm, "what an awful thing for you to have to discover. Are you all right? Would you like me to drive up?"

Darina liked the feeling of being cherished but said quickly, "Of course not, I'm fine, I'm going to have a stiff drink and some supper then go to bed."

"Tell me again exactly what happened."

Darina went through the events of the day, finishing with an account of her visit to Eve and Joshua.

"And you're going into The Wooden Spoon tomorrow morning?"

"After I've been to see Clive Thompson."

"Who?"

"A big City chap who was at the celebration lunch and had a conversation with Elizabeth at the funeral. I have a feeling he's wrapped up in all this somewhere. If I call early, at breakfast time, I should just catch him before he leaves for his office. I'm sure I can get him to talk."

There was silence from the other end of the telephone.

"William?"

"Useless, I suppose, for me to say leave it to the police?"

"Useless. But I will tell them if he says anything important, promise."

"You're the most infuriating girl I've ever met."

"I know," Darina said smugly, safe in the knowledge that he was nearly 150 miles away. "I'll ring you tomorrow evening, will you be home?" She rang off, went and poured herself a single-malt whisky, cooked some scrambled eggs, and consumed both untroubled by misgivings, her mind busy trying to fit Clive Thompson into her latest theory.

Nearly 150 miles away William also sat with a glass of whisky and gazed at the telephone. He had definite misgivings. He ran once again over the various details Darina had told him and cursed himself for not paying more attention to her chatter the previous day. The more he thought the less happy he became. Finally he sighed and reached for the telephone.

CHAPTER TWENTY-FOUR

When Darina arrived at The Wooden Spoon on Monday morning, she found Eve pleading with a C.I.D. officer to be allowed to continue the catering business.

"Elizabeth didn't even belong to the company, you can't connect her death with us." She was neatly dressed in her working clothes, her hair tied back under a triangle of linen but the very air around her quivered with electricity and her eyes bored into those of the policeman.

The officer returned her impassioned gaze stoically, "She died at your cottage, Mrs. Tarrant, of what looks like food poisoning and there has already been a poisoning connected with your food. You understand we have to safeguard the public."

The two of them were in Eve's office. As Darina entered, she saw Jo was also there, standing quietly by the desk but listening intently. "I don't think," the other girl said now, "you actually have the authority to close us. Isn't that up to the Environmental Health Officer?"

The policeman turned to her. "As you say, miss, and I don't suppose it will be long before he is round here."

"Well, until he is, we shall continue fulfilling our contracts. I'm sure you don't want a bride to do without her wedding breakfast tomorrow."

"Very well," he sighed. "In the meantime, I and my officers will be searching these premises. We have the necessary authority." He produced his warrant. Jo looked at it carefully then handed it back.

"Come on," she said to Eve, "Let's leave them to it."

All three girls went to the catering kitchen and started work.

Darina began preparing a basic pastry for barquettes to be filled with fruits, finding the process of pinching the butter, egg and sugar together soothing whilst her mind worked on the details she had obtained from a puzzled Clive Thompson that morning. It had been surprisingly easy to talk to him, she only had to mention Claire's name to get his full co-operation and their conversation hadn't taken long, she was no more than a few minutes late arriving at The Wooden Spoon. But what he had told her had once again upended a theory. Now she was busy placing the jigsaw pieces she had gathered together over the past two weeks into a new pattern, one that was beginning to emerge with a fatal and distressing clarity.

They were working on a finger buffet for a large wedding the next day down on the south coast, it called for an early start and everything had to be ready before they left that evening: the food placed in the cold store, all the equipment, the deep fryer for the raw scampi and the filo cheese and spinach parcels, the fan ovens for reheating the tiny tarts and meat balls and grilling the bacon wrapped scallops and chicken satays, the boiler for hot water, the working tables, all the drink and glasses, they all had to be assembled and left for instant loading early the following day.

By mid-morning they were in full swing.

Darina stopped at one stage for a mug of coffee and looked round the kitchen, thinking Kenneth should really be there to capture some of the delights of the preparation. The choux pastry balls, so beautifully risen and golden brown, the Swedish meat balls, round and succulent, the tiny leek and anchovy tartlets, golden topped. A jug held a muslin-lined sieve through which was dripping freshly squeezed orange juice for little jellies studded with small segments of orange; she had just finished freeing these from their overcoats of pith and membrane and they sat in a glass bowl glowing like the sun. As did the dripping juice. Even the muslin was scenic. It looked like a bridal veil, little squares had been cut out of one corner at some stage and it hung in folds reminding Darina of the bride at the previous wedding they had done, was it only ten days ago?

She had looked so young yet so confident standing hand in hand with her stout new husband, now on his second wife. He had made up in personality what he lacked in looks. Throughout the reception, wherever the loudest laughter was, there were the bride and groom. When it came to his speech it had been one of the wittiest Darina had heard but finally he had turned to his wife, looked into her eyes and raised his glass, "You know what they say, a second wedding is a triumph of hope over experience; I can only say that Robin carries all my hopes and I offer her all my experience." His voice was full of raillery but the look he gave her explained his success with women.

"Hey," said Jo, "Have you gone on strike?"

Darina brought her attention back to the present but her hands moved mechanically at their task. The last little detail she had been looking for had slotted into place. The picture was complete.

They had finished preparing the food and were checking wine bottles in the drink store when Darina looked at Jo and said, "Have you given Eve the good news about your partnership in The Wooden Spoon?"

Both girls stopped what they were doing and gazed at her, Eve as though Darina had suddenly started speaking a foreign language, Jo with one eyebrow quizzically raised. "No," she said, "I haven't."

"Partnership in The Wooden Spoon? What *do* you mean, darling, surely *Jo* hasn't the money to invest in us?"

"She is now your equal partner, Claire left her her shares." Darina sat back on her heels beside the stack of champagne boxes and watched the effect of her words.

Eve looked as though she had had the breath knocked out of her. "I don't believe you," she said at last.

"It's true," said Jo levelly, "The lawyer confirmed it to me on Friday. We are partners."

"The hell we are." Eve sprang to her feet and stood, her breath coming in quick little rasps, "Claire was going to leave those shares to me. You must have had some sort of hold over her, what did you do to make her change her mind?"

Jo rose majestically, two spots of red flaming on her cheek bones. "Now, look, I know you don't like it but there's no need to make nasty innuendoes. Claire decided it would be fairer to leave the shares to me, that's all there was to it."

"Fairer! *Fairer!* What's fair about it? *I* started the company. Where do you think it would have got without me?"

"Claire and you started the company," corrected Jo quietly. "And without me the catering would have failed the moment you moved away from Putney and started the courses."

"Oh, you think you're so bloody marvellous. Let me tell you, if there had been anyone else, you'd have been fired without a moment's hesitation. I was only waiting until we had time to look around for a suitable replacement." Eve thrust her hand up into her hair, dislodging the triangle of white linen that held the bush of curls away from a face distorted with anger.

"I don't think Claire would have been very happy if you'd tried that." Jo was maintaining her calm but Darina could see her chest rising and falling with suppressed emotion.

"Don't you?" Eve's voice was heavy with sarcasm, "But then you don't know how she and I would laugh at you and your funny ways." She darted behind the pile of wine boxes as Jo's control slipped and she hit out with the flat of her hand. Darina scrambled to her feet and got out of the way.

"Hah!" said Eve from behind the barricade of champagne, "That's got you, hasn't it, you don't like to hear that!" There was a triumphant note in her voice.

Jo's hand fell to her side, "You're making it up, I don't believe Claire would laugh at me."

Eve's hair, released from its restraint, made a wild bush that echoed the wildness in her eyes as she gazed at the girl who claimed to have become her partner. Several times she made to speak, failed to find words, then turned on her heel and walked back into the kitchen to stand trembling before one of the work surfaces, her gaze fastened blindly on a collection of misshapen or broken items of food that were stacked in neat piles on the white surface.

Jo followed her. "Can't you see," she had regained her control and her voice was almost normal, "that with me you have a chance of making a real go of this company?"

"It's too late," said Darina, coming up to stand between the two girls. "If you hadn't picked and cooked a poisonous mushroom and added it so carefully to that plate at the anniversary lunch, maybe something could have been saved from the wreck. If Claire had realised exactly what was wrong with her, perhaps even then it might have been possible. But now it's a case of murder. And not just one." Both girls turned towards her, neither said a word.

"But it wasn't just a case of finances, was it?" Darina continued, "Claire was having an affair with Joshua."

Eve gave a cry and wiped her shaking hands down the front of her white, hussar-style overall, then repeated the action over and over again. "How dare you say that. He couldn't have been in love with her, he loves me, *me!*"

Jo had gone white. "So it was true?" she whispered. "I couldn't believe it yet somehow I knew, I just wouldn't admit it."

"There was no money," Darina's voice continued inexorably, "Ralph had turned you down, both as a woman and an investment prospect and Joshua was in love with Claire. It must have seemed you were going to be left with nothing. Then the mushroom walk came along. When did the idea of a poisonous fungi present itself? How much planning did you do? Or was it a spontaneous decision?"

Jo was gazing at Eve with horror, "You couldn't have done, not to *Claire.*"

Eve looked at her with blank eyes. Her right hand reached out sideways to the rejected food. She picked up a broken tart and brought it to her mouth. Gently her teeth nibbled at the pastry, then she dug their pearly whiteness greedily into the filling.

"You made it look as though the mushroom had been meant for you and you concocted that story of the car that nearly ran you over to suggest someone was out to murder you. And, God knows, I found any number of people who could have wanted to."

Eve reached for a broken choux pastry and crammed it into her mouth.

"You must have thought you were safe, that nobody could prove anything, then you saw Elizabeth talking to Clive Thompson at Claire's funeral. Clive Thompson who had sat next to Claire at that luncheon party. What did Elizabeth say that gave you the impression he'd alerted her to the possibility you were the murderer?"

"Elizabeth," the word hissed out from a mouth stuffed with pastries. "She was making love to Joshua. I saw them together at the funeral. She thought with Claire out of the way she could get him back, I know her."

She grabbed at the food with both hands, eating as fast as she could, stuffing first one item then another into her mouth as the other two girls stood riveted in front of her.

"And she looked at me in such a way, I knew what she'd been talking to Clive about. But you can't prove I killed her. She died of natural causes." She gave a strangled laugh edged with hysteria. "Natural causes, nature at work!"

"Hemlock tea, wasn't it?" Darina's voice was unemotional though her eyes were watchful. "It was the muslin that made everything clear. You came in here on Saturday morning, cut the squares, drove down to Sussex, dug up one of the plants outside your cottage, shredded the leaves and tied them up in the material, just like your herbal tea bags, did you add something else, just in case Elizabeth noticed an odd flavour?"

Eve's eyes glittered, their gaze slid around the kitchen but her hands never stopped their ceaseless task of conveying food to her mouth.

"What excuse did you give her for calling in? Something you wanted to collect? How easy was it to switch the tea bags? Did you offer to make a couple of mugs whilst she went on working, using one of the original bags for yourself? If Elizabeth hadn't been eating, the hemlock would have started to work quite quickly. I don't suppose you stayed long after that but before leaving you sabotaged the telephone so she couldn't get help."

"You can't prove any of it, any of it," panted Eve, crumbs falling from her overstuffed mouth down the front of her overall.

"Can't I?" Darina's voice maintained its calm, "That muslin roll was cut in a straight line when I checked all the stores on Friday. On your own admission you were in here on Saturday. I'm willing to place a large bet that it can be proved the tea bags in the cottage waste bin are made from hemlock wrapped in pieces of that roll. And Clive Thompson will make a statement that Claire told him it was you who told her to sit in your place, not the other way round. It was you who organised the place switch to make it look as though the mushroom had been intended for you if there was any question that it hadn't got included accidentally. The ironic thing is that Elizabeth never mentioned the lunch to Clive on Friday, she had guessed he was making a bid for Ralph Cox's company and was trying to get him to confirm it. He refused, of course, but reckons she didn't believe his denials."

"Eve." None of the girls had noticed two men enter the kitchen. Now Joshua's cry drew all their eyes towards the door where he stood looking at his wife forcing food recklessly into her mouth, her cheeks bulging with half chewed morsels, fragments clinging to her face and front. "Eve, what is it? What's happening?"

His wife turned, her eyes vacant, then she reached out a hand towards him, a tartlet falling to the floor, "Josh, help me." The voice was no more than a whisper, the words hardly distinguishable through the food-filled mouth.

But Jo, suddenly casting off her immobility, rushed at Eve, grabbed her by the shoulders and shook her, thrusting an angry face at the shapeless visage before her, "You murdered Claire? You killed my darling? How could you? Oh, you are a devil, a devil, a devil." Eve was flung backwards and forwards, her body unresisting, unswallowed pieces of food erupting from her mouth with the force of the attack.

Darina grabbed Jo, forced the strong fingers to open their grasp on the birdlike frame and pulled the distracted girl back. She held her until the shudders running through Jo's body gradually stilled. Then she turned in time to see Eve sink down to the floor, looking at the remnants of food strewn all around. Her eyes filled with horror, she frantically brushed at her overall and her face, rubbing her fingers to dislodge the clinging crumbs.

Joshua came and sank down on his haunches in front of her. "Eve, what's happened, what have you done?" His voice was tortured, he gazed at her with eyes that refused to accept what was before him.

"I must go to the loo, I must go to the loo," her voice became frantic, she clutched at him, "take me, Josh, take me to the loo."

He instinctively recoiled then brought himself to grasp her hands, speaking firmly in a no-nonsense way. "No, you don't need to, Eve. Come on, stand up." She resisted his efforts to make her rise with cries that mixed pain with a childish outrage.

Once again the kitchen door opened and Darina saw William re-enter with the police officer that had been in Eve's office that morning. Though her mind had registered William's presence behind Joshua, she had been so involved with Eve and Jo she hadn't noticed him leave. Now he came and stood beside her as the officer helped Joshua force Eve to her feet and then proceeded to arrest her for the murder of Elizabeth Chesney.

CHAPTER TWENTY-FIVE

The next few hours were confused. Police seemed to be everywhere. Eve was taken to a station with Joshua holding her hand. She hardly spoke beyond moaning every now and then that she wanted to go to the lavatory.

"All she wants is to make herself sick," said Jo brutally when Darina couldn't understand why Joshua wouldn't let go. "Eve can't handle her relationship with food. She's either eating almost nothing or stuffing herself as she did just now. Then she vomits it all up again. She's terrified of putting on weight."

Darina looked at the girl now being removed from the kitchen between two policemen and remembered Honor's account of her anorexia.

"Claire told me all about it. Eve normally never binges in front of others, today was the first time I've seen her eat anything but the tiniest of morsels. She's completely unbalanced, she should be seeing someone."

"I think she did at one time."

"Why ever did she give up, she can't think she's normal?"

There was nothing to say to that. Darina turned to William, "What on earth are you doing here?"

He gave her a wry smile. "I was worried about you. After our conversation last night it seemed to me you were dealing with a murderer who'd killed a second time to cover his or her tracks and you could be putting yourself in danger."

Darina dismissed the possibility, "I could handle Eve once I knew what had happened. She's not the type to grab a kitchen knife and stick it in you, much more devious. But," she paused and gave him a brilliant smile, "I do appreciate the concern, how did you get the time off?"

"I persuaded my inspector I could have today in lieu of yesterday. I should have been here much earlier but I had a blow out on the motorway."

There followed interminable hours at the station for both Jo and Darina before the point was reached where statements could be signed. William left, promising to return for the weekend, then the girls were told they would not be allowed back into The Wooden Spoon the next day. Neither girl would accept this. They must, they said, be allowed to take all the food they'd prepared for the wedding.

"Look," said Darina at last, "You've got the muslin, I carefully saved that for you. There's nothing else in that kitchen that can possibly help you. Think of that poor bride with two hundred people coming to the greatest day of her life and finding there's no food or drink? Have a heart."

They gave in and after a few short hours sleep, she and Jo got the waitresses, barmen, food and drink organised in two vans and various cars and after a successful function managed to get staff and equipment back again before parting too tired to exchange more than the odd word.

It was, Darina told William after lunch at her house on the Saturday, not until Wednesday that they could face up to trying to sort out the tangle that was The Wooden Spoon's affairs.

"Jo's been marvellous. I've put her in touch with Frances, the girl I handed my business over to, they'll make a good team. Frances can do with some help and Jo thinks she can take enough business with her to make the partnership pay."

"What's going to happen to the Marylebone premises?" William stretched out his long legs in the fireside chair that now seemed to be his.

"The company's being dissolved and Joshua's trying to raise enough money to settle all the debts. He thought he would have to sell up entirely but it appears that Elizabeth left him everything under a will she made before he married Eve and never changed. And apparently after she left the funeral on Friday afternoon, she instructed her stockbroker to buy a large holding in Ralph's company. Now that Clive Thompson's consortium has made an official offer for Cox's Fruit and Vegetables, the shares are whooping up. She had some other capital and her house is worth quite a lot. But Joshua says Eve's defence will probably take any money left over after the liquidation of The Wooden Spoon and he may yet have to sell both the Putney house and the cottage."

"How is Eve?" William drank some more of the wine left over from the lunch Darina had cooked, boned trout in filo pastry with lemon thyme flavoured mayonnaise followed by an unpasteurised brie with fresh oat cakes and grapes.

Darina looked moodily at the pattern of flames from the gas log fire, wishing it could have been the real thing she enjoyed down in Somerset. "Not good. She's under psychiatric care. Joshua's solicitor thinks there's a possibility they can plead diminished responsibility. She seems to have no real understanding of what she has done and apparently was convinced that when Claire didn't die immediately, the mushroom hadn't worked. She says that she never really thought it would anyway and it must have been something else that killed her. She's just like a child who blames every misdeed on someone else. Did you find out anything about the police case?''

"Not a lot. Unless Eve pleads guilty, I think they're doubtful they can pin Claire's murder on her, all the evidence is circumstantial.''

"But she lied, told us all it had been Claire who said they should change places, she made it look as though the mushroom had been intended for her, not Claire.''

"We only have Clive Thompson's word that it was the other way around and a good defence lawyer could very well make out that he had misunderstood what she said.''

Darina was silent for a moment.

"What about Elizabeth's murder?'' she asked finally.

"Ah, there they're on surer ground. It *was* hemlock in the tea bags, mixed with a little peppermint herbal tea, and it seems a plant was dug up outside the cottage, they found the remains in the ditch a little further along the lane, with most of the leaves stripped off and some of the stalk gone as well. She seems to have sat in her car, shredded the leaves, cut up the piece of stalk, added the peppermint and tied it all up in the muslin squares. Tiny plant fragments have been found on the floor of the car, they think it was given a good brush out but you can never get rid of everything. An unused square was found in the pocket of one of her jackets and the lab boys seem to be satisfied the muslin is identical to the roll in The Wooden Spoon. Joshua has made a statement that he didn't see her all Saturday until he went down to the kitchen sometime after six o'clock. He has no idea exactly what time she got back but says it definitely wasn't until late afternoon because he looked for her around five in case she wanted some tea. The case seems pretty clear cut.''

"What about the telephone?''

"The telephone?''

"The one at the cottage, had it been interfered with?''

"Ah, yes, of course. The cord had been ripped out of the junction box, it was one of those old fashioned ones, installed before jacks came along and never updated.''

"You see,'' Darina exclaimed triumphantly, "I knew she had made sure Elizabeth would not be able to call a doctor or an ambulance.'' Her face clouded, "What a terrible mixture of complexes that girl is. To carry out two such cold blooded murders and yet in other ways to be so vulnerable. Joshua says he couldn't bring himself to tell her that Claire and he were in love as he thought it might destroy her. She treated him as a sort of anchor, the person who would always be there no matter what happened. It must have been a devastating blow when she discovered about the affair."

"How did she?"

"She won't say, Joshua reckons she found a letter on his word processor that he'd forgotten to erase, she used it every now and then for recipes."

"What did he think about her fling with Ralph, or didn't he know?"

"He suspected but reckoned she'd been given her marching orders, that was why she was so down."

"Didn't he mind?"

"Says he felt guilty that he hadn't been able to help her more. He knew how insecure she was, it wasn't just the anorexia, she'd grown up in a family of brilliant minds feeling she was of no value, her one talent held for nothing. Perhaps it was no wonder she felt guilty at being so involved with food. Joshua had reached the end of his ability to cope but couldn't bring himself to make the final break."

"Claire must have been a delightfully relaxing contrast."

"Hmmn, I wonder if she wouldn't have bored him after a little, once he'd recovered from the battle scars of life with Eve? I don't think he'd have written the love of his life that letter I found in her file."

"What made you decide it was from Joshua rather than Ralph?"

Darina smiled, "Quite apart from the fact I felt Ralph would never have allowed matters to go that far, I was sure he would never have put anything in writing. Think how Eve would have used them if he'd written any to her."

"And what finally convinced you the murderer was Eve?"

"It was talking to her and Joshua after Elizabeth's death. Until then I felt it could have been Jo."

"But she loved Claire."

"Ah, she could have thought she was adding Amanita phalloides to Eve's plate. She knew the menu, the seating plan, all about the mushroom walk. When she was called home, it could have seemed a heaven-sent opportunity to get rid of Eve, which would allow her and Claire to run the company properly. All she had to do was find a mushroom, there was a book on them in her flat, slip into the house on Sunday morning via the side door when no one was looking, doctor Eve's plate and be off up north. She would have known nothing about the switched places until she came back, which she did immediately she heard Claire had been ill. She could equally well have doctored the herbal tea bags in the cottage sometime during the week, there was a spare key in Jackie's drawer.

"But that night I realised Jo had seen Eve give the cottage keys to Elizabeth. And Eve seemed very keen to play down the fact that Elizabeth had been talking to Clive Thompson and then refused to tell them what they had talked about. So I started to think again. Someone may well have wanted Elizabeth out of the way before she could tell what it was Clive and she had discussed or, as it turned out, what it was someone thought they had discussed."

"There's one thing I don't understand," William frowned at his wine glass, "it's been worrying at me ever since Monday."

"What's that?" Darina reached over and poured more chablis into his glass.

"Well, you spoke to Clive Thompson before you arrived at The Wooden Spoon, you must have known then that Eve was the murderer, why did you wait until the afternoon before doing anything?"

"Ah, that. Two reasons really; in the first place it wasn't until I saw the orange juice draining through the muslin that I understood how she had persuaded Elizabeth to take the hemlock and without that I didn't see I had much more detail to give the police. The second reason," she stopped and grinned at him, "can't you guess?"

He shook his head.

"How were we going to get the wedding breakfast done if Eve had been arrested in the morning?" Darina said triumphantly.

William threw his head back and roared with laughter. "Not that I'm really surprised, I don't think anything you did could startle me now, I'm only amazed you didn't wait until after the wedding."

"Nonsense," Darina was indignant, "I know where my duty lies."

"What do you think will happen to Joshua? The poor chap's lost his wife, mistress and ex-lover."

"Oh, I think he's pretty tough. He's got his work and none of those women was quite right for him, Eve was too neurotic, Claire not intelligent enough and Elizabeth too old. I expect he'll write another book, plunge into a few affairs then get caught by a pretty face and end up with another unsatisfactory marriage."

"You seem pretty cynical," he said quietly.

Darina shifted uneasily on her sofa. "I think I've become disillusioned about relationships. Everyone seems to be after something, nobody seems to care about anyone else's feelings, not even the person they're in love with, sex is allowed to justify anything. Look at Eve, Ralph, Joshua, even Claire, all tangled in liaisons, ruining perfectly good existing relationships. And think what love and sex did to Jo. After her father had finished with her, she couldn't look at men. And when she did fall in love, it was with a girl involved in a clandestine affair. I tell you, William, love's a dangerous business."

"Is that why you so firmly refuse to consider the possibility yourself?" he asked quietly.

The question slipped under her guard and exploded in her mind. She looked at him, relaxed in the chair, affecting a detached concern but with an inner watchfulness that betrayed a deeper involvement.

"Don't look so startled," he said, "you can't deny you have veered away from any emotional response to me ever since we met. I would think it my personal freshness except you show no disinclination for my company, particularly if it's to discuss some murder case or other."

Darina toyed with her empty wine glass then took a deep breath, "William, I've not been fair with you. I'm sorry, it's not that I don't like you, I do, more than anyone else. I don't know why I'm afraid of letting myself feel more than that."

"For God's sake," he said, "I'm not asking for some great emotional commitment, I'm not even asking for a full blown affair, just that . . ."

"Just that we explore some of the possibilities?" Darina gave him the ghost of a smile.

He let out his breath in a long sigh, "When you relax, when you forget about the "dangers of sexuality," you're so warm, so responsive, I want to sweep you up, start kissing your eyes and end with your toes, lingering over every gorgeous inch on the way."

"Every inch! You'd be bored before you reached my chin!"

"There you go again, sliding away from the issue, turning it into a joke. Why do you do it?"

"A disinclination to lay myself open to a battered heart, I suppose," she said flippantly.

"Which supposes you have suffered that way in the past?"

She dropped her gaze before the intensity in his eyes. There was no way she could avoid this.

"When I first came to London, I met someone. I thought he felt the same way I did. But he left me for someone else."

"And?" he prompted when she fell silent.

"And?"

"And who else? Apart from your cousin, that is?"

"Digby?"

"Do you have other charismatic cousins I don't know about? Did you think I was unaware what a powerful attraction he had for you?"

Darina sighed, "Yes, I suppose you're right, I was emotionally involved with him, even though I hardly realised it until he was dead."

"And?"

"What do you mean, 'and'?"

"And who else?"

"No-one."

"No-one?"

"No-one."

"You mean to tell me one unhappy affair and a still-born relationship with Digby has turned you off men for life?"

"No." Darina was angry, he made her sound like some frustrated spinster knitting her repressions into mail armour. "Of course not, it's just that I've been too busy."

"Cooking?"

"Yes, cooking. It's . . . it's very time consuming." She looked across at him, daring him to laugh.

It was no good; his gaze held hers for a long moment, then his face crumpled and all the emotional intensity that had lain behind his questioning dissolved in another great shout of laughter.

Just for a second she was furious, how dare he not take her seriously, then she, too, was caught up in the absurdity of it.

Helpless with hilarity they gave themselves up to laughter. Several times it died, only for one to catch the other's eye and the mirth to bubble up again. Finally, with a few hiccupping catches of breath, Darina wiped her eyes of the tears that had squeezed through.

"I suppose it is funny, really," she said, "making roulades instead of having a roll in the hay." She gave another gurgle of laughter and replaced the handkerchief up the sleeve of her jumper, looked up—and found herself, all guards down, completely unprepared, ensnared by a new light in the silvery eyes of the man sitting opposite her.

Her breath caught on a last hiccup that seemed to clutch at her soul. Every life-giving force was poised, waiting. She watched as his expression changed, an eager question rose in his eyes and he moved quietly and efficiently onto the sofa beside her.

Then all defences fell as she forgot the dangers of letting your emotions take charge. The wine glass fell onto the carpet and the coffee cooled beside the fire.